DARK PAWN

A.B. COHEN & JP RINDFLEISCH IX

For J & Zach, our mentors.

Tree of Life

Divine One
Keter
Holy
Timekeeper
Binah
Time
Traveler
Chochmah
Space
Elemental
Gevurah
Nature
Lover
Chesed
Heal
Seer
Tiferet
Vision
Invulnerable
Netzach
Sheild
Pacifist
Hod
Hold
Bonded
Yesod
Link
Warrior
Malchut
Push

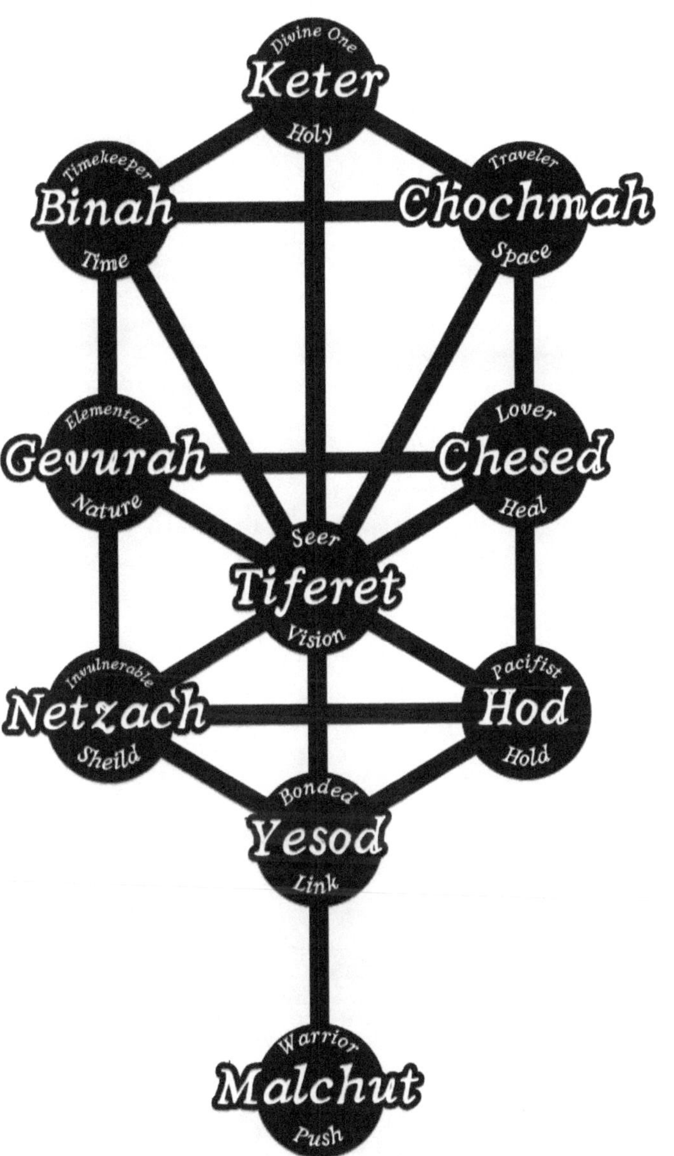

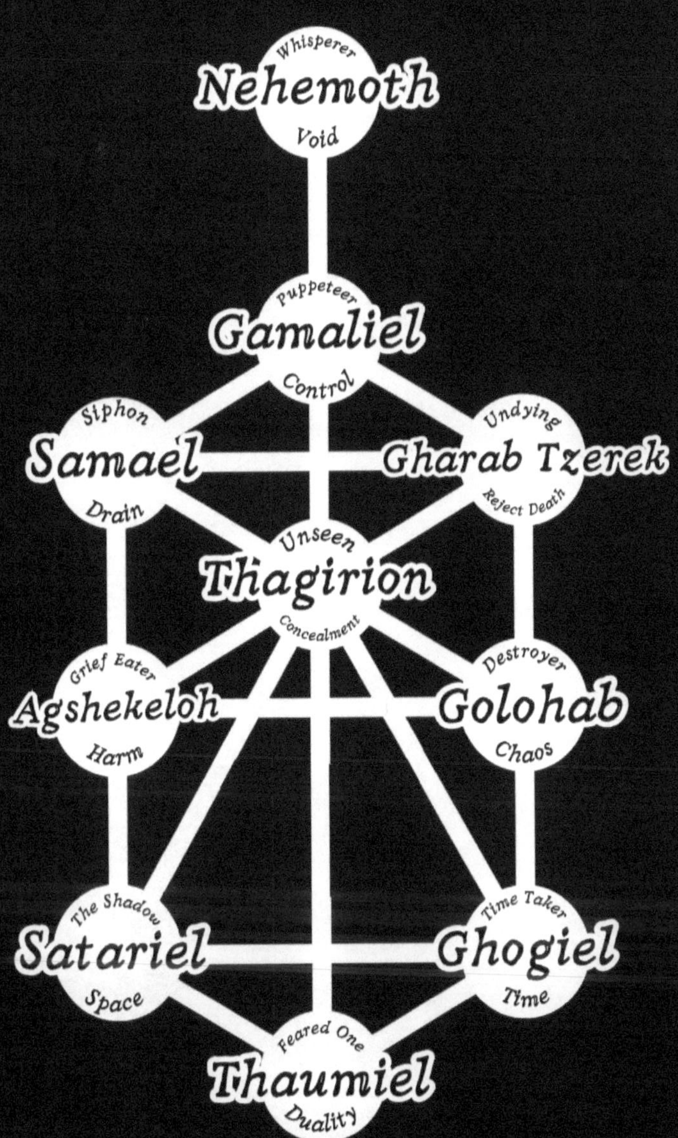

Tree of Death

The Infinity Board

 King

 White Queen

 Black Queen

 White Rook / Sage

 Black Rook

 White Bishop

 White Knight

 Black Bishop

 Black Knight

 White Pawn

 Black Pawn

 Square

CHAPTER I

AN UNEXPECTED VISITOR

Shadows stretched across the floor, trailing past Leah's translucent legs and up the tall wool curtains that blocked light from outside. She still wore her pink plaid pajamas and had no memory of how she got there. Where were her parents? Had they even noticed she wasn't lying in bed anymore?

Cold air brushed past her unkempt auburn hair. She turned, spotting large flakes of ash falling like snowflakes onto a mahogany desk. Behind the desk sat a high-backed leather chair, facing away from Leah and toward a massive stone fireplace that streamed light out into the room.

Leah looked down through her ghostly hands and onto the floor below. Was she dead? Panic flooded her, and she darted her eyes left and right, looking for any sign of where she was. She stepped in front of the fire, hoping something on the desk might give her a clue.

The scent of caramel and smoky pine stopped her in her tracks, the pungent scent of scotch filling her nose. An image of her father, rosy-cheeked and laughing, holding his favorite drink, came to mind.

Maybe he's here, too.

A long-fingered pale hand stretched out from the leather chair and placed an empty glass on the desk. The thrum of Leah's heart pounded heavy in her ears.

That's not him.

A soft, melodic voice sounded from behind the chair. "There is only a handful outside our grasp. I doubt they'll even be a threat."

A chill ran up Leah's spine, and she backed away, moving deeper into the shadows. She couldn't make out the voice, but she shuffled along the wall beside the desk and leaned to peer around the leather chair. Dark shadows clung to the figure unnaturally, forming a blackened silhouette that rested their head in their hands.

A gravelly voice resonated out from each corner of the room. The voice weighed down Leah and sent a shock drilling into her jaw as it echoed all around her. "They need to be dealt with. I won't have us taking any chances."

Leah whipped her head around the room, trying to trace the sound's origin. Shadows danced and stretched, concealing any hint of another in the room.

"Very well," the dark figure said, wrapping their long fingers around the arms of the chair. "But there isn't much I can do. The ritual keeps their locations secret for a reason."

"Leave that to me." The other voice took in a raspy breath, more like a growl than anything else. "I have the right candidate. Remember Asmodeus? Who was it that defeated him?"

Pressure built around Leah, a tension that grew heavy in the room. The figure in the chair swiveled around, peering out from behind the desk. Shadows coalesced around their face, obscuring it from Leah's vision as they rested their elbows on the desk, crossing their arms. "Elizabeth Mizrahi?"

The harder Leah tried to focus on the face, the more the

shadows blurred her vision. Yet she somehow knew beyond the darkness that thing had locked its eyes on her.

"Ah, yes. Might be good to give him another try, don't you think?"

The shadowed figure spoke, their voice breaking. "I don't think that's a good idea. What about her—"

The raspy voice resonated around the room, louder this time. "Seems we have a spy in our midst. Little girl, don't you know it's rude to eavesdrop?"

Leah jumped back, her head spinning like on a swivel. Unseen eyes pierced through her.

The dark figure turned their face toward Leah. A pressure threw Leah up against the wall, squeezing her tight and stealing all the air from her lungs. The sound of chains rattled around her, and she strained to breathe, gasping for air like a fish pulled from the sea.

Darkness crept into the edges of her vision, and the soft orange light from the fireplace shrank to the flickering kindling of a dying candle. The raspy voice let out a shrill that stabbed Leah's ears before the figure waved their hand and plunged Leah into darkness, pulling her down into unknown depths.

CHAPTER 2
BAD DREAMS

Leah lurched up out of bed, gasping for air and sweat pouring down her face.

A cool hand pressed against her head. "Hey, it's okay. Just a bad dream. Yeah?" David Ackerman, her father, sat on the bed with her, his blue eyes staring into Leah's. He turned to the tall woman standing next to him, an older image of Leah right down to her honey-colored eyes. "Liz, could you get a damp washcloth?"

Her mother, Elizabeth Mizrahi, nodded, averting her eyes from Leah before stepping out into the hallway.

Leah propped herself up on her elbows, wiping away the cold sweat with shaky hands. "What . . . What happened? Why are you two in here?"

"You were screaming. We thought someone broke in." He ran his hand through his graying brown hair and chuckled. "Nearly took a dive headfirst into the dresser trying to get out of bed."

Her mother stepped back into the room carrying a damp cloth that she rested against Leah's head. She lifted her daughter's chin with thin, delicate fingers and studied Leah's eyes. "So, what was this dream, love?"

"I . . . I don't remember . . ." She pulled away from her mother and held her head in her hands, rubbing her eyes. Goosebumps travelled across her skin, and sweat beaded again on her forehead. "It was dark, and I was alone. I was sinking."

Her mother took her hands. "You're okay now, love. Just another bad dream, that's all."

"But why do I keep having them?"

Her father shrugged and looked at Elizabeth, his voice dropping low. "Do you think it could do with p—" He paused, stuttering over the word while her mother shot him a warning look.

Leah shifted on the bed, pulling the covers up to create a barrier between her and whatever her father was about to say. Her anxiety-addled brain was too afraid of the next thing to come out of his mouth.

Could it be one of the many secrets her parents seemed to keep from her? Both rarely spoke about their past. They never told her how they met or what Mother did before Leah was born. She didn't know anyone on her mother's side of the family. No grandparents. No aunts. She slowly looked up at her father, waiting for an answer.

Her father's concerned face flushed red as he said, "Puberty?"

Leah felt her cheeks grow hot, and she dropped her head into her hands. "Don't you think it's a little late for that? I'm fifteen." She shook her head, angry she even thought for a second that they'd tell her something of value. "I'm not having this conversation with Dad in the room."

Elizabeth swatted at her husband's arm and leaned close to Leah. "Your dad is headed to the doghouse tonight." She paused and looked at David, who feigned a pout and rubbed his arm. "Maybe his terrible jokes cause your nightmares." Her mother tucked one of Leah's brunette strands behind her ear and turned to David. "She's right, maybe you could you get a glass of water while us girls talk."

David stood and faked a salute to Elizabeth. "I see my services are no longer needed, Captain. Guess I'll walk the plank. Maybe the fishes will find me funny." He turned and walked cautiously toward Leah's door, placing one foot in front of the other like balancing on a plank.

"Hey, Dad. What's a pirate's favorite exercise?"

He paused and looked up at the ceiling, tapping his finger to his chin. His eyes lit up, and he closed one eye and made a hook out of his finger. "Arr, be it the plank?" He turned his back to them and stiffened before falling out of her room and into a pushup position. Then he hopped up and headed to the stairs, bellowing a song about Davy Jones.

Leah let out a half-hearted laugh and Elizabeth shook her head. "You know you encourage him, right? Now he'll be up all night testing pirate jokes on me." Elizabeth repositioned herself on the edge of Leah's bed. "If you want to talk about . . ."

"No," Leah said. "I don't."

Elizabeth raised her hands. "Alright, I won't push you on it. But, in that case, mind if I try something?"

Leah nodded, and her mother continued.

"Then, close your eyes."

Leah shut them and felt her mother's fingers press gently on her temples, moving them in slow circles.

"What are you doing?" she asked, her eyes still closed. The question remained unanswered as her mother's fingertips stopped moving, pressing gently on Leah's temples. Leah cracked open her eyes and saw her mother frowning. "Mom?" Leah asked. "You okay?"

Her mother fluttered her eyes open, and she straightened her back before shaking her head and smiling. "Yeah, everything's—"

"I've got one gin and tonic for the pirate queen," her father said, stepping back into the room carrying a tall glass. He handed it to Leah, and she eyed it. She knew he was only joking, but she still sipped it carefully, confirming it was just water before drinking the rest.

Leah looked back at her mother. "Everything's what?"

"Fine, everything's fine." She stifled a yawn and patted Leah's knee. "My mom did that when I had bad dreams. Pressure points for nightmares." She smiled and shrugged. "That's what she said, at least."

David brought his hands to his temples and squeezed his eyes shut. "I've been rubbing my temples for years, and that old nightmare is still around."

Elizabeth rolled her eyes and sighed. "You could try being nice to her for a change."

"Never." David looked over at Leah and laughed.

Elizabeth leaned back and stood up. "Well, that's enough excitement for tonight." She pulled up Leah's covers and pecked her daughter on the forehead. "Back to bed." She turned and slammed her hip directly into Leah's desk, letting out a small gasp and holding her hand to her hip.

"Everything alright?" Leah asked.

"I'm fine. My leg must have fallen asleep or something."

David eyed his wife before looking at Leah, pointing to her glass and miming drinking. Leah chuckled, wondering if they had gotten into the wine after she had gone to sleep.

Elizabeth hit his arm. "You two are terrible." She sauntered to the door, muttering, "Why didn't I marry that doctor my mother wanted?" before flicking off the lights. "Night, love. Pleasant dreams only, yeah?" She left the room with David, the two of them whispering and giggling all the way back to their room.

Leah laid back and closed her eyes. The darkness behind her eyelids forced her to snap her eyes open, staring up at the ceiling. A few green stars she had yet to pull down glowed back at her. She flicked on the lamp next to her bed and closed her eyes, a soft light behind her eyelids keeping the dark at bay.

CHAPTER 3
FAMILY

Sunlight beamed onto Leah's face as she woke. Not a single dream echoed in her mind, only a fog of exhaustion numbing her senses. She pulled herself out of bed and wrenched open the window, hoping a cool morning breeze would liven her senses. Instead, humid summer air rolled in. As she shut the window, she spotted her neighbor Derick, a junior at her high school, shirtless and mowing the yard. Her eyes stayed on him longer than she'd intended, and he looked up, catching Leah's gaze and startling her as she jerked back away from the window. She turned to the vanity opposite her bed to assess what sort of sleep monster her neighbor had seen.

She tied back her mess of auburn hair and rubbed the sleep from her face. After that, her morning routine began with an array of cleansers and moisturizers while she periodically sucked in her cheeks and posed in the mirror. Her face still looked so young compared to her friends. They claimed their "baby fat" just up and vanished one day, but she remained looking like an eighth grader posing to be a freshman. She supposed all the makeup and crop tops her friends wore to show off their midriffs also contributed, seeing as her mom still flipped out if she even dabbed eyeshadow on.

Her phone dinged, pulling her away from her trance at the mirror. The touchscreen was still foreign to her, another thing her friends got to experience for almost a year before she got her own. She unlocked the screen and saw that Ashley sent her the usual five texts that she could have summed up into one, asking if Leah was still game for the party tonight. Leah's fingers hovered over the keys, not sure how she was going to ask her parents yet, before she sent back a fervent *Hell yeah*. She got up and dressed before heading down to the kitchen.

Her mother sat at the table, a cup of black coffee left untouched on the table next to her and her nose buried deep in the paper. Her father turned from the stove, wearing a ridiculous apron meant for Elizabeth, lacy frills and all. "Good morning, sunshine. How'd you sleep?"

"Fine, I guess." Leah stifled a yawn.

Her mother pushed the mug of coffee toward Leah. "Here, have the rest." She eyed her husband with an eyebrow raised. "He's making scrambled eggs, I think."

David raised a metal bowl to them, as if to show off the eggs, and started whisking away, the sound of metal scraping metal echoing in the house. Elizabeth put down the paper and pinched the bridge of her nose. Dark circles lined her mother's eyes, and Leah wondered if she'd ever gone back to sleep after the incident the previous night.

Leah paused, wanting to ask, but a twinge of guilt stopped her. Did she really want to know if her mother had stayed up all night, worried that Leah might have another fit? Leah decided it was better not to ask and instead wrapped her hands around the coffee and took a sip. The bitter taste flooded her senses, and she wondered how her mother drank plain black coffee before grabbing the sugar off the table and nearly drowning the cup in white crystals. Either the caffeine or the sugar washed over her in an instant, the exhaustion melting away.

David poured the eggs into the skillet, and soon enough, he walked over and scooped the slightly burned eggs onto Leah's plate. "So, any fun plans for your first day of summer? I know the lawn misses you."

Leah stared down at her plate, rolling the chunks of egg around. "Well, I actually was wondering . . . Ashley invited me and the girls over for the night. Would you care if I went?"

Her mother peered over the newspaper and shot a glare at Leah. "And why are you asking now? Do you remember we have your father's cousin's wedding tomorrow?"

Leah locked her eyes onto her plate, not ready to meet her mother's gaze. "I know. I'd still be home in time for us to go. You're cool with it, right?"

Elizabeth set the newspaper down. Leah felt certain her parents were about to plunge into another lecture on why Leah consistently kept them out of the loop until the last minute so she could get her way. Her mother drew in a breath, holding up a finger to Leah. Then the doorbell rang.

David raced to set the pan down and shouted, "I'll get it," before rushing to the front door.

Leah's mother strained to keep her voice low as she hissed, "You need to stop doing this. It's not considerate. Ask us when we actually have time to think it over, especially when you know we already have plans like a wedding tomorrow."

David shouted from the door. "Uh, Elizabeth, can you come here for a sec?"

Elizabeth raised an eyebrow and stared through the wall, her gaze directed to the front door. Leah had seen her do this before, like she thought she had x-ray vision or something. Her mother rolled her eyes and stood. "Wait here."

Leah had no interest in waiting. She listened for her mother's footsteps to fade, and she spun off her chair, peering out of the half wall separating the kitchen from the living room and across the hallway.

She spotted her mother reaching for the door and step out, closing the screen door behind her. Leah leaned through the vestibule as much as she could but couldn't catch a glimpse of the visitor. She tiptoed through the living room to get a better view, climbing onto the sofa and peeking out onto the inlet porch through the curtain.

A man wearing a black leather jacket over a white shirt stood in front of her parents. He had a chiseled jaw covered in unkempt scruff that matched his chestnut hair. Placing her hand on the window, Leah quietly cracked it open.

". . . wouldn't show up if it wasn't serious," the man said. "Discovering that Asmodeus is back seemed serious enough." His voice was deep, and something familiar chimed in the back of Leah's mind.

David waved his hands in the air, stepping between Elizabeth and the man. "So, what? She's out of all that. And we're protected."

Elizabeth rested a hand on David's shoulder and gently pulled him back. "You're right, love, but it matters. It involved me, which means we just need to keep an eye out." She paused and turned to the man and hugged him. "Thanks, Eric, really. But . . . look at you. When was the last time you slept?"

The man, Eric, nodded and stepped back before sighing loudly. "Things are—" He cut himself off, rubbing his forehead and looking back up at them, a half-smile pulled across his face. "It's been a lot, that's all." He fished around in his pocket and pulled out a small piece of paper, along with a wad of cash and a pack of cigarettes. "This is the number to my room. I'm at the Motel 6 in Prospect Heights for a few days, in case anything happens. Call me, okay?" He handed them the paper and stepped back off the front porch. "It'd be good to catch up. Maybe when I'm not on a case."

His light brown eyes flicked over to the window where Leah sat. Her heart skipped a beat, and she leaped back, racing out of the room.

Leah found her seat back at the kitchen table as the front door closed. Shortly after, her parents rejoined her. Her mother pulled the paper back up to cover her face, and her father pushed around cold scrambled eggs on his plate.

"So, who was that?" Leah asked, shifting her eyes between her parents.

"A relative," Elizabeth said, her newspaper still hiding her expression.

Her father picked up a piece of toast buried under a mound of eggs and tried to shovel it into his mouth, pieces of egg falling onto his plate.

"I think it is best for you to stay home tonight." Her mother turned another page.

"What? Why?" Anger bubbled up inside Leah before she could even think to stop it.

"Listen to your mother, Leah," her father said before dropping his gaze and hopping up out of his seat, stepping into the kitchen. "Anyone want more toast? I'll make more toast."

"Why won't you just tell me why? Is it because some lunatic named Asmodeus is on the loose?"

Her mom slammed the paper down onto the table. "Leah Ackerman, I told you to wait in the kitchen!"

Leah pushed herself up from the table. "Dad said we're protected, whatever that means. How would this

Asmodeus even know who I am? You've never mentioned him before. Am I supposed to believe he knows where Ashley lives, too?"

"There are things you don't understand. Bad things, and bad people who take what they want. What else did you hear?" her mother said.

"Then why aren't you calling the police? You two just sat back down at the table like nothing happened. If it were bad enough, you'd call the cops." She crossed her arms and tilted her head at her mother. *Checkmate.* Leah grabbed her glass of orange juice for a victory sip.

Smoke rolled up out of the toaster and caught Leah's eye. Her father jumped into action and unplugged the toaster, fishing out the burnt piece of toast.

"Tell me what else you heard." Her mother spoke through gritted teeth.

"Or, what? I'm not telling you shit!" Leah yelled, feeling the rage course through her. The glass in her hand cracked with an audible snap, and the remaining orange juice poured out onto the table.

Her mother took in a sharp breath, likely rearing up for another argument with her daughter. Instead, she glowered at the glass as she let her breath out slowly, the anger in her eyes dissipating.

David jumped out from behind the counter with a towel and soaked up the mess on the table. "I don't know where you get that language from. Definitely not me. But can we not have a shouting match this early in the morning?"

Her mother pursed her lips and returned to the paper, pulling it up again to form a barrier. She muttered something under her breath.

Leah balled her fists and turned, stomping out of the room. "Another great talk, Mom!" she yelled, before reaching the stairs.

She slammed her bedroom door and threw herself onto her bed, looking up at the ceiling. This wasn't the first time her mom diverted a conversation, putting the blame on Leah while keeping things from her and coming up with excuses for what she did before Leah was born. Her father never talked about her mother's past, either, or how they met. *Why can't they just tell me? All they ever do is lie and change the subject, but the moment I ask a question, they both turn on me. How is that fair?*

Leah's face grew hot, and her chest constricted as pressure built from inside. She reached for her phone on her nightstand, but before she could grab it, it slid across the table, crashing down onto the floor. *That's weird. I wonder what would—*

A light knock sounded at her door, pulling her away from her thoughts. "Hey, it's Dad. I just want to say I'm sorry. We're sorry." He paused, and for a moment Leah thought he'd left. Then she heard him again. "Could I come in?"

"Go away," Leah said, her hands balling into fists.

"Please don't be like that, Leah. I just want to help." He jiggled the handle.

Her face flushed. Leah prepared to yell at her dad when a thought popped into her mind, and with it, the constraint around her chest melted away. "Cramps, Dad. I have cramps. Please, leave me alone."

The jiggling stopped immediately, and her father's voice dropped to a low whisper. "Oh, okay, I, um, I . . ."

Footsteps faded away from the door, and Leah sighed, rubbing her temples. Moments later, she heard footsteps again that stopped in front of her door. She sat up, clutching her abdomen from the pain. "Dad, I said go away."

"I know, I just . . . here." A white packaged cylinder

slipped under the door, followed by a few supplies from under her bathroom sink. "I didn't know which one you needed. I also grabbed your mother's Motrin, a glass of water, and some chocolate. If you are anything like her, we're going to need more chocolate. So, uh, yeah, I'll just leave them here."

Leah listened to his footsteps recede before creeping to the door and cracking it open, not missing out on the chance to indulge in some chocolate. She grabbed the other contents too, downing a Motrin and chugging some water before tearing open the chocolate bag. She picked her phone off the floor and hopped into bed, putting on head-phones to drown out any noise that might come out from the hall.

CHAPTER 4

RELATIVE

Candy wrappers accumulated beside her while she flipped through her phone, scrolling through all the fun everyone else was having today while she sequestered herself off in her room. Ashley kept her busy by updating her on the plans for tonight. Like Leah suspected, Ashley's parents were out of town for the weekend, and Ashley's brother, a senior when the school year picked up in the fall, took the bait. Leah wondered if any of the boys she knew would be there—specifically, if Steven would be there.

Another knock came at her door, and Leah looked at the clock. Afternoon had already come, and with it a mound of chocolate wrappers.

"Leah," her mother said, "would you let me in, please? Listen, I didn't mean to lash out. There are simply things I can't tell you yet."

Leah peered at the door, considering opening it for a moment, wondering if she had finally chipped enough away that her mother would confess something, anything, to why she was so secretive.

"You'll understand one day," her mother added.

Leah grabbed her headphones and turned up her music, crossing the room and opening the door. She met her mother's eyes and saw her trying to say something, but the music in Leah's ear drowned it out. Leah shuffled past her and down the stairs, music blasting while she put on her shoes and stepped out into the backyard. She stomped across the yard and into the shed, pulling out the push mower and yanking on the pull cord, roaring it to life. Her eyes remained on the lawn in front of her, certain they'd leave her alone if she were doing chores.

After the lawn had met its match, Leah showered and laid back down on her bed. By the time she settled in, another knock disrupted her silent protest. Without waiting for her to give him permission to enter, her father stepped into the room holding a bowl.

"I can't have you eating just chocolate all day. What would the neighbors say? I made your favorite: homemade mac and cheese."

Leah's stomach growled, and she couldn't pretend she wasn't hungry. "Fine. Thanks, Dad."

He handed her the bowl before starting. "So, I know you're mad at Mom. And I get it, I really do. To be honest, she didn't even tell me about what your uncle did, or what she did, for a living until recently. And, I've got to say, you might be better off not knowing. The stuff she did . . . it gives you nightmares if you let it."

"Uncle? She said he was a relative. I have an uncle?"

David looked at the door and back, his face turning pale. "Uh, yeah. They don't talk much. Not anymore."

Leah furrowed her eyebrows and stabbed several noodles with her fork. "So, what is she then, a spy? Why can't she just tell me? It's not like I need all the details."

Her father tousled her hair and smirked. "The problem is you eavesdropped, and she's not ready to tell you. We know this wasn't the first time you did it, either."

"But why do you get to know about it and I don't?"

He stepped back and crossed his arms, taking in a deep breath. "I almost left a few years back." Leah interrupted with a sharp gasp, but he continued. "You were two, and I just couldn't deal with it. All the lies and secrets. She kept disappearing, no explanation. We fought a lot about it, but eventually I found out."

The thought of her parents almost going through a divorce, a seemingly happy couple who still giggled at each other's jokes, overwhelmed Leah. Her thoughts spiraled. The idea of living in two separate houses, two holidays for everything. Her father spoke again, his voice pulling her out from under the void.

"It isn't easy, not knowing. I realize that more than anyone. But she has her reasons, and you need to respect that, okay? Now, can my girls get along for just a little while longer?"

"I can try." Leah sighed.

Her father rested his hands on her shoulders and squeezed. "That's my girl." He kissed her on the forehead. "Alright, I promise we'll leave you alone tonight. But, please, make sure you get to bed early. We all need to be dressed and out the door by ten if we want to beat traffic."

Leah rolled her eyes and smiled. "Oh, great, I can't wait."

"Sleep tight, don't let the bedbugs bite." He closed the door behind him, leaving Leah to be alone once again.

She picked up the bowl of mac and cheese and devoured it. Placing the bowl on the floor, she smiled and crossed the room, pushing in the lock on her door before pulling out a pair of jeans from her dresser. She eyed the window and grinned. "Sleep tight."

CHAPTER 5
OUIJA BOARD

Leah lay in bed, eyeing the glow of the dark stars on her ceiling. She waited for the rest of the house to be silent, certain then that her parents would be asleep. She pulled her blankets off and, under dim lamplight, quickly brushed her hair and dabbed on gold eyeshadow around her eyes. After scanning herself in the mirror, noticing the striking resemblance to her mother with the addition of makeup, she zipped a hoodie up over her white blouse and quietly opened her window.

She lowered herself down onto the half-banister on the front porch and then jumped onto the ground. Looking back at the house, she wondered if her parents knew how easy it was to get on and off the roof. She'd done it so many times before without getting caught.

Leah headed out of the cul-de-sac and into the lit streets of Lincolnwood, Illinois.

She could walk to Ashley's house blindfolded, the path worn into her memory, but then she'd miss out on the extravagant mini mansions that her neighbors constantly changed in some unspoken competition against each other. Stones imported from who knows where lined a fence to her left, a new fountain dribbled water to her right, and up ahead was a miniature statue that mimicked Michelangelo's David. Luckily, her parents never tried to compete, else she was certain they'd be bankrupt in a day.

More and more cars packed the sides of the streets as she came closer, all leading up to Ashley's. Leah's heart leaped into her throat. She hadn't expected so many people, especially so many who could drive. Had Ashley invited the whole school?

She mustered the willpower to open the front door, and a wall of music met her on the other side. She squeezed in through a crowd of people huddled in the foyer and pulled off her hoodie, clutching her elbow as she passed by the juniors and seniors.

"Leah, you're finally here!" Ashley's voice tore through the music, and Leah turned to see a wave of blond curls come rushing toward her. Ashley stood much taller and carried all the right assets to make any other girl jealous. Not that Leah was jealous, just that Leah knew she'd never outshine Ashley, and that was fine by her.

Leah wrapped her arms around Ashley and spoke in her ear. "How did you pull this off?"

Ashley pulled back and shrugged. "Parents are out of town. My brother did all the legwork. I'm just glad he let me invite friends instead of locking me in my room like last time. Better yet, his friend Tyler hooked us up with some booze." She grinned and handed Leah a cup. "Want some punch?"

Leah bit her lip. The memory of her parents almost catching her the last time she sneaked back into the house after drinking. Her chest tightened, and she stared at the cup. They'd be so mad if they found out. She shook her head and let out a deep sigh, taking a good gulp of the punch.

It was awful, burning all the way down her throat. "Ugh, what's in this?"

"I didn't say it was *good* booze." Ashley shrugged before the grin on her face turned into laughter. She glanced at the clock. "Finish that. I've got a surprise upstairs, and I don't want to leave them too long up there."

Leah threw back the last of the punch, trying not to think of the awful taste. She wiped her mouth. "What are you scheming?"

Ashley tilted her head and tapped her finger to her lips. "Well, Steven and Tyler are in my room. He's been asking if you'd be coming tonight, you know."

Leah felt the heat flush in her face. Steven, the junior track star she'd had a crush on since the third grade, was here, in Ashley's room, and asking about her?

"OMG, your face is so red," Ashley squealed, pinching Leah's cheek. "Come on, before you chicken out."

Leah batted away the hand. "Shut up! How do I know you don't have a troll like Jimmy up there waiting?"

Ashley feigned shock. "Leah Ackerman, I'd never." She grinned. "At least, I'd never to you, I swear. I have Steve and Tyler trapped in my room. They said they wanted to play a game, but they needed at least four to play. I'm hoping it's Spin the Bottle!" Ashley grabbed Leah's hand and pulled her toward the stairs.

They waded through the crowd, up the stairs, and into Ashley's room. Leah met Steven's gaze with a smile as her face felt red hot. Ashley hadn't lied. Both Tyler and Steven were there, sitting on Ashley's bed.

"All hail Queen Ashley!" Tyler slurred out while raising his beer before finishing it and tossing it into the small garbage pail beside Ashley's bed. His Cubs hat sat slightly tilted on his head, and the first three buttons of his flannel were undone, revealing the interior of his smooth chest.

Leah could definitely see Ashley's appeal toward him, even if he thought he held his liquor better than he actually did.

Steven was the polar opposite of Tyler, his hair coiffed and wearing a fitted polo against well-toned muscles. Leah could barely keep her eyes off him as he stood and slid a hand into the pocket of his black jeans. He smirked, a dimple forming on his cheek as he awkwardly waved at Leah. "What up?"

Leah locked onto Steven's green eyes and gave a slight smile. "Not much." She nodded at his can. "Have one for me?"

Ashley had warned Leah he was a player, but Leah just didn't see it. Steven was always kind to her, and shy. She was pretty sure her friends told Leah those things about Steven so he'd seem less desirable, or something. Either way, she wouldn't risk a shot at finding out for herself. She wrapped her finger around her hair and smiled.

"Make room for me!" Ashley jumped onto the bed, taking Steven's spot and cuddling up against Tyler. "You know, a queen's gotta have a king, right?"

Tyler grinned and leaned in to plant a long kiss on Ashley's lips before pulling away, leaving her frozen in stunned silence. "You ladies are in luck. We snuck an entire case of beer up here, undetected." He pulled the case out from under Ashley's bed. "I think we could survive the entire night up here if we had to."

Tyler picked one up and tossed it to Leah, and she cracked it open and took a sip. She did her best to mask her reaction to the taste, raising her can to Steven as he cracked open another and drank.

Steven hopped into the giant beanbag across from Ashley's bed and made room for Leah. Her heart pounded as she sat next to him, his arm wrapping around her.

Leah looked over at Ashley and Tyler to see the two of

them kissing again, certain Ashley was swinging for a home run with Tyler. She felt Steven's heart racing, and before she knew what she was doing, she cleared her throat. "So, uh, what was this game you were so excited about?"

Tyler practically threw Ashley off him. A big smile stretched across his face. "Oh yeah! I picked it up at my mom's thrift store." He paused, looking between Leah and Ashley. "Rules are that neither of you can chicken out. Got it?"

Ashley shook her head immediately and stared at Leah, waiting for her to say something.

"Bring it on," Leah said, anxiety shooting through her like ice cold needles.

Tyler pulled a long box from behind Ashley's pillow. "I can't believe my mom wanted to burn this."

Leah tilted her head, expecting a bottle, but he pulled out a long black and white box. She recognized it was a Ouija board right away, the familiar markings the same as the ones in the movies her mother always turned off. She leaned in, a grin spreading across her face, relieved it wasn't a bottle.

"Well, I see one of you is excited," Tyler said, shifting off the bed to be level with Leah and Steven on the floor before pulling on Ashley's leg to join him.

Ashley ran over to the door and dimmed the lights before finding her place next to Tyler. Everyone looked at her, and she shrugged. "What? It sets the mood." She helped Tyler pull the board from the box. Ashley held up the planchette, looking through the small magnifying glass in the center. "Which one of you wants to go first?"

No one spoke. The two boys looked over at Leah, and she heard the voice of her mother in her ear, warning her against Ouija boards. She nodded. "I'll start."

Steven and Leah moved off the beanbag and sat cross-legged on the floor around the board, forming a circle with Tyler and Ashley.

"So, uh, how do we start?" Leah asked.

Tyler held up the heart-shaped object with the hole in it. "This is called a planchette." He placed the planchette on the board. "Put your fingers lightly on the edge of it, like this."

Leah placed her fingers on it and looked around the room.

Tyler continued. "Then you just need to ask for someone from the other side and see if they answer."

Ashley and Steven joined in, Steven nuzzling his pinky against Leah's. Leah looked up at Ashley's ceiling. "Okay. Well, is someone here?" Her fingers felt a flush of warmth, and she looked back down at the planchette. It hadn't moved. She left out a quick laugh.

"Guess not," Steven said.

The planchette jerked on the board, sliding an inch before Ashley pulled away. She let out a scream, and Tyler laughed. Ashley hit him on the arm. "It's not funny, guys! One of you is pushing it!"

"I'm not doing anything," Tyler said. "I swear!"

Leah looked back down at the planchette, and it continued to drift toward *Yes*, the magnifying glass hovering over it.

"Dude, we've got contact," Tyler whispered. "Ash, put your fingers back on. It won't bite, I promise."

She huffed before returning her fingers to the planchette.

"Don't move it again," Steven said to Tyler.

Tyler groaned. "I swear on my mother's life that I didn't."

They all sat in silence as the party downstairs roared on. Leah frowned. "So, what should I ask it?"

Ashley leaned in and shouldered Tyler. "I've got a question." She cleared her through and closed her eyes. "Oh, spirit from the other side, is this the best party ever?"

The planchette circled around the board before coming to a halt.

"No," they said in unison.

Ashley let go of the planchette and crossed her arms. "Well, this ghost is rude." She huffed and elbowed Tyler. "If you are the one moving it, I swear you are in for a beating."

"Come on, guys, it isn't me. I promise. Put your fingers back on the planchette."

Ashley rolled her eyes, uncrossing her arms and placing her fingers back on the planchette. "Who's next?"

"I'll go." Steven leaned into the board. "I need to know what makes them think this party isn't awesome." He cleared his throat. "Um, spirit. How are you?"

Leah cocked her head and eyed Steven. "How are you? Um, they're dead. So probably—"

The planchette slipped away from *No* and drew a straight line from letter to letter. Leah spoke the letters as the planchette stopped.

"C,"

"O,"

"L,"

"D,"

"Cold?" Ashley scoffed. "Well, me too, Ghosty."

A chill bore down Leah's spine, like an icy finger tracing down her back. She jumped and turned around, glancing at the space behind her.

"You alright?" Ashley asked.

Leah turned back, rubbing her forehead. "Yeah. Fine. Just thought I felt something."

"You've got your work cut out for you if there's a pervy ghost attracted to Leah," Tyler said to Steven.

Steven nodded at Leah. "Why don't you ask it a question? Maybe you'll get something good out of it."

Leah focused back on the Ouija board. "Are you alone?"

Her fingertips grew warm again, and for a moment she thought the noise from the party had become louder. She focused on the sound and realized it wasn't coming from the party. Whispers sounded throughout the room, nibbling at her ears with an inaudible track.

The planchette stopped moving.

"No."

"Okay, so the pervy ghost has a pervy army. Great." Tyler muttered.

Leah's stomach churned, and she shrunk into herself. The whispers stopped, but she felt a pressure surrounding her, like icy hands resting on her shoulders.

"Can we stop? I don't like this," Leah said, pulling her fingers from the planchette.

"Aw come on, we're just getting started," Tyler said.

Steven bumped his shoulder into Leah and smiled. "I'll keep you safe."

Leah smirked and met Ashley's stare. "Fine, okay, whatever," she said, placing her fingers back onto the planchette.

"Okay. How about this then? Oh spirit, what is your name?" Ashley asked.

The whispers grew in Leah's ears, and this time she could hear small bits and pieces.

Kill them. Tear them apart. Wear their skin. Be the flesh. Warm. Blood.

The planchette streaked across the board, thrusting their arms above letters before zipping to another letter. Ashley tried to follow along, shouting the letters as they stopped.

"A,"

"S,"

"M,"

"O,"

"D,"

"E,"

"U,"

"S."

Darkness closed in around Leah, the whispers ebbing at her ears. She needed to be free. She leaped back, and the light above them popped, casting them in darkness. Leah felt the fear close in all around her. She heard the bookshelf rumble and the closet door slam shut.

Ashley screamed before flipping on her bedside lamp.

"What the fuck was that?" Ashley shouted.

Leah looked around the room. Glass scattered across the board, books and other knickknacks fell off the shelves.

"An earthquake, maybe?" Steven rubbed his hands, his face pale.

"Sure, Steven, keep telling yourself that." Tyler said.

How could it have spelled that name? Leah felt her knees trembling. She shook her head and looked over at Ashley. "I have to go."

"No, don't go, please. We can play something else. Something less," Ashely shot a glare at Tyler, "terrifying."

"I . . . I'm sorry. I just . . . I need to go." Leah left the room, racing down the hall and out of the house, ignoring the shouts from Steven asking to walk her home.

CHAPTER 6

MORNING DELAYS

"Leah," a voice whispered, breath hot in her ear. "Leah."

An icy chill drew down Leah's back. She sat up, the pounding at her door matching her heartbeat. Her father shouted from the other side. "Leah! Get up! It's almost ten, and we need to be on the road by noon."

She groaned and stretched, enjoying the comfort of her bed. She wished she could stay there, wrapped in covers all day.

"Are you up? Don't make me come in there and dump a bucket of water on you."

She rubbed her eyes, trying to ignore the room as it spun. "I'm up, I'm up. Just give me a minute." She uncapped the half-full bottle of water she'd grabbed from the fridge before crawling into bed last night. Grabbing her phone off the nightstand, the battery light flashed red, and she noticed the charging cable wasn't plugged into the wall. She shoved the cord into the wall and laid back, staring at the ceiling.

Images of the Ouija board surfaced in her memory, the planchette spelling out the name *Asmodeus*, and she shivered. The whispers hadn't vanished when she'd left the room. They followed her, chasing her all the way home, calling from the shadows. It wasn't until she had slipped inside the house that the sounds had stopped altogether.

"Hurry up! We're leaving in two hours!" her mother shouted from the other side of the door before Leah heard her footsteps trailing down the stairs.

"Alright!" Leah shouted, standing up and clutching to her bed post for balance. She crossed the room and peeked out into the hallway. All clear. She tiptoed to the bathroom, brushing her teeth and sneaking two ibuprofens before jumping into the shower.

Wrapped in a towel, Leah hovered over two dresses laid out on her bed, unsure if she wanted to wear the cute black dress or if it was too somber for a wedding.

Her mother slipped into the room with a quiet knock. "Can we talk now, please? So that neither of us end up making a scene at the wedding?"

"Mom!" Leah shouted, tightening her towel. "We don't have time for this now. You know, the wedding."

"Listen, I know you don't want to talk to me, but you went to Ashley's last night, didn't you?"

Leah felt her heart leap out of her chest. She knew. Somehow, this time Leah didn't get away with it. She nodded and looked down at the floor. "It was only for a couple of hours. I promise. I—"

Her mother cut her off. "I meant what I said yesterday. We need to be careful, and I asked you not to leave. It's simple, Leah; I ask you to do something, and you do it. Why do you have to defy me every time?"

"Maybe I wouldn't if you just told me something for once instead of lying to me!" Leah stepped forward in her mother's face.

Her mother pointed a finger at Leah, a vein pulsing out of her neck. The anger emanated off her in waves, and Leah winced, holding her breath for the moment her mother exploded.

Her mother spoke through gritted her teeth. "Don't you use that tone with me, young lady! I have every right to withhold what I want. It's to protect you. Do you think this is just a little game? Grow up before you get someone hurt!"

Guilt washed over Leah, her stomach tying into knots, and she wanted to apologize, but the words didn't come out. She wanted to tell her everything about the whispers and the Ouija board, but the words melted away on the tip of her tongue.

"What the hell are we all shouting about?" her father said, stepping into the room, fully dressed and ready, wearing a blue suit and red tie.

"Ask your daughter. Maybe she'll tell you about her little adventure to Ashley's last night."

Her father huffed. "Leah! Really?" His face drooped, exhibiting the look of disappointment Leah hated to see.

"But Dad . . ."

Shaking his head, Leah's father looked at his watch. "We don't have time for this, Elizabeth. We've got to get going if we are going to make it at all." He turned back to Leah and looked past her, eyeing the dresses on the bed. "I'd say wear the light blue one. That's my favorite." He left the room.

Her mother groaned, following her husband as she hollered back, "Great, Leah. Now we're both in the doghouse tonight. Happy?"

Leah chewed her lip before studying the dresses. Her

insides cramped again, and she reached for the black one, just in case. She knew it would be the icing on the cake for her father. He'd understand, she hoped. She brushed out her hair quickly, dabbed on a little makeup, and eyed the Star of David pendant hanging at her desk.

She used to love wearing it, playing with the interlaced lines in class. Then her friends had made fun of her, pointing out that it wasn't a cross. Bringing attention to her being different, having opposing beliefs than them. The longer she looked at it, the more terrible memories surfaced. Shaking her head, she stood and headed downstairs.

A familiar voice sounded from the living room. ". . . telling me how to do my job. I get results, and that's what matters . . ."

The voice died off, and her mother spoke from the living room. "Leah, come here, please."

Leah stepped into the room, spotting the same handsome man she'd seen at the door yesterday.

Her mother rested a hand on the man's shoulder. "Leah, this is your uncle, Eric."

Leah tilted her head and narrowed her eyes as she gawked at the two of them.

Her mother continued, "He doesn't come around much because he's usually so busy with work. You're too young to remember the last time he was here."

Eric smirked and shrugged. "Yeah, work keeps me busy. Too busy. It's good to see you all grown up, though." He stepped up and wrapped his arms around her, a wave of nausea hitting Leah as the scent of alcohol wafted from his clothes.

"Uh, yeah," Leah said, peeling herself away from him and stepping back. "Good to see you too." She mumbled, not sure what else to say. "So, what brings you here?"

Eric glanced over at Elizabeth. "I picked up some work here in Chicago. Figured I'd stop by when I got the chance."

Elizabeth clasped her hands. "And I asked your father if he could come along to Ariel's wedding. To catch up on old times."

Leah eyed his clothes, certain they were the same ones he had worn yesterday. "And Dad's letting him go dressed like that?"

"Apologies. She's been having a rude streak." Elizabeth studied Eric's attire. "Although, she has a point. David should have something upstairs for you to wear. Might be tight in the arms, but you can't go looking like that."

"I'd rather not," Eric said. "I'm fine with—"

She waved her arm, and David stepped into the room, a piece of toast hanging from his mouth. "Okay, we need to leave. Eric, are you are still certain you want to follow us? I have room."

Eric shook his head. "No, that fine. I'm still on the clock, so I should drive myself in case I need to duck out early."

Elizabeth shook her head and looked at David, pushing Eric forward. "Whatever. Give me five minutes. I'll turn my slob of a brother into something presentable to your family."

David let out a long breath. "Fine, but make it quick."

He stood at the base of the stairs, tapping his foot and eyeing his watch.

CHAPTER 7
WEDDINGS AND DRINKS

Silence dominated the drive to the synagogue. Leah's father white knuckled the steering wheel, any hint of sound leading him into a spiral of muttering about how late they'd end up being.

They reached the synagogue in record time.

David's uncle, Moses, greeted them as they got out of the car. Leah slung her purse over her shoulder and leaped into his arms, knocking down his cane, and gave her great-uncle Moses a big hug. She was certain that her father got all his excellent jokes from him.

Her great-uncle smiled and looked down at her, his blue eyes peering over a bushy beard. She let go of him and reached down for the cane. Leah knew his limp wasn't from old age, but from something that had happened a time long ago. From the same place he received the tattooed numbers on his arm, hidden now by his blazer.

Her father came diving in for a big bear hug, practically lifting poor Moses off his feet. Leah knew how much Moses meant to her father. He had taken his nephew in after David's father died.

Leah didn't know her father's parents, and Moses had been more like a grandpa to her than them.

Elizabeth gave Moses a hug and kept her arm wrapped around him as they approached the synagogue. She turned, spotting Eric catching up to them after parking his car off at the other end of the lot.

The light inside struck Leah, and she took in the beautiful stained glass windows and chandeliers of fine crystal shining down on the blue and white flowers throughout the space. Her mother steered her to the left, leading her to the women's side as her father, Eric, and Moses headed right. She and her mother sat among distant aunts and cousins. Leah wasn't sure who she was actually related to as she waited quietly for the ceremony to begin.

Leah turned and spotted her father across the hall, seated a few rows back. The rabbi started down the aisle, followed by the smiling faces of the groomsmen. The man her cousin, Moses's youngest daughter Ariel, was about to marry anchored the line. He was handsome. With a perfect jaw and bright smile, Leah could barely keep her eyes off him.

Then a hum deafened her ears, filling in like white noise and drowning out the other sounds around her. She rubbed at them, but instead of silencing, the whispers started.

You're weak. Worthless. Kill them. Kill everyone. Blood. Flesh. Death.

Not again, she thought.

The whispers grew louder, and she reached up to cover her ears. Her eyes locked onto her arms, where several things seemed to wriggle just beneath her skin, trying to claw their way out.

She flailed her arms, brushing them before realizing they, and the whispers, had vanished.

Her mother grabbed onto her arm and mouthed, "What are you doing?"

Leah shook her head, eyeing her arms one last time before looking away toward the rabbi standing beneath the chuppah. It was designed as four beautifully illuminated trees, interlocking branches into a canopy at the front of the room. She traced the branches and breathed, trying to calm down.

The rabbi opened his arms, and everyone in the room turned to watch the wedding party as they entered.

Bridesmaids trailed past her, collecting at the front on the other side of the groomsman, all looking down toward the entrance.

Then the organ changed tune, and Ariel, dressed in a beautiful white gown, walked down the aisle locked arm and arm with her parents.

The crowd settled back into their seats, and the couple reached the chuppah. Whispers flowed back into Leah's ears, speaking in harsh chittering tones that cut at her ears, gibberish, foreign tongues.

She focused on them, drowning out the rest of the synagogue, trying to piece out the foreign words.

Names mixed in with the whispers. Names like Michael, Sarah, Helena. Why was she hearing all these names?

Her attention drifted back to the surrounding space, and she turned back toward her father and uncle.

Eric looked around the room, a stern look on his face. Leah wondered what was wrong with him, but then something pulled her attention to her father. As she stared at him, he sweat profusely. The humid temperature inside the synagogue didn't justify the amount of perspiration on her father. He wiped his forehead on an already doused handkerchief, and Eric leaned in to ask him something, to which he shook his head no. He stuffed the wet handkerchief back into his pockets and locked his eyes on the ceremony ahead.

Cold bore into Leah, and her eyes fell back on Eric, who stared directly at her.

She felt him staring right through her, the same look her mother gave her from time to time.

Leah shifted, averting Eric's gaze and trying to focus on the ceremony, the whispers quietly chittering in the back of her mind. She rubbed her palms, pushing hard into them with her thumbs, trying to ignore the voices.

The surrounding noise quieted to where she felt like she was the only person in the room. A whisper sounded in her ear, and she could feel the fiery breath rolling over her. *"Asmodeus."*

"Mazal Tov!" shouts exploded around her as the crowd stood up and clapped.

Ariel's husband had just stepped on the glass cup and was now pulling Ariel into his arms and dipping her, planting a kiss on her lips.

Leah couldn't hold it in anymore. She stood and pushed past the row of cheering people.

"Leah?" Elizabeth shouted behind her. "Leah! Where are you going?"

Leah's chest tightened as she pushed past the people, gasping for air as she stumbled into the center aisle.

She raced down the aisle, ignoring the stares as those that were cheering saw her. Leah broke out into the open air and took in the hot summer air.

"Leah! What's wrong?" her mother asked, pushing through the doors.

"Nothing. I just. I needed air," Leah said.

"I don't buy it, what happened—"

Her mother was cut off as the door behind her opened and the wedding party filtered out the doors.

Leah's father spotted them standing to the side and raced up to them, a smile wide across his face. "That was a beautiful ceremony, and Ariel is so astonishing in that dress, don't you think?" Her dad reached for Elizabeth's hand and added, "Not as astonishing as you, though, my love." He gestured to a separate building across the parking lot. "The Hora should start soon. Let's go grab some food while we can."

Elizabeth smiled at her husband and looked back at Leah. "We'll talk about this later."

They crossed the parking lot with the crowd and stepped inside. More white and blue flowers lined the walls and tables, along with drapes and streamers of the same colors. The scent of cured salmon and herbed goat cheese from the hors d'oeuvre table filled Leah's nostrils, but the knot inside her stomach turned those scents sour.

She gently wrapped her arm around her mother and pulled. "Mom, can we talk now?"

"No, they're going to start any minute. Your father won't be happy if his girls miss this."

Leah squeezed on her mother's arm. "Please. It's important. About last night. I . . . I did something—"

A song blasted over the speakers, drowning out Leah's voice as groomsmen entered the room, carrying chairs with the newly wedded couple seated on top.

They set them down at the center of the dance floor, and Leah's dad turned, grabbing onto both Leah and her mother, pulling them to the dance floor.

Her mother stretched out her other arm and wrapped it around Eric. Leah heard him shout, "No, no, I can't dance," but her mother held on with an iron grip and the four of them joined the circle around the newlyweds.

Ariel and her husband stood and slow danced while those surrounding them smiled with a gleam in their eyes.

The song ended, fading into the next track with a more up-tempo beat. People flooded the newlyweds, pulling them apart. Leah joined her mother and the other women as they surrounded Ariel and started a slow dance with her. Eric and Leah's dad joined the men, who pulled the groom away from his bride and interlocked arms with him, forming a massive circle around the women. They started dancing around the women, moving faster and faster around them as the music picked up speed. Soon enough, they were dangerously flinging around the couple, trying to keep up with the fast pace of the music. Others joined in, the circle growing, and Leah lost track of where her parents or Eric ended up.

Then the circle broke, and groomsmen forced the groom back into the center with his bride. Seconds passed, and the bride and groom were lifted out of the crowd on chairs while shouts erupted above the music.

Leah broke free from the dance and sneaked off the dance floor, finding a place to sit.

She spotted Eric nursing a flask he'd pulled from his jacket pocket. Apparently, he was even faster at fleeing dances than her.

"Not much of a dancer either?" he asked.

"Not anymore." Leah sat down next to him and sipped on a glass of ice water.

"You and me both." He raised his flask and waited for Leah to respond with hers. She toasted him with her glass of water, smiling awkwardly and giving it another sip while she eyed his flask. It was an old and tarnished thing with an intricate Celtic knot etched into the side.

"What's in that?"

Eric drowned another gulp, then shook the metal container. "Scotch . . . mostly."

Leah tilted her head. "Mostly?"

Eric shrugged. "I like my drinks with a little kick."

"But isn't scotch just straight booze? How can you have more of a kick?" Leah asked.

"When you drink to forget, you'll take what you can get," Eric said with a pitiful half-smile.

Leah looked at his knuckles, noting several scars and fresh cuts that trailed up his hands and under his sleeves. She didn't want to ask him directly why, but settled on, "So, what is it you do for a living?"

Eric looked at her and dropped his smile. He leaned back in his chair and straightened his shirt. "If I tell you, I might have to kill you."

Leah rolled her eyes, and Eric snorted out a laugh. Her uncle waved his hand and said, "No, really, I'm what you'd call a private detective, I guess. No real roots anywhere, just go where the boss points me. What about you? What do . . . thirteen? Thirteen-year-olds do around here?"

Leah pursed her lips and crossed her arms. "I'm fifteen."

Eric raised both hands. "Hey, no offense meant. So, no job? Then how's school?"

Leah shrugged. "No job. And I can't complain about school, I guess. Just finished freshman year."

Her uncle's eyes widened, and he ran a hand through his hair. "Freshman year. That's gotta be rough. Drama, hormones, and everyone berating you about your future." He chuckled. "I always tell Jade that . . ."

His voice caught in his throat as he stared off, then dropped his gaze to the table.

Leah frowned. "Who's Jade?"

Eric shook his head and looked at Leah. "No one. Just a bad memory. Never mind." He tipped his flask to his lips, paused, and shook it. He let out a sigh. "Need a refill."

Without another word, her uncle stood up and walked toward the bar. He left Leah with only her thoughts, and she wondered who this Jade was. An ex-girlfriend? Someone else? Eric was her uncle, but he'd lived a whole life Leah knew nothing about. A life that might answer who her parents were before she was born.

Leah's parents continued cutting a rug on the dance floor for what felt like an hour, weaving in and out of the undulating crowd. She grabbed herself a plate of appetizers and settled into her seat, picking at the small square of smoked salmon and beets. Eric, now on his third refill of scotch, leaned back in his chair, finally looking relaxed.

The music shifted from the frantic celebratory melody to another slow ballad, and the dancers moved apart, grabbing partners and making space on the dance floor.

Leah spotted her parents, her father laughing and stumbling, even more sweaty than before, buttons on his shirt torn open as Elizabeth helped him back to the table.

"Your father apparently got a little too adventurous and tried to keep up with the others," Elizabeth said.

"Come on, she's basically my sister. What do you expect?" Her father's words slurred together, and he slumped into the chair beside Leah. She could smell alcohol permeating off him, certain she had seen a few groomsmen handing out shots in the middle of all the dancing.

"Eric, I'm sorry to ask, but this one overdid himself," Elizabeth said. "We aren't too far from home. He needs to sober up and get a new shirt. Do you mind staying with Leah?"

"We could go with. There's something I wanted—"

"No, Leah. Stay, mingle with some of your cousins. Ariel would love it if you talked to her," her mother playfully swatted at Leah's knee. "Have fun! Dance with your great-uncle Moses."

Eric took a sip of water and looked at his sister. "You sure we don't need to come with?"

Elizabeth shook her head. "No, please. Someone should have fun. We'll be back, I promise."

Leah dropped her head. "Sure, yeah, fine. Take your time."

"Great, that's settled, then. We'll be back in a few." She turned to her husband. "And you're having water for the rest of the night, you hear me?"

Elizabeth pulled David up out of his chair. Leah watched her mother all but carry her father to the front doors before she looked back at Leah and smiled, nodding to her and the dance floor. Leah smirked and waved her mom off, watching her leave the ballroom, leaving Leah with her estranged and increasingly intoxicated uncle.

CHAPTER 8
SOMBER NIGHT

The pressure in the room lifted the moment her parents left, as if whatever stress Leah had been feeling uncoiled. The tension in her chest fled and, even more jarring, that small nagging whisper in the back of her mind silenced.

She furrowed her eyebrows. Were the voices related to her parents somehow?

The scents of roasted halibut and buttery potatoes hovered in the air, melting her thoughts away as she focused on the table of food.

Her stomach growled, and she eyed the line, thinking of grabbing a plate.

No, something's wrong. The voices had to be connected to her parents, and she never had a chance to tell her mother. They were the same voices she'd heard last night. The same voices that have both said and spelled *Asmodeus*.

It was all connected, and now it followed her parents. Fear overwhelmed her, and her hunger fled. She had to get out. She had to warn them, *now*.

Leah shifted in her chair and glanced over at the exit.

Her uncle put his glass down and scratched his head.

"Well, I suppose now is as good as any for food. Want some?"

She chewed her lip, smelling the alcohol rolling off him. *He's too drunk. He'll only hold me up.*

"No, I'm good," she lied. "Go ahead. I'll grab some in a bit."

He raised an eyebrow. "You sure? You've barely eaten since I showed up at your parents."

She nodded. "I had some appetizers, besides . . ." Her stomach growled loudly, and she winced. "Uh, cramps. You know?"

He took the bait, widening his eyes and leaning back. "Oh, right. Well, I think I'll grab myself some grub. You sure you don't want anything?"

"I think I just need to use the ladies' room. Maybe you could grab me a plate of halibut and some ratatouille before it all goes away?"

Eric nodded and stood. "It'll be waiting for you when you get back."

Leah stood up and crossed the room, walking down the hall toward the bathroom.

If she was fast enough, she could catch them in the parking lot.

Leah didn't know what these whispers were, but with all the secrets her mother kept from her, there was no doubt now it was dangerous.

She slipped out the side exit, taking off her heels and racing into the parking lot.

The spot where they had parked was empty. She was too late. Leah scanned the parking lot, but there were no taillights leaving either.

She stared up at the sky and huffed. *Just my luck. Half-hour walk if I go fast, cut through a few alleys and parks,* she told herself. Leah paused. *Am I crazy? Maybe a little para-*

noid? Nothing responded.

She pulled out her phone from her purse and noted the black screen. *Dead.* She shook her head and clutched on to her shoes, marching out of the parking lot toward home.

I am crazy; she kept repeating to herself as she crossed through streets, following the path over bridges. *I'm getting worked up over nothing, and by the time I get home, they'll probably have left to come back to the party. Any minute, a car is going to pull over and my mom is going to wave me down.*

No matter how much she wished for it, no such car came. Fear continued to form knots inside her.

Clouds covered the moon by the time she reached the front of her house, darkness casting elongated shadows onto the front of her otherwise welcoming home.

She spotted the car in the driveway and frowned.

The lights inside the house looked off. *That makes no sense. What are they doing?*

She bit her lip. Her stomach churned, and something in the back of her mind screamed for her to run back to the reception and wait. *This is a bad idea,* she thought, as she walked up to the door of her house.

Leah grabbed onto the handle and the whispers surfaced again, a breathy hiss and a laugh ebbing at the back of her mind.

You're dead.

She turned the handle, and it clicked open. *Odd, the lights are off and the door's unlocked?*

Thick, hot air rolled past her as she stepped into the pitch-black house. The hair on the back of her neck rose, and she opened her eyes wide to catch any hint of light that might help her see.

She flipped the switches on and off and on again, but no light illuminated the entry hall. *Did they blow a fuse?*

"Mom?" Her voice echoed through the house. "Dad? Are you guys home?"

She walked farther into the house, stopping to wipe her feet on the rug. She held her heels in both hands, pointy ends aimed out, just in case.

The whispers continued to drown out any other sound as she stepped into the kitchen. She flipped the light switch, but again, nothing happened.

She stepped forward, and the air grew dense, a thick miasma wrapping around her.

Leah reached into the junk drawer and dug around until her hands wrapped around the flashlight. The light beamed for a moment before flickering out.

"Stupid thing," she said, hitting it before it failed altogether.

Leah sighed and looked out the patio door. *This is stupid. Just go back to the reception. Get out of this house and wait for them to come back.*

She nodded to herself and swallowed hard, crossing the room and putting her hand on the door handle.

A whimper sounded in the entrance to the living room, and Leah felt a freezing shock shoot through her entire body. The voice whimpered again, this time loud enough for her to hear. "I didn't mean to . . . I didn't want to."

Leah's hand froze over the door handle, and she turned. The whispers echoed loudly. ". . . didn't mean to. Dead. Mistake. Mean to."

She turned, and the moon broke free from the clouds, casting silvery light into the living room. A beam of light drew the silhouette of a person sitting on the couch in the living room.

She took a deep breath and dropped her hand, turning and walking toward the silhouette. As she stepped closer, the silhouette became recognizable. "Mom?" Leah whispered. "Mom, are you okay?"

Leah stepped closer, the miasma of air growing thicker. The scent of metal filled her nose. She grabbed onto her mother's shoulder, wet and sticky.

Her mother collapsed. Leah stumbled back. Her face was cut to shreds, her lifeless eyes fixed on something beyond Leah.

Leah's entire world collapsed into an infinitesimally small echo of what had once been Leah Ackerman.

What did this mean?

"M. . . Mom?"

Her world shattered before her eyes. Moments became eternity, and she fell to her knees, staring down at the remains of her mother.

It couldn't be real. It can't be real.

She glanced around the room, her eyes settling on a figure in the corner. Her father stared down at his hands, which were dripping with a dark substance.

"Dad? What happened? What did you . . .?" Her voice was not her own, ripped from her throat and replaced with a high shrill.

Her father limped forward, moving erratically, his arms twitching and contorting.

A smile stretched across his face so wide that his lips split from the strain. He cocked his head sideways and stared at her.

"Hello, child."

The voice was guttural and breathy all at once, but Leah recognized it. It spoke with the same tone as the whispers.

The fear untangled inside her, flowing into every corner of her being.

She had no time to think, only to run.

Leah leaped back toward the kitchen and back door, but

icy fingers wrapped around her left arm. Pain seared through her arm, boring all the way down to her bone and sending a shock that made her see stars.

A voice resonated from her father's throat. "You're mine now."

She stumbled back, tripping, knees slamming onto kitchen tile. She flipped and crawled backward on her elbows, the fear surging into every corner of her body.

Her father stepped over her, reddish spittle dripping from his mouth.

The fear turned into a pressure, tearing at her skin, begging to be free.

She finally let out a scream, one that tore at her vocal chords as all her fear and rage was directed at her father in an explosive force.

Everything around her faded away into darkness.

CHAPTER 9

ROUGH JOURNEY

A cool breeze blew across Leah's face, carrying with it small drops of cold mist that dampened her hair.

She blinked, staring up at the night sky. Her body ached, and every joint in her body protested.

Leah propped herself on her elbows, feeling the carpet beneath her and squinting to focus on the surrounding ground.

She couldn't process the remnants of her home scattered about in heaps of rubble. The living room, kitchen, and her parents' room above were completely leveled. A small part of the second floor remained, half of her room torn apart as if by a vicious tornado. It creaked and teetered on whatever remaining support it had.

Sound creeped back into her ears, the melodic sirens of several car alarms filling them.

The memory of her mother, torn to shreds and staring lifelessly at Leah, resurfaced in her mind. She turned her head, peeking over the rubble where her mother had been and spotting the arm protruding out of the heap next to her.

"No, no, no!" Leah whimpered, rolling over onto her

stomach and crawling closer to the heap, the aches in her body fighting against her.

"Mom, no. Please, please, no."

She grabbed onto the stiff hand, tears blinding her vision.

"I . . . Mom . . . We were supposed to talk. You said you'd be right back. Mom? Mom!"

A flash of the smile surfaced in her mind, the lips of her father stretching inhumanly across his face.

She rolled onto her back and stared at the heaps of rubble.

Did I kill him? The question resonated inside her tightening chest, squeezing on her ribs. Pressure popped in her ears as the horror and agony blinded her vision with tears.

The pressure snapped like a rubber band, and all her joints burned. Rubble around her shifted and rolled away while she writhed and screamed from the pain.

The voice of her father played again in her head.

"I didn't mean."

He'd killed his wife, and he was going to hurt Leah too. What happened? Why would he do that?

A voice shouted out from behind the rubble. "Leah!"

Her eyes widened. The thought of her father calling out to her, looking to do the same he did to her mother crossed her mind.

Someone approached, climbing over the rubble.

She grabbed onto a broken chair leg, pointing the sharpened end out. Protection against whoever crawled over the rubble.

Her heart pounded, and a silhouette stepped over the debris. Her eyes adjusted, and the fear of her father coming back for more vanished when the form came into view, revealing it was Eric.

"Leah, are you hurt? Your mother, is she here?"

His eyes dropped onto the arm sticking out of the rubble.

"No," he whispered, dropping to his knees and grabbing the hand from the rubble. "Lizzy, no."

Leah trembled, pain emanating from him like small waves.

He sniffled and looked up, cocking his head, hearing the sirens off in the distance.

He wiped his tears on his coat sleeve and grabbed Leah's arm. "We need to leave."

"What? No!" Leah shook her head and looked back at her mother's hand. "I can't leave her here."

"Listen to me, Leah. We can't stay here. The thing that did this could be back any minute." Eric looked around. "And if you end up with the police, he'll know where you are."

"But I can't leave her." The words burned as she spoke.

Eric lowered his head. "I know. But she left you with me, and right now you need to trust me. You can't stay here, not with the police on their way. They can't protect you from . . . him."

His breath smelled of whiskey, but he looked far from drunk, his eyes piercing through her. Fear bubbled up inside her again, and she looked around, worried that her dad could rise out of the rubble.

Her vision settled on a small picture frame, cracked, but the photo inside was still intact. She reached for it and pulled the picture free. A younger version of herself stared back, a face full of spaghetti. Her parents stood behind her, her father looking lovingly at his mother instead of at the camera.

That smile was his, not the twisted grin burned into her memory.

She looked up at Eric. "That wasn't my father. He couldn't do that. He wouldn't do that."

Eric scanned the rubble. He drew a breath and reached for her. "I know. It wasn't him."

Leah stared at him, the man she'd never met until today. His eyes were her mother's eyes. *He knew it couldn't have been him.*

The sirens grew closer, and Eric shook his head, pulling on Leah's arm. "We have to go, now."

Leah nodded, folding the picture and squeezing it in her hand.

She let him pull her up, the warmth of his hand breathing life into her.

He wrapped her arm around his shoulder and helped her up over the heap of debris.

She looked back, catching one last glimpse of her mother's hand before stepping over the mound of wreckage.

Eric helped her into the car, her mind still in the rubble, still next to her mother, holding her hand.

The engine roared to life, and she ran a finger along the picture. Wishing she could be back in that highchair, laughing with her parents in front of a plate full of spaghetti.

The car pulled away, blurring the homes as Leah's neighbors started peering outside to see what happened. Flashing lights passed by the car, the emergency workers unaware Leah and Eric were involved.

"I didn't mean to."

The voice echoed in her head, the strain of her father's voice wrapped in the guttural, raspy whisper. The intertwined voices played over and over.

Her uncle sighed and ran his fingers through his hair. "Leah, I can't understand what you're feeling, but—"

"You're right, so just don't." The barrier within her,

the mix of fear and anger, built again. A wall she never wanted to tear down. He didn't deserve to be let in. No one did.

Eric sighed, staring forward on the road for a long moment before starting again. "She was my sister."

His voice cracked, and guilt poured into Leah for a moment. He was in pain too, but the wall Leah built didn't waver.

He cleared his throat. "I need you to decide something, and I need an answer now."

Leah turned to look at him, eyeing the sweat on his brow.

"I could take you to your great-aunt and uncle, Moses and Miriam. From what I saw at the wedding, they are good people. I could explain enough of what happened so they can keep you safe. You'll be with family, and I'll do what I can to protect you, but I can't guarantee that." He took in a deep breath, exhaling the strong scotch stench. "Or you come with me. I'll take you to a place. Somewhere that will help explain what happened tonight. You'd learn the secrets your mother kept. The skills she had, and the abilities you have."

She raised an eyebrow. "Abilities?"

Eric waved his arms around. "How do you think half your house exploded? They'll say it was a gas leak. If you're lucky, they'll mention swamp gas, but either way, it was you."

She let out a hysterical laugh, turning to look out the window. "That's ridiculous." But the feeling inside her knew he wasn't lying. "No, that can't be. That's not a thing."

"It is, and you'll learn way more than that if you come with me." He turned to Leah before focusing on the road again. "So, stay with your grandparents, forget what happened, and have a hopefully normal life? Or come with me? I need an answer now."

Leah pulled the picture out of her pocket and unfolded it, staring down at it as the lights on the highway passed by.

The secrets her mother had kept. The whispers. Could she really leave all that unanswered? She looked out into the dark. "I need to know what happened."

Eric nodded and held out his hand. "Hand over the phone. I need to check something."

"I . . . I left it in the rubble, inside my purse."

"Even better. Alright, try to get some sleep. We've got a long way ahead of us."

CHAPTER 10

FROZEN

Leah stood again inside a darkened home, a faint yellow streetlight beaming in just enough light to see the home wasn't her own. Small shoes lined the wall below a framed photo of a young, happy couple standing in the middle of a field.

She breathed, then gagged, the stale air dense with the taste of metal.

Not again.

Her translucent hand wrapped around the handle of the front door, but it wouldn't budge. She tried the lock, but even that was stuck in place, as if glued down.

She was trapped inside a home that wasn't hers, the scent of blood heavy in the air.

Her heart thrummed in her chest, pounding in her ears. She had to move forward and find a different way out.

She took a step, her eyes wide, peering into the dark. A snap sounded at her feet.

Her foot hovered, the sound echoing out from the room next to her. She turned her head, trying to locate the source.

Another snap, followed by another. They mixed with

another sound she couldn't put her finger on, something akin to a pile of wet clothes dropping to the ground.

A silhouette stood up in the center of the room, towering over the space.

Pins and needles shot through Leah. The silhouette's eyes locked on her as a raspy voice echoed out, "Leah."

Whispers rose in her ear, foreign tongues clawing at her mind.

The silhouette stepped forward, outstretching bloodied arms.

The light above her flickered on and off, and the silhouette laughed, the face of her father staring wild-eyed at her. "I see you."

He reached forward, wrapping his hand around her arm.

Pain seared in her mind, mixed with the scent of burned flesh.

She screamed.

He laughed.

Everything went dark.

Leah jolted, a beam of headlights shining into her eyes. She winced and wiped the sleep from her eyes.

The picture lay open on her lap, showing a once-happy family now broken.

Her parents gone, dead.

Pressure welled up inside her, the fear uncoiling and enrapturing her body.

The car swerved, and she heard her uncle shout, "Leah! Listen to my voice, come out of it."

Her uncle sounded miles away, muffled by the blood throbbing in her ears.

A force pounded against her chest, radiating like waves down her spine to her toes and fingers.

Whispers started again, and she squeezed her eyes shut and cupped her hands over her ears. But the voices continued. "He comes. Use it. Let it consume you."

Images of her home collapsing around her and power flowing out of her, tearing apart floorboards and disintegrating walls, flooded her mind. The voices were right; she should use that power, whatever destroyed her home. Using it again could destroy everything around her. Leah could let the world feel the pain she felt.

A loud crack sounded next to her.

She opened her eyes and saw the passenger side window shaking. A spidery fracture formed across it, spreading to the corners of the window. The car shook, and the radio phased in and out, the sound of Johnny Cash drowning out the whispers.

Her uncle's knuckles were white against the steering wheel as he shouted, "Stay with me! Focus. Breathe. Don't let it consume you. You don't want it to happen again. Please, stay with me. Breathe. In and out. You've got this."

He weaved through the lanes, an unseen force pushing the car.

Another wave emanated from her chest, and she heard a loud thud as Eric's head slammed into the side window. The car swerved again, and blood dripped from his temple.

He lost control, and the car spun out, racing toward the middle of the road and into oncoming traffic.

Eric clapped his hands and shouted, "Stop!"

Everything froze. The car, Leah, Eric, even the empty cans of coke hovering midair.

Eric turned to Leah, her eyes shifting about, her body locked in place and unable to move.

She met his strangely calm eyes, pupils dilated larger than they should be.

"Snap out of it," Eric said. "I know it hurts. I know it feels like everything is collapsing around you, but you need to breathe. Let go of that feeling in your chest."

Her breathing slowed, his voice pulling her back from the encroaching void. The whispers deadened, and the darkness faded.

The catch in her chest unwound, and the fear inside her uncoiled into a small snake, slithering back from where it came.

Eric sighed. "Good. Now, just keep breathing, in and out, like I said before. We'll be there in a few hours if I still have a car by then. The Bishop, your instructor, will do a better job than I'd be able to. Give you a sense of control. Okay?"

She nodded, and Eric let go of her face, turning back to the steering wheel.

Leah looked through the windshield and spotted the other car, frozen still, the driver's face beat red with tears streaming down their face. She was certain they were about to have a head on collision.

Eric let out a long sigh, and the hold over Leah vanished. The airborne trash fell straight down onto Leah's lap, the trajectory completely stopped in their tracks.

Eric shifted the car back into park before turning over the ignition of the killed engine. It roared to life, and he turned the wheel, driving off. The driver in front of them slammed their hand on the horn, screaming inside their car.

"We're lucky there was only one. No one will believe them," Eric said.

Leah waited until the other car was long lost in the rearview mirror before she spoke again. "Where are we going?"

Her uncle turned off the highway and onto a gravel road. "Somewhere quiet and safe."

CHAPTER II

PIT STOP

The rays of the early morning sun broke through the horizon as Eric shut off the ignition. Eric let out a yawn before looking at Leah. "Good, you're up. We're halfway there, and I brought us to my favorite donut shop, Flyby's."

Leah looked to the small building, blue and gray lined with a bright yellow sign that spelled out Flyby Donuts around a strange drawing of a donut with wings.

She rubbed her eyes and noted two large empty coffees in the cupholder already, and another cup lying on the floor.

Eric opened his door and unbuckled. "I figured we could get out and have a stretch."

She adjusted herself, wincing from the stiffness in her back. "Where are we?"

Eric glanced over at Leah, bloodshot eyes scanning her. "We've been headed west for over five hundred miles. We passed into South Dakota about half an hour ago."

Leah looked outside the car again. A few others had lined up outside the donut shop before it opened. She unbuckled and hopped out of the car, along with Eric, and stretched. "What's in South Dakota?"

"You'll see." He nodded to the building beside the donut shop with the name Scooter's Drive-Thru Coffee written on the front. "Mind getting me a large black coffee? Oh, and a box of donuts. I want to check our tires quick. You can get whatever, then head back here."

He pulled out a wad of cash from his pocket and picked out a twenty and handed it over. "Don't go wild. We still have a long drive ahead of us."

Leah dropped her head and smoothed her dress as much as she could, a dirtied remnant of the night before. The sweet scent of donuts wafted over her, and her stomach growled. But the idea of food sickened her. She took in a slow breath, holding back tears. Her parents were dead; how was she supposed to just get donuts like everything was okay?

She met eyes with the clerk, a large woman, who immediately scanned Leah up and down.

"Oh, my God. Are you okay?" the woman asked.

Leah bit her lip and nodded. "I just want two coffees and a box of donuts. I don't care what kind. Surprise me."

The clerk glanced out the window, spotting Eric at the car. "Do you need me to call someone? I can keep you in back, hun."

Leah shook her head. "He's family." Tears rolled down her cheeks. "I promise I'd take you up on your offer if I didn't feel safe."

The woman looked at her a moment longer, then started on her order. When she handed over the receipt, she wrote a number down at the bottom. "If you're ever . . . not okay . . . call this number. Okay, hun?"

Leah gave the woman a half-smile and took her things, leaving without another word.

Leah found Eric seated at the only outside table. She handed him the coffee and change, and he opened a small box of donuts and grabbed a chocolate glazed one.

After taking a bite, Eric said, "Eat."

"I'm not hungry," she whispered.

"I know, but you need to eat. Come on."

Leah took a deep breath as her eyes fell on a blueberry glazed. She scooped it up and began picking it apart and popping it into her mouth.

After a moment of silence, she looked at Eric. "So, where are we going then?"

He took in the morning air and looked out west, away from the oranges and yellows covering the predawn sky. "There's a Square outpost in Mystic, South Dakota. It's the closest one I know of that I can drop you off at. You'll be safe there."

Leah raised an eyebrow. "Square outpost? What's that?"

"Somewhere you can learn."

Leah looked down at her food. "Oh."

"What is it?"

"I just thought that you would take me in. I didn't know you were dropping me off at some daycare."

Eric shook his head. "It's not like that. I can't teach you right now. Not permitted. We have others who do that. You have to learn how to control what you did." He looked back to his car, eyeing the cracked glass. "Preferably somewhere far away from my car."

"Not permitted? So, what is this, some kind of cult?"

Eric laughed and picked up another donut, tearing it in half. "No. More like spies, or the military, if you wanted to relate it to something. I'm more like a soldier, and you need an instructor. Think of it like boot camp."

Leah looked out past Eric and to the road, where cars and buses began filling the streets the longer they sat. "Great. I've always wanted to be shipped off, away from my friends, and go to boot camp. That's *exactly* what I wanted to hear. Anything else I can get out of you before you ditch me?"

Eric sat back and brushed off his hands, grabbing his coffee and standing. "It won't be easy, but it'll be worth it. Trust me. And I'm not leaving you. I'll take a post nearby and figure out what's next. Work on some cases and try to get some answers. I'll stop by and check in."

Leah cleaned off the table and tossed the trash into the garbage. Light from inside the donut shop caught her eye. She looked up to see her face, plastered on the screen of the morning news, alongside the pictures of her mother and father, with the headline: Gas Explosion Near Chicago Kills Three."

Something rose inside her—a fear settling in her throat, tearing to get out. Her heart raced as images of her home flashed all over the television.

She turned and raced past Eric, hopping into the seat and crossing her arms.

He got into the car, looking at her. "You alright?"

"Yeah. Just go. Please."

Shaking his head, Eric started the car. "Ok then."

CHAPTER 12
MALCHUT

Thoughts kept poking at Leah's mind as they drove back onto the highway. She was dead; the authorities had declared her as such, along with both her parents. There would be a funeral for her. Within days, there'd be a stone in a graveyard somewhere to remember her by. How would her friends react? What would it be like for Leah to go see her own tombstone?

They even claimed her father was dead, though she didn't believe so. Even Eric still considered him to be alive, hiding somewhere. Waiting to leap out from the shadows.

"Could we talk about something? Anything. Please?"

Eric turned down the radio. "Like what?"

Leah shook her head. "Anything that will let me know what I am getting into. Like this thing I did. What is it? Where did it come from?"

Eric looked at the clock and then at a few road signs. At first, Leah thought he had just ignored her, and the feeling inside her clawed at her insides. Then he spoke, his gaze still forward. "It's a connection. One that I, and your mother, have. It lets you do things. Other things. The more you train, the better control you have."

Leah furrowed her brows. "What kind of things?"

Eric shook his head and tightened his grip on the wheel. "I shouldn't be telling you any of this. We have rules."

She took in a sharp breath. "Please answer me before I do it again. It'll help keep my mind off this feeling in my chest."

He looked at her, and for a second Leah thought she saw a glimmer in his eye, the same as when her mother had been worried about her. "Fine. If it will help." He took in a breath and looked back at the road. "It lets you do things like push things away with your mind. You have a connection to what some call the Astral world. Basically, your spirit. Last night you called on that connection. Which is how your house blew up. You accessed the first energy, *Malchut*, the Warrior."

The catch in her chest came unhinged. "Are there others like us? Did they blow their homes up?"

Eric shook his head. "Few have the awakening that you did. You and I are called Mystics. I am part of a secret organization that calls themselves the Infinity Board. We keep the balance between things like demons, who try to knock the scales."

The word 'demons' ignited a memory in her. His face looking back at her. That smile across his face. She shook her head. "Secret organization? That's just—"

He looked over at her. "You saw what we're up against. There are plenty more where that came from, and something needs to keep them in check."

Leah clenched her fists, feeling her nails dig into her palms. That smile still ebbed in the back of her mind, duplicating over and over again, thousands of toothy grins torn out from helpless faces staring back at her. "I can't. I can't do this."

Eric hit the steering wheel. "Dammit, this is why I'm

not the instructor! Look, it's a lot. It's weird, even." He shook his head and muttered the next bit under his breath. "I should have just kept my mouth shut and left it to the Bishops."

She wanted to ask more, but she rolled her window down instead, taking in deep breaths of cool morning air, allowing time for her mind to slow.

The image of her mother surfaced from the sea of dark surrounding her vision. The warm glow of her face pulled her free from her thoughts, drawing her back from the abyss she'd spiraled into.

She closed the window and looked down at her fingernails, picking at them. "What happened to my parents? My dad, the way he whimpered and smiled. It felt all wrong. He . . . He wouldn't do that. He loved her. He couldn't . . ."

Eric shifted in his seat, rubbing his neck with his hand.

"I don't know, Leah. I don't think this is something I can . . ."

"The demon. It was Asmodeus, right?"

Eric tightened his grip on the steering wheel. "You overheard us?"

Leah pulled the folded picture from the center counsel and looked down at it.

Finishing his coffee, Eric cleared his throat. "I don't know for sure, but it looks like it. The Board would have to give me access to some more info before I could make that call."

Leah raised an eyebrow. "But you knew he was coming. You warned her. Didn't this Infinity Board give you information on it?"

Eric shook his head. "I came on my own after I heard."

Leah clenched her jaw. He knew about it. He'd known Asmodeus was coming. "Why didn't you call then? You could have told her sooner."

"Phones can be tapped. I wasn't supposed to be there."

"But—"

Eric shot a glare at Leah. "Don't you think I would have wanted to call? Enough! Your Bishop will fill you in on what you need to know. No more questions."

"I just want the truth," she said, looking out the window. "I want to know. Why me? Why her?"

"And you will, in time." Eric reached for Leah, his warm, callused hand resting on hers for a moment before he brought it back to the wheel. "Lizzy was my big sister, you know. It may not be as hard as it is for you. Even so, I have to follow protocol. And you will too, if you want to learn what happened to your parents. If you want justice for them."

Justice.

That piqued her interest . . . something she could at least hold on to.

CHAPTER 13

OUTPOST

The badlands turned to forest, and more gravel covered the roads as they rode on. Woods towered over them, and hours passed, the sun obscured by the trees.

Eric turned a corner and slowed the car. Ahead, Leah spotted three wooden buildings with boarded-up windows like a scene from a horror movie.

"Welcome to Black Hills Outpost. Home sweet home, for now," Eric said.

Leah peered into the dense woods. "So, where's Jason?"

"Who?" Eric asked.

Leah rolled her eyes. "You're kidding me, right? Hockey mask. Kills campers."

Eric laughed. "Should be here any minute to see you off. Leatherface should be around somewhere too."

"Ha. Ha. Real funny." Leah looked back toward the buildings. "It's, uh, quaint."

"This town was abandoned about fifty years ago. Not sure why, but either way, it still has electricity, so that makes it one of the better outposts. There's no one around for miles. It makes an ideal place for exploding things, if you ask me."

Leah stared at the crack in the windshield. "I'm sorry, by the way. I'll pay for it."

"Sure, I'll invoice you later." He smirked. "For what you went through, that's a small price to pay. Hopefully, here you can gain a little more control. Maybe enough that I'll let you ride in here again."

"Hilarious." Leah half-smiled. She paused, her hands cold, and the thought of the fear boiling inside her surfaced again. "But what if I can't?"

"You'll be in excellent hands. Black Bishop Sachs trained me, and I turned out alright." He paused. "Well, alright enough. She's strict, though. Especially for hard-heads like us."

Leah wasn't sure if she should take offense, but something else caught her attention. "Black Bishop?"

"Her title. We all get one. You'll be a Square to start, but she'll tell you all that." He hopped out of the car. "Let's do this."

Leah stepped out and stretched, her legs and back straining to be free from sitting. She took in the scent of the surrounding woods, a rich pine scent that reminded her of the time her parents drove her up to the Wisconsin Dells.

Eric led her up to the building, the wooden porch groaning and popping as they crossed it. He knocked on the door once, waited a few seconds, then knocked twice.

Footsteps approached, and a voice spoke on the other side. "Who's there?"

"It's B8," Eric said. "I'm bringing in a potential piece for the Board."

"Who am I to care?" The voice sounded soft and kind, but commanding.

Eric continued. "You are C8, shaper of potential pieces into sevens."

The door opened, revealing a tall woman, thin with high cheekbones, black hair, and thick eyeliner bringing out her striking dark eyes.

"Eric Mizrahi, what a pleasure." Her lips pursed, and she looked down at Leah. Her eyes shimmered yellow for a second, then she raised her eyebrows and looked back at Eric. "This outpost is far from your jurisdiction."

"Black Bishop Sachs," Eric said, dropping his gaze to the floor. "I apologize, but we had nowhere else to go."

She clicked her tongue. "Call me Alma, Eric. You don't need to be cordial with me. Care to explain why you are here?" She spoke coldly, her eyes piercing through Eric.

"This is my niece, Leah Ackerman."

"Ah. Daughter of Elizabeth Mizrahi?"

Eric nodded.

"The Mizrahi bloodline still shines, I see." She glanced over at Leah. Her gaze softened, and she almost smiled. "I'm afraid I have no vacancies for a new Square at the moment."

Dread filled Leah. Something inside told her this was her one and only chance to get the answers she wanted. Her heart raced, and she blurted out, "Look, we've been driving for hours down dirt roads in the middle of nowhere. I don't know what this is all about, but I just want some answers. I need to know what happened to my parents. And why Asmodeus—"

Fingers dug into her shoulder, while Eric hissed. "Silence, Leah!"

Alma raised her eyebrow. "I see you've been busy filling her head with many things you shouldn't be."

Eric pulled Leah back. "She's suffered a great trauma. It

woke inside her before I spotted it. Her mother . . . my sister . . ."

Alma dropped her stern posture, a great sadness washing over her face. "Say no more."

She stepped toward Leah and rested a hand on her shoulder. "I wish we could have met on better terms. Tell me, what do you know of what has woken inside you?"

Leah lost control of the words as they spilled from her mouth. "It was my house. There was . . . My father, he was . . . He was going to hurt me. Something happened. When I woke, the house was gone."

Alma nodded. "That would do it. Some of the most painful trauma comes from family."

"But it wasn't my father. The smile, it wasn't his," Leah said.

Alma paused, staring at Leah for a long time, before turning to Eric. "You will transfer to this jurisdiction at once. I will not put my other students in danger without the additional protections."

Eric nodded. "Yes, I'll call the Board."

"I presume you haven't notified them of our fallen former White Knight? You will do that as well. She may have defected, but she deserves as much recognition as the rest of us. Maybe even more." Alma turned back to Leah. "I am sorry for your loss, child. A Knight assigned to recruitment should have collected you and brought you to your appropriate outpost. Your uncle is not a recruiter, and we are already two months into training." She began pacing the porch before she continued. "However, from the sound of it, you may have a target on your back. This would make it dangerous for you to be traveling. The path ahead will be difficult. I am strict, and I expect my pupils to become respectable Black Pawns for the Academy." She turned to

Leah and crossed her arms. "You will not receive special treatment. Do you still want this?"

Leah shifted on her feet before speaking as clearly as she could. "Yes, I do. I want to learn. I want to fight. I want justice for what happened."

"Justice or revenge? Either way, it'll pull at your heart and make you unpredictable and chaotic." Alma tapped her finger to her chin, her other hand behind her back. "Before we can move forward, you must relinquish all possessions of your previous life. Consider it your first test, or your entry exam. The Infinity Board can grant you answers to questions you never knew you had, but first you must prove you will give up everything."

Leah looked down at the porch. "I have nothing left. I destroyed my home. I have nothing to go back to."

Alma frowned. "You are telling me you left everything behind except the clothes on your back?"

Leah squeezed her hand, feeling the edges of the photo press up against her hand. "Not everything." She unfolded it slowly, the dim light enough to see the image of her family.

"That will suffice, then." Alma stood tall, linking her hands in front of her and staring at Leah.

Leah traced the image of her mother with her finger. She brought her hands to the corner of the image, pulled slowly, and felt it tear.

Her fingers grew numb, and the smiling look on her mother's face flashed back to the image of her on the sofa. She locked eyes on the image. On the memory of her mother from a better time. "I . . . I can't. Not this."

"Then I can't teach you. Not until you can show me you are willing to set aside your emotions and relinquish your possessions."

Leah pursed her lips, mimicking Alma. "Then forget it."

CHAPTER 14

PAIN & KINDNESS

Leah hopped into the passenger seat and slammed the door behind her, ignoring her uncle's protests. She looked down at the picture in her hand, the image of a happy family, of a time long before things turned sour. How could she give that up, and why would she?

Eric unlocked and opened the door. "Leah, get out of the car."

"No!" She crossed her arms and stared forward.

"You're being a brat! It's just a picture. She isn't taking your memories." After realizing Leah wouldn't respond, Eric's voice hardened. "I warned you, this wouldn't be easy. You want answers, right?"

"I'm not giving this up. I gave up everything else."

Eric huffed and slammed the door, walking around the car and plopping into the driver's seat. "Listen, I asked you if you wanted this life. I told you there would be sacrifices. I know this is hard, and that picture means a lot to you, but this is part of the process. Hold on to the memories you have, all the other times this picture doesn't capture."

Leah looked out toward the building. "I think I made a

mistake. I should be with my grandparents. I shouldn't have agreed to come."

"You already made that choice. It's too late now. The Board knows you exist, and I can't hide you from them."

"So what? What would they do?"

"Lock you up, at the very least. A young Mystic, unwilling to learn. You'd be a liability."

Leah fought back tears. "Why me? Why did it have to . . ." Tears dropped onto the picture, blurring the smile on Leah's younger self.

They sat in the car for a long time, neither speaking, while Leah cried. The realization that her parents were gone hit her, and the pain finally burst free from her.

Eventually, Eric broke into her sobs, his voice gentler than before. "The Infinity Board will give you your answers. I wish she wouldn't ask you to give this up, but she's testing you. Seeing if you are ready. We all have to make sacrifices eventually, and I guess she needs to see what you are willing to—"

Eric stopped mid-sentence, catching Alma's gaze as she stood at the edge of the porch, her hands clasped behind her back.

"But for now, I can't stay out here with you. I have business to take care, now that I'm caught up in Black Bishop Sachs's . . . I mean Alma's game too. I hope you'll come around and join us."

Eric pocketed the keys and hopped out of the car, leaving Leah alone on the graveled road with nothing but a burned-out streetlight keeping her company.

Leah sat in the car for hours, the seat leaned as far back as it could as she watched the sky turn from a pale red to purple. Lights from within the building turned on, and she could see movement from inside. Was anyone looking for her? Would anyone find her if they even tried?

Someone tapped on the window, and she jumped. A girl with dark copper skin, two large brown eyes, and a mass of long, black, tightly curled hair stared at her from the window.

She reached for the lock, a primal fear rising that someone or something was trying to get in, trying to take her.

Dark copper hands pulled back the curled hair, and Leah caught sight of a girl, not much older than her, smiling back at her.

With her hair out of the way, Leah saw the girl wasn't alone. Behind her was a younger pale boy, his green eyes wide as he kept glancing back toward the building.

The girl rolled her hand in a circular motion and pointed to the door. Leah rolled down the window a small crack in response.

"Well, pardon my French, but you look like shit," the girl said, pressing her face closer to the window. "Did he even feed you? The Knight who brought me at least stopped a few times to let me eat."

"Sarah! Be nice!" the boy hissed.

Sarah smirked. "Ah, yeah, sorry. I don't really have a filter. You look terrible, though." Sarah paused, likely waiting for a rude comment back from Leah, but Leah didn't take the bait. Sarah pressed on. "So, yeah, I'm Sarah. And this is Isaac."

Isaac smiled and waved before turning to look back at the building again.

"Uh, I'm Leah."

"We've got a talker!" Isaac said. "We just wanted to see who we should be thanking."

Leah raised her eyebrow. "Thanking? For what?"

"You showed up in the middle of evening drills," Sarah said. "Alma dismissed us out of nowhere. Strange, since it was one of her punishments. Anyway, Isaac here tailed her, and that's when we saw you and that guy. He's a Black Knight, right?"

Leah shrugged. "I don't know. Is that a bad thing?"

"No," Isaac said. "It's just a status thing. He's probably a Black Knight if he's reporting to Alma."

"Oh. Then, I guess so?" Leah said.

"We had to wait until night to come out here, or else Alma might have our heads." Sarah smiled and leaned back. "So, you're one of us, right?"

Leah sighed. "I don't know what I am. Tired, for one."

They both laughed, and Isaac stepped closer to the car, his green eyes reflecting the moon like gemstones. "You really don't look all that great. You alright?"

"Just a rough couple of nights. Sleeping in a car probably doesn't help either." Leah looked down at the picture, folding it up.

She popped open the door and stepped out, stretching her arms high above her.

Sarah stepped back and waved her hand at her face. "Phew, maybe a shower, too?"

Leah dropped her arms to her sides immediately and stepped back from them.

Isaac elbowed Sarah. "Stop being rude." He looked at Leah. "It's not that bad."

Sarah shrugged him off and added, "We've had a few rough nights, too."

Leah crossed her arms. "Oh, really?"

"Yeah." She leaned in closer and whispered, "Black Bishop Sachs can be a real bitch sometimes."

Leah let out a laugh, and the other two whipped their heads behind them before shushing her, giggling as they did.

Sarah caught her breath and looked up at Leah, a broad smile across her face. "She's strict, but still better than any teacher I've ever had, that's for sure."

"Are there others here like you two?" Leah asked.

Isaac nodded. "There's eight of us here. We've been here about two months now. From what Alma's been teaching us about the society, I'm surprised you're even here. They seem pretty strict about starting outposts together."

"I think my uncle tried to make a special case for it. It doesn't matter though, 'cause I'm not joining." Leah's arms dropped, and she kicked the gravel.

"Why not? You've got powers, right?" Sarah asked.

"Energy," Isaac said, correcting Sarah. "Alma calls it energy."

"Oh, whatever! You know what I'm talking about."

Leah nodded and looked back at the cracked windshield. "Yeah, you could say I've got something."

"Then why wouldn't you join? We literally learn to throw things with our minds. That's pretty badass, right?"

Leah smirked and ran her fingers along the picture. The thought of letting it go crossed her mind, but it quickly faded. She shouldn't have to. They shouldn't force her to.

Isaac cleared his throat and looked at Sarah. "Maybe she's not ready. We shouldn't pressure her." He stepped closer to Leah. "Sorry. We didn't mean to bother you. We were curious, that's all. Especially since that guy and Alma have been arguing all night." He turned back to Sarah. "We should get going before we get caught out here."

Sarah frowned but didn't protest as Isaac started toward the building. She followed him a few paces before turning. "You hungry?"

Leah's stomach growled loudly. "Yeah. I am."

Sarah turned and smiled. "I figured. Stay put. We'll try to get you something after dinner. If you're still out here, that is." The two stepped into the building and shut the door behind them, Isaac looking back out the window at Leah, who leaned against the car, looking up at the purple night sky.

Darkness engulfed the surrounding forest, the only light coming from the dim incandescent lamp outside the front porch. Cold air blew past her and she shivered. She eyed the building, thinking about the warmth and food inside. Her stomach growled again.

Leah couldn't give Alma her picture. The thought of Alma ripping it up in front of her crossed her mind, and she couldn't bear it. She gritted her teeth, unsure how she could muster the strength to face Alma, knowing she'd have to give up the one thing left of her parents. *Why couldn't they understand?* This was all she had left, the only thing that seemed to pull the image of that stretched smile out of her head. The image of her dad in the corner, waiting for her to come home.

If Leah didn't have to give up everything, then she'd join Alma and the others. But she didn't know them. Sarah and Isaac seemed all right, but they were still strangers. Still, the thought of learning more about her energy, as Isaac had called it, intrigued her. The idea of meeting others like her, who could even potentially become friends, interested her.

An idea surfaced, and Leah looked in the car. She opened the door and grabbed a plastic bag from Flyby Donuts, lying on the floor.

She eyed the cabin, making sure no one peeked out from inside, and she crossed the gravel road.

Leah stepped into the forest, the trees looming over her and drowning out any light shining from the building. After her eyes adjusted enough to make out the shapes of the trees, they fell on a knotted tree, different from the others.

She unfolded the picture once more, trying to see the image and hold it in her mind. "I'm sorry." She placed it in the plastic bag, wrapping it tight.

Leah dug at the base of the tree with her fingers, creating a small hole.

With the bag in her hand, tears rolling down her face, she whispered, "Goodbye, Mom and Dad. I promise I'll be back for this."

She placed the bag in the hole and shoveled the dirt over it with her hand, covering it back up with leaves and pine needles. She then placed a large rock over it as a marker.

She stood over the burial site, the only one she could have of her parents, and let her tears fall. Time stretched on to eternity, her tears the only measure.

Then her stomach rumbled, uncaring of her grief and pulling her back to reality. She turned, rubbing the dirt from her hands onto her dress before stepping back out onto the gravel road.

Leah approached the car as two figures, one pale and the other dark, stepped out from the side of the house, dashing through the grass. She ducked behind the car, unsure what to expect, before the shapes turned into Sarah and Isaac. Sarah carried a small bowl, steam rising from it.

"Parmesan chicken and spaghetti. Nothing amazing, but Gabe at least knows how to cook. Alma couldn't cook if you handed her—why are you covered in dirt?" Sarah handed Leah the bowl, scanning her soiled dress.

Leah nearly ripped it from her hand, stabbing the entire chicken with her fork and biting off mouthfuls. "What do you mean, nothing amazing? This is delicious!"

"Wow, okay. I guess you really *were* starving," Sarah said. "I didn't think a couple of hours in the woods would turn you feral."

Isaac and Sarah stood bewildered long enough for Leah to devour the food, then Isaac broke the silence. "So, have you reconsidered? If you liked that, then you're going to love the pizza rolls."

Leah smirked and wiped away the red sauce on her cheek. "I thought it over."

"And?" Sarah raised an eyebrow.

Leah eyed the wooden building. "And no one will even tell me what I'm getting into. What do you guys do all day?"

Sarah shook her head. "We can't tell you much. But it's what I pictured boot camp would be, only with more crazy mind stuff."

Leah looked from the building to the two of them. "Can everyone do it, then? Break things?"

Isaac looked at the cracked windshield and shrugged. "Maybe not as much as this, yet. But yeah. I think Sarah here is getting real good at *Mal*—"

Sarah elbowed him in the ribs, and he hunched over, clutching his side.

"Dude, you wanna get us in trouble?" Sarah said, turning back to Leah. "We better get back before anyone notices."

A deep, male voice shouted out beyond Sarah and Isaac. "Leah!"

All three of them jumped, turning to see Eric standing about thirty feet away at the edge of the porch.

"Shit! You think he'll rat us out for bringing her food?" Sarah hissed.

Leah stepped past them, staring at Eric as Alma stepped onto the porch and stood next to him. Eric fidgeted while Alma stood firm, her arms interlaced in front of her, eyeing Leah.

Alma's mouth opened, but before she could speak, Leah stomped forward, cutting their distance in half, and chimed in. "Before either of you say anything, I . . . I'm ready to join."

Eric blinked a few times, his eyes wide. Alma barely moved while she spoke. "And are you ready to abolish all your possessions?"

Leah stepped onto the porch, standing in front of Alma. "The photo's gone."

Alma's eyes seemed to glow as they looked Leah up and down.

She stood in silence for a long while, before saying, "I see. Then, as a representative of the Board, I will accept you as my Square." She glanced at Eric. "I'm still displeased with the circumstances. In all my years as a Black Bishop, I've never inducted a Square two months late. You have a lot of catching up to do, including private lessons with me in the morning and evening, atop daily training." She wagged her finger. "And don't think you'll get out of daily chores. The path ahead will be hard. Can I expect you to do so with your head held high?"

Leah nodded. "Yes, Black Bishop Sachs."

There was a twitch in the corner of Alma's mouth, the faintest hint of a smile, before she nodded. "Then let's get you a shower and your new uniform. You will be up before dawn until you've caught up, and you will obey all the rules of this outpost. Is that clear?"

"Yes, ma'am," Leah said.

Alma stepped aside and opened her arm to the outpost entrance. "Very well. Sarah, you will wait here to escort Miss Ackerman to bed after I am done talking with her. Isaac, you are dismissed. Expect to have some extra chores on both of your lists tomorrow."

Alma looked at Eric and nodded. He smiled and patted Leah on the shoulder, and she passed by into the outpost.

CHAPTER 15

THE TREE OF LIFE

Three large leather couches surrounded a low table in the center of the living room Leah stood in. She eyed the enormous stone fireplace, wondering how cold the house got during the winter.

She'd entered the house and followed Alma down the hallway, passing by closed doors on her left before entering the living room to her right.

It looked more like an oversized log cabin to her, with walls composed of light-colored logs and a high ceiling above her. However, something felt off, like it was stale or devoid of life. Then it clicked.

There was nothing on the walls. No pictures, artwork, or even mirrors. They were completely bare.

Alma cleared her throat and said, "Follow me."

Leah followed her, Eric trailing behind as they crossed the living room into another space with two long tables and a sliding glass door leading outside. Leah spotted the opening to the kitchen while Alma rounded left, guiding them up wooden stairs that creaked and groaned all the way up. They turned and walked down the hallway, entering the last room on the left before the hallway turned.

A dark mahogany desk stretched across the room, papers neatly piled atop it. Books lined one wall, and three closets were on the other. Alma crossed the room, opening the closet farthest from Leah.

Leah noticed the massive painting that took up the wall behind the desk. It was the first painting she had seen in the house, and it featured a tree with two spheres floating behind it, one black and the other white.

Alma pulled her attention away from the canvas. "Clothing and shoe sizes?"

"Uh, medium, and seven."

Alma opened a wardrobe filled with clothes and shoes, and pulled a stack of neatly folded gray clothes, topping them with a pair of white sneakers. "We only have seven and a half, so you will have to make do for now. One of the other girls may need a larger size and be able to trade."

She held out a stack comprising her clothes, shoes, a towel, packaged undergarments, and socks. "You'll find toiletries and feminine products in the bathrooms."

She looked past Leah and snapped her fingers.

Sarah stood at attention and said on cue, "Yes, Black Bishop Sachs?"

"Show Miss Ackerman to the rooms and the bathrooms." She turned back to Leah. "Shower and head to bed. I'll need you rested when I collect you in the morning for private lessons before the day begins."

"What should I do with my clothes?" Leah asked, looking down at her dirtied dress.

"Throw them out. You don't need them anymore." Alma waved her off and looked down at her desk.

Leah looked down at her dress, running her fingers over the skirt. Her mom bought her this dress. Last summer, for a distant relative's bar mitzvah. It had happy memories lingering in the threads, now stained with her mother's blood. "Fine," she said.

"Any other questions, Miss Ackerman?"

"No. No more questions," Leah said.

"Good, then you may leave." She looked back at her desk and sat down.

Leah turned to the door and faced Eric. He looked down at her and smiled. "I don't know if your mom wanted this life for you, but I think she'd be proud, regardless. I'll help you find him. I promise." His eyes were still bloodshot, and she wondered how long it had been since he slept.

"Thanks. For everything" She forced a smile, and he nodded.

"See, it's not all that bad," Sarah said as she led Leah back down the hall toward the stairs. She cracked open the door and pressed her finger to her lips, leading Leah into the girls' dormitory.

It was dark, but Leah made out five beds lined along the walls, small lockers at the foot of each. Sarah took her to the end of the room, near a large window.

"It's a little drafty, but Alma had us pull it from storage and put it here. Drop your stuff, and I'll show you the showers."

Leah nodded and placed her things in the lockers, trying her best not to make any noise.

Someone turned over in one bed and hissed, "Geez, Sarah, could you be any louder? What are you even doing, trying to sneak into one of our beds?"

"Shut up, Paige," Sarah hissed and grabbed Leah's arm,

leading her back out of the rooms. Outside, she shook her head and glared inside. "I'd keep away from her if I were you."

"Why?" Leah asked.

Sarah glared at the door. "She acts like the queen bee and even has the platinum blond hair to match."

Leah wavered where she stood, ready to pass out from exhaustion. Sarah pointed to the restrooms down the hall, a clear placard for the girl's room, and farther down, another marking the boy's room.

Leah took the hint and walked down the hallway alone, into the bathroom, and into an empty shower stall. The scalding water sunk into her muscles and unwound the lingering tension built up inside her, carrying with it the dirt and dust that had caked on her. Memories washed away too. The blood and grime dripping off her numbed the memories of the past few days.

She toweled off and looked at her reflection in the foggy mirror. Only a few cuts and scrapes remained from the previous night. That, and the stained dress and heels piled up on the floor. Her old life was over. The person staring back at her wasn't even familiar, bags under her eyes and a stare Leah had never seen on her face before.

She turned and picked up her old clothes and dumped them in the trash, finding them easier to dispose of than the picture tucked safely away under the rock. She then slipped on a pair of gray shorts and a tank top, wrapped her hair in a towel, and crept back into the dormitory, tiptoeing over to her bed at the window.

The lumpy mattress recoiled against her, but she soon settled, feeling the exhaustion drag her away.

Sarah whispered near her head, "I'm glad you stayed."

Leah sighed, the world around her fading quick. "Me, too."

Cold pavement froze her ghostly toes as she stood in the middle of a foggy street.

Leah looked around, the streetlight above her flickering on and off. The homes were all dark and dilapidated, several with smashed windows or boarded up with spray paint defacing the brick walls. The street was empty. No other lights on, no homes lit up.

She turned again, ready to stare down an empty street, when a man in a long brown trench coat appeared. His face was smooth, and his ginger hair was short and cropped. He studied her with bright green eyes. The scent of incense wafted off him, and he sighed, speaking with a slight foreign accent. "Oh, it's you. Too bad we didn't get to you sooner. You could have been a great addition." He smiled, his toothy grin large and too familiar for Leah.

Fear uncoiled inside her. *Get to you sooner? He must be talking about Asmodeus.* The familiar serpent wrapped itself around her chest. Cold sweat broke from her brow, and she turned and ran.

He shouted out behind her, "No, wait!" But she was already gone, rounding the corner.

Her feet thudded hard against the ice-cold pavement as she raced down the street, finding more and more abandoned homes. After traveling a couple of blocks, she stopped to catch her breath, her heart pounding in her chest, goosebumps running down her arms.

Then a voice whispered in the distance. Not the man's voice, but the voice she hoped she wouldn't hear. Her father's breath tickling her ear. "Leah."

She whipped her head around, expecting to see that grotesquely stretched smile. Instead, the road was empty.

The voice sounded behind her again. "Where are you?"

Again, nothing as she turned.

Her breathing quickened, and she couldn't slow it down, a pain emanating in her chest. "What? What do you want?" she gasped.

Her echoes bounced off the homes, reverberating back at her and dying slowly in the deafening silence.

Then he sounded again, "You," as a fiery hand grabbed at her left arm, searing her flesh.

Leah took in a sharp breath, ready to scream as one hand squeezed her arm and another pressed against her mouth. Her eyes flung open to a darkened room, and she clawed at the hand around her arm, the one that had seared her flesh.

Her senses came rushing back to her, and the burning pain vanished. Instead, she looked down at a woman's hand. Tracing it back, Leah found Alma's stern look on her face, illuminated by the pale orange of the pre-dawn sky seeping in through the windows.

Alma waited patiently for Leah to calm her breathing and released her mouth from her grip, gesturing for Leah to get out of bed.

Outside, Alma spoke softly, as if Leah clawing at her hadn't phased her. "Wash up, get dressed, and meet me in the living room. Lessons start in ten minutes."

She shakily nodded, her heart still racing. Leah changed out of her sweat-soaked pajamas and into gray sweatpants, a gray shirt, and white sneakers before walking to the bathroom.

After splashing cold water onto her face, she studied the insignia on her left chest. Four squares were stacked to make one larger square, colored in alternating black and white, making what Leah assumed was a chessboard.

Chess again, she thought, wondering what the obsession was all about.

She walked down the stairs and into the living room, spotting the bundled blanket haphazardly thrown in the couch's corner. Glancing outside the window, she saw the empty spot where Eric's car should have been.

He already left. Without even a goodbye.

"I sent him away. If that is what you were thinking," Alma said. "After I had him transferred to my region, I was able to put him on a case that has been stumping my Knights for a while." Alma sat on a couch behind Leah, sipping on a cup of coffee. She stood and pointed to a set of closed doors across the room.

He'd said it would be like this. Said that he wouldn't be around. Even so, Leah hadn't thought he'd leave so soon. She still had many questions for him.

Leah headed into a classroom as large as the living room with desks placed in the middle of the room and a large green chalkboard in the front. Alma placed her cup of coffee down at the desk in the room's front and gestured to the smaller desks.

"Sit."

Leah dragged her feet, thinking of how little interest she had in being in a classroom. She passed by the first row of desks, only to be stopped by the sound of Alma clearing her throat.

"Up here, please." She gestured to the front row.

Leah obliged, sitting at an old desk at the front and center of the room. She looked down, noting the dozens of carvings on the desk from what looked like decades of use. One carving was both deep and well worn. Written, like calligraphy, stating, "Nicholas was here." Next to that was a poorly carved heart with "E+N" carved in the center. She also noticed a slew of dates, chiseled all the way back to the seventies.

"Something you're looking for?" Alma asked.

Leah looked up, then back down at her desk. "Yes, actually. Pen and paper?"

Alma shook her head. "We write nothing down here. All documents relating to the things I am about to tell you are maintained within the Infinity Board. All other notes would be immediately destroyed."

Leah nodded and folded her hands on her desk.

Alma clasped her hands. "Alright, first off, you're a Square."

"Eric mentioned that."

"Well then, as you know, it's a term we use for potential members. So, get used to it. And I am a Bishop. So, members of the Infinity Board expect you to refer to me as Black Bishop Sachs during lessons and trainings. Outside that, I allow the use of Alma, my first name."

Leah traced the etchings on her desk before shifting her gaze to Alma. "And that makes my uncle Black Knight Mizrahi. What about my mom? She was a knight as well?"

Alma nodded. "She was a White Knight before she left, a rank higher than Black Knight. But that isn't what we are here to talk about."

She paced the room, grabbing her cup of coffee and looking at the various maps and strange markings lining the walls.

"We keep you all safe, training groups of students at different outposts before you go to an academy for the trials. This one is called the Black Hills Outpost. It's best you become friends with the peers here, since it will only get harder from here on out."

Leah shifted in her chair. The idea of having to make

friends all over again seemed like a distant concern. She took in a breath and asked, "Did my mother come through here?"

Alma sipped her coffee. "You sacrificed your life before, to come to this outpost to learn. That includes answers about your mother. For now, you may know that it was my first year of teaching as a Black Bishop when I trained Elizabeth. That is all I will say on the subject. We have things we need to go over. Most importantly, I do not permit my Squares using their abilities without my supervision. None of you are trained enough for the control and discipline it takes to wield *Malchut.*"

Leah leaned forward in her seat. "You trained her? What was she like?"

Alma shot Leah a glare. "I said I was done discussing that subject."

Leah felt her face grow hot. She needed to know more about her mother, to know what she was like as a Mystic. Alma paused and stared at Leah, her lips pursed, waiting. Leah remained silent, obedient, certain that another question about her mother now wouldn't bode well.

Alma continued. "Great, then we will begin with the basics."

She turned around and unrolled a chart above the chalkboard, revealing a tree marked with an intricate set of spheres connected by lines written in Hebrew text. The title of the chart was printed in bold black letters at the top. "The Tree of Life."

Alma pointed to the bottom sphere, connected by one line to the sphere above it. Black text filled the bottom circle.

מַלְכוּת

Leah thought back to her memory of Hebrew, recognizing the text from what Isaac had said the night before and Alma just now. *Malchut.*

Alma stepped out of the way. "The tree is where everything starts and ends. It connects every living thing together within a vast river of energy, creating and destroying within a web of different energies working together to form natural balance."

Leah nodded. "Eric said we were Mystics."

Alma raised an eyebrow. "Did he? And what other things did he discuss with you?"

Leah shook her head. "Nothing. I was about to have another . . . episode, and I made him talk about it. Tried to keep my mind elsewhere."

"Well, Black Knight Mizrahi wasn't wrong. We are Mystics, yes." She pointed to the symbol of the Tree of Life. "Each of these represents different energies we could connect to, given proper training and time."

Leah nodded. "Eric . . . uh, Black Knight Mizrahi . . . he clapped his hands together, and everything sort of froze. Is that the energy you're talking about?"

Alma smirked. "Yes. He used a different energy, one that can stop movement."

Leah nodded and eyed the chart, following the ten spheres through their intersecting lines. "So, I could do it too? One day?"

Alma smiled. "With enough will, any student can access the full energies of the tree." She peered down her long, thin nose. "Very few have the will. Don't fool yourself into believing strength equals ability. What use is power if you cannot control it?" She pointed to the base of the image, the single sphere Leah knew as *Malchut.* "But for now, you are here, at the base of the tree. The point at which all who come to wield the power of the Tree start: *Malchut,* The Warrior." She traced her finger up the single line, connecting *Malchut* to the next sphere. "And this is *Yesod*, meaning The Bonded, connects you to everything else. But, for now, prove your control over *Malchut*, and we will consider bonding you to the Board."

Leah stared at the chart, following the intersecting lines up the Tree of Life, and staring at each node. "How far did she get?" Leah asked, speaking again of her mother. "You said with enough will . . ."

Alma clenched her jaw. "I said I was done speaking of your mother. You may have questions, but she left the Infinity Board so she could start a family without the Board's influence. I'm not interested in further discussion, and if you choose to bring her up again, you will get more than your daily drills today."

Leah averted her eyes from Alma's gaze, anger and frustration bubbling up inside her again. She wasn't going to get answers. She never was.

"It starts as a pressure in your chest, right? A feeling that comes after a moment of anxiety and spreads outward to the edge of your skin before bursting out?"

Leah turned back to Alma and took in a deep breath, feeling the catch in her chest unhinge and relax.

Alma pointed to the bottom circle, tapping on the letters מַלְכוּת. "*Malchut*, the first well. In Hebrew it means kingdom. In the old texts, it refers to the physical plane, the material world, what we see and feel. The energy from this well comes as a force or wave of energy that bursts from within and can destroy what it touches."

Leah leaned forward in her seat. "So, can we use it as a weapon?"

"Yes, nearly all the wells can be used as such once a Mystic learns to control them. However, all these powers also have equal opposites. Trying to access the energy too fast and without proper training will tempt you to use a different, more dangerous energy."

Leah took another breath, and the feeling in her chest all but vanished.

Alma grabbed a piece of chalk, drawing a cube onto the board. "Now, my last point to make is where this energy comes from. It should help in understanding how to use it."

Alma continued, but Leah stopped listening, her mind still focused on her mother. She wondered why she'd left. Her mother never spoke about the Board to her, never mentioning if it was a bad thing or not. Yet Leah wondered if she had made the right choice to join. What had she gotten herself into?

"Square Ackerman." Alma's voice pulled her from her thoughts.

Leah shook her head. "I'm sorry."

"Focus. The cube. Now again I'll ask, if everything we know exists within this cube, then what exists outside of it?"

Leah eyed the cube, which did not indicate what Alma was looking for. "Um, well, if the cube is the world, then the universe?"

Alma shook her head. "Not quite. The cube is the universe. Outside that cube is where the Tree of Life exists. It exists outside our understanding of the actual world. It's something more . . . metaphysical."

Leah raised an eyebrow and perked up. "My uncle said it was on the astral plane. That we call it over into the physical plane. Is that the same thing?"

"So, *he* did tell you more than he should." Alma sighed. "Yes, that is a simple way of putting it, but I teach my students to think beyond just the idea of spirit and physical. The Tree of Life exists on another plane, or dimension.

That will mean more as you come to fully understand it, but for now, you just need to know it exists elsewhere."

Alma grabbed her mug of coffee and took one last swig. "Well, that is all for this morning. I've oversimplified, more than I would have liked, but I need you to understand a few things before practical tests today. For now, go get some breakfast with the others." Alma headed toward the door.

Leah thought of something she had heard, a hint she believed she almost had. "Black Bishop Sachs?"

Alma turned. "Yes?"

"This idea of other planes. You said it was important to view it like that. Is that where this demon, Asmodeus, comes from? Or is that somewhere else?"

A smile flashed across Alma's face, and she nodded. "The tree is one of many rivers and the one that gives us life. Nothing says there aren't other trees out there in the unknown. Other rivers may exist, and even worse, others may have dried up."

Leah raised her eyebrow, opening her mouth for more questions.

"This lesson is over for now," Alma said. "Take some time to think over all we have discussed today. Head off to breakfast; your training will begin afterward." Alma stepped out of the room and headed toward the kitchen, leaving Leah alone with her thoughts.

CHAPTER 16

THE TREE OF DEATH

Sarah caught Leah's gaze as she stepped into the dining room and waved her over. "Come sit with us."

Leah saw others working in the kitchen and frowned. "Shouldn't we be helping?"

"No," Isaac said. "We've got cleanup duty."

As Leah sat next to Sarah, a tall boy with freckles and ashy hair carried a large pot, setting it at the head of the table. He shot her a smile. "Hey, I'm Gabe."

Before she could reply, she lost him among the others, who stepped in front of the pot and began filling bowls and passing them around the table. Leah then noticed another boy, with golden brown skin and buzzed hair, who dropped the bowl he was holding, splattering it all over a taller boy with tan skin and wavy hair.

The wavy-haired boy glared, picking the oatmeal out of his hair. "Buck! Come on, dude."

Buck scooped a clump of oatmeal off the guy's shirt and back into the bowl. "Good as new. Who doesn't like eau de Harry in their oatmeal, right, Emma?"

Harry looked toward the girl entering the kitchen before

his face quickly turned pale and he glanced away. The first person who entered was a pale white girl with short black hair. Her wide eyes darted away from Harry as she raced to the table. Two other girls followed, snickering and pointing at Harry's shirt. One of them looked just like Buck if he had been a girl. The other had her blond hair in a bun and had a razor-sharp chin that cut through the air as she looked over at Leah before sitting at the other table.

Harry and Buck resumed their duties, haphazardly passing bowls around to everyone else. The scent of cinnamon and raisins filled Leah's senses as a steaming bowl arrived in front of her. She wasn't sure her father had ever made oatmeal that smelled as good as this did. The thought crept in, and his malevolent smile permeated her thoughts. She balled her hands into fists and focused on the bowl. A few more deep breaths, and her stomach growled, pushing the thought back down into the abyss.

She picked up her spoon, ready to dig in when Sarah elbowed her. Leah followed Sarah's gaze and spotted Alma standing at the head of the table.

"Good morning, Squares."

Everyone else moved in unison around Leah, saluting and saying, "Good morning, Black Bishop Sachs."

Leah quickly muttered after them, "Good Morning . . . Black Bishop."

Alma looked at Leah, then nodded and sat down at the head of the table, picking up her spoon and digging in.

The others followed suit, eating their breakfast.

Between large mouthfuls, Sarah asked Leah, "How'd you sleep?"

Leah toyed with the oatmeal and stretched her back against the chair. "I think I could have slept on a pile of dirt and it would have been better than that car."

Sarah laughed. "Well, it's no Hilton, but at least we've

got somewhere to sleep. Some of the others have nothing to go back to."

Leah bit her lip. Images of her home in ruins surfaced, followed by the icy feeling of her mother's hand. Then that smile. Stretched across her father's face.

Her chest grew heavy, and the fear riled itself awake, uncoiling and stretching inside her.

She felt a hand grab her shoulder. "Leah? Leah, are you okay?" Isaac asked.

The bowl had slid a few inches away from her. She blinked and looked up into Isaac's green eyes before noticing Alma, her lips pursed, and her gaze piercing through Leah.

"Yeah, I'm okay. Thanks."

Alma cleared her throat. "Miss Ackerman, have you had a chance to introduce yourself?"

Leah looked up from the table, meeting the eyes of everyone else staring back at her. She raised her hand slowly and waved. "Oh, no. Uh, hi. I'm Leah . . . Leah Ackerman."

Her cheeks burned as everyone's eyes stayed on her way longer than she'd wanted. Alma remained quiet, then rose from the table and passed her gaze over the others. "Lessons begin in fifteen minutes." She picked up her bowl and left toward the stairs.

Leah took a few bites of her oatmeal, but the stares from everyone vanquished her appetite. A couple of spoonfuls later, she pushed the bowl away.

She was about to excuse herself when the blond girl, pale with blue eyes, butted in between her and Isaac.

"So, is this your new girlfriend, small fry?"

"She's not my girlfriend," Isaac said, his face glowing red.

Leah sat up straight and met the girl's stare. "And who are you?"

The girl focused her stare on Leah and smiled. "Paige." She shot a thumb backward at the two other girls at the table behind her. "And that's Serena and Emma."

Leah shot a glance at the girls, who were badly pretending like they weren't listening. She looked at Serena, and back to Buck, before opening her mouth. "Are she and Buck—"

"Twins?" Paige finished. "Yup. Except Buck's a colossal idiot, and Serena clearly got all the looks."

Buck turned around, nearly slipping out of his seat while shooting a glare at Paige. "Hey, who're you calling an idiot?"

Paige rolled her eyes and looked at Leah. "So what, you a transfer?"

Leah shook her head. "No, I'm just . . . new."

Paige raised an eyebrow. "Huh? Alma told us this was it, that no one else is allowed to join once we've started. You must be really special, or really screwed up." She looked at her nails before glancing at Gabe.

Leah shrugged, figuring Paige had already lost interest. "Guess you'll have to wait and see."

Paige rested her chin on her hands. "You must have done something *really* bad then. What did you do? Kill someone?"

"Lay off, Paige," Sarah said, flicking a raisin into Paige's hair.

Paige leaped back and glared at Sarah. "Oh, so she's your girlfriend? I didn't picture someone like her as your type."

"Wow, insecure much?" Leah blurted. She didn't know Paige, but already, she knew they wouldn't be friends anytime soon.

Paige scoffed. "Wow. So, the new girl is stupid *and* she's a bitch."

Everyone at the tables stopped talking and focused their attention on the two girls.

Leah felt the pressure build up inside of her, more anger than fear, pushing for release. "I'm not the bitch here. Maybe if you looked in the mirror, you'd figure that out."

Paige huffed, red forming around her cheeks. "This is stupid." She got up and sat at the other table.

The pressure subsided in Leah, and she let out a long breath.

Sarah patted Leah on the back and laughed. "Nicely done."

Isaac looked at Sarah and shook his head. "She's as crazy as you."

"No, not crazy," Leah said. "Just not in the mood." She jabbed her spoon into her oatmeal, her hunger raging back with a voracious force.

As the last of the bowls settled in the cupboard, washed and dried, Alma descended the stairs. "Squares, to formation!"

She clicked a stopwatch, and all the Squares leaped into action and raced outside. Sarah locked arms with a confused Leah and dragged her out and onto the patio.

They stood shoulder to shoulder, facing out to the yard. Leah noticed that the forest enveloped the large practice yard that looked more like an outside CrossFit gym than anything, but mostly covered in dried pine needles.

She noted the rows of stuffed practice dummies,

battered and broken. Several massive tires lay across the yard, and knotted ropes hung from the trees. A sweat broke out on her brow as she wondered what she had gotten herself into.

The nine Squares stood in a line on the bottom steps leading up to the patio. Sarah turned to Leah, trying her best to get Leah's back straight and chin up to match her posture.

Alma walked behind them, swatting her hand at several of the boys, correcting their posture.

She paused behind Leah.

Leah looked at Sarah from the corner of her eye and adjusted her stance accordingly, straightening her back even more than she thought possible.

After a quiet, "hmm", from Alma, she stepped out in front of the Squares.

Alma raised a hand to Leah. "Come, stand by my side."

Leah felt a lump in her throat but did as she was told and stepped out of line, standing at Alma's side.

The Bishop looked up at the other students. "Square Ackerman has arrived to us late, but this makes her no more or less special than the rest of you. She has a lot of catching up to do if she wishes to join you all at the Academy. We all work together, understand? You are not in a competition. So, I expect you to keep her in line."

Paige rolled her eyes before locking them back on Leah. Something told her that the blondie wasn't about to make things any easier for her.

Alma pulled out her stopwatch and clicked it. "Five laps to the bend in the road and back. Move!"

They moved in unison, jogging out from behind the building and onto the gravel road. Leah staggered behind, trying to keep up.

They ran past two log cabin buildings Leah had seen the night before, which were far more dilapidated than she expected in the morning light. They were covered in a dark green moss, one even with half the roof caved in and a tree growing out from the hole in the roof. Birds sang in the trees as they ran, and the morning air was cool and filled with the scent of cedar trees.

As they approached the bend in the road, Leah could see a fourth house, boarded up like all the rest. She held her side, doing all she could to not throw up as Sarah and Isaac fell out of line and came to her side.

Sarah smiled, not a drop of sweat on her brow. "You've got this. We'll just do four more of these, to and from this house."

Leah gulped in air. "I'm trying. Do you . . . do this . . . every day?"

"Every morning," Isaac said.

Sarah ran ahead of Leah and faced her, jogging backwards. "If it makes you feel any better, Paige threw up on her first day. Right about here. She refused to jog anymore. That was until she got the look from Alma, then she had to run laps that whole night."

Leah laughed, wincing from the stitch at her side. "So, I just have to beat her and not whine." She gulped in the cool morning air, focused on the line in front of her.

"That's it," Isaac said. "It sucked our first day too, but you'll get used to it."

They finally stopped in the backyard, and Leah clutched onto her knees for dear life.

Isaac came to her side and handed her a bottle of water, which she chugged, and the nausea subsided.

"Squares, formation!" Alma said, stepping off the porch.

Everyone rushed to their positions. "Square Jones, please show Square Ackerman position one."

"Yes, Black Bishop Sachs." Paige stepped forward, her tight bun shining in the sunlight. She planted her feet firm on the ground and placed her hands behind her back, making a triangle, pointing down, with the tip of her index finger and thumb.

"Square Tate, can you explain why this position is important?"

"With proper posture and hands placed behind your back," Gabe said, "the release of *Malchut* will be unhindered, and the Mystic can focus all efforts on the intent of *Malchut*."

"Good," Alma said. "Fall back in line, Square Jones." She paced around them. "We will continue practical demonstrations using *Malchut* at a distance today. Square Ackerman, you are to remain in position one during practice. The rest of you may attempt the other positions once you have passed my evaluation. Understood?"

"Yes, Black Bishop Alma," the group said together.

"*Malchut* is your key to entering the Infinity Board. It will be the primary well they will test you on at the Academy, and the one energy that will determine your bonds and your future within the Infinity Board. Keep that engrained in your head. I expect all my students to succeed." Her eyes landed on Isaac. "The weakest among you reflects poorly on my teaching, but also on your teamwork. We must rise together."

Alma led them to the practice dummies, each lined up five feet apart. Everyone paired up, facing off against a dummy. Leah ended up beside Gabe, giving him a slight smile.

Alma started. "*Malchut* is the key to the rest of the Tree of Life. I have shown you how to collect it within the arms. However, in order to access its full potential during combat, you must first guide this feeling downward, to the feet. You have to be grounded, like a statue, pulling that force downward before releasing the wave of energy. Only then can it grow and travel far enough to hit your targets."

Alma faced a practice dummy, taking position one, and drawing in a deep breath. She barely slipped her foot forward, and in that instant the dummy in front of her slid several feet backward, gouging deep lines into the dirt. The other dummies beside it were untouched, the power solely directed at the dummy in front of her.

She turned and paced in front of the squares. "That is why we use position one, and why we direct it to our feet. When facing an enemy, it's dangerous to unleash *Malchut* without control, or else you may collapse entire buildings, missing your target and allowing the opposing force to take control."

Paige scoffed. "Tear down an entire building? Like any of us could do that."

Leah felt her face flush, noting the others didn't realize what *Malchut* could really do, or what had happened with her.

Alma passed her gaze over each Square, falling slightly longer on Leah and demanding everyone's silence. "Many of you first experienced *Malchut* as a slight push, a way to have an upper hand in a fight, or to fend off from someone attacking you. Others don't have it as easy. *Malchut* turns to *Nehemoth*, and it nearly consumes them, and that force destroys everything in its path." She paused, allowing her words to sink in before saying, "Be grateful, Square Jones, that your energy didn't harm anyone when it woke inside you."

Paige looked Leah up and down before rolling her eyes and focusing on Alma.

Alma clasped her hands together. "Now, everyone, shift

to position one and take turns practicing on your dummies."

The Squares stood at attention and said in unison, "Yes, Black Bishop Sachs," before breaking off into their small groups.

Leah looked over at Gabe, and he smiled. "I'll go first. Watch me, and see if you can copy what I do."

He took on the position, and Leah noted how well defined his back muscles were through his tight gray shirt. She shook her head, shifting her focus to the dummy.

"That feeling in your chest," he said, "I imagine mine almost like a snake. I think of something scary to wake it up. Once it unwinds, that's when I push it down to my feet and then . . ." He kicked his foot forward, much more prominent than Alma's slight twitch, and the dummies in front of him shook.

Leah, not sure what else to do, clapped her hands softly. Gabe smiled at her.

"Remember to keep your focus," Alma said to Gabe. "With more focus, you can push farther. Your mind should only be on the dummy in front of you, nothing else."

Gabe nodded, his face turning red as his eyes flicked to Leah.

Alma nodded at Leah. "Your turn. I'd like to see what you've got."

Leah closed her eyes and mimicked Gabe's stance, planting her feet firmly on the ground and touching her index fingers and thumbs behind her back. She felt Alma tapping at her feet, straightening out the stance before pulling back her shoulders.

"Alright, when you are ready," Alma said. "Remember, push it down to your feet."

Leah tried to wake the feeling inside her chest—the snake, as Gabe had put it—but nothing happened.

She thought of her father's smile, her mother's hand, but nothing came. Leah stood still for what felt like an eternity before a ring sounded from inside the cabin.

"What's that?" Leah asked.

"Phone call. From one of the Knights on a mission," Gabe said.

Alma looked toward the cabin and spoke loud enough for everyone to hear. "Practice your stances and breathing. Imagine your mind traveling with your breath from your chest to your toes. This shouldn't take long, but there is to be no *Malchut* practice until I've returned. Understood?"

"Yes, Black Bishop Sachs."

She nodded and hurried back to the cabin.

Leah heard murmurs from Paige's direction. That quickly died down as the group began practicing in silence. Leah felt useless, standing there and simply breathing, unsure if she should feel any different.

Paige crossed her arms and huffed. "Well, this is boring. I was looking forward to taking down a few dummies."

Leah realized Paige was looking directly at Sarah and Isaac, and not the practice dummies.

Sarah stepped forward, and Isaac grabbed her by the wrist to hold her back.

"She's not worth it," he said.

Sarah shook off his arm, glaring at Paige for a moment before walking over to Leah and nodding her head at Gabe. "I'm not feeling anything. What about you, Leah?"

Leah shook her head. "Nothing, but Gabe made a few dummies shake when Alma was watching."

Paige stepped out from behind Sarah and said, "Oh, what's this? Lover's quarrel? I wouldn't get in between these two, Gabe. I'm pretty sure Sarah's got a thing for her. She might not even be into boys."

Sarah clenched her fists. "One more word from you and I'll break your jaw."

The others dropped their meditation practice quickly to form a circle around the two.

Paige glanced at her two cronies, who looked at the cabin and nodded to Paige. Paige then said to Sarah, "I'd like to see you try."

Leah grabbed Sarah's arm to stop her. She felt something vibrating beneath Sarah's copper skin, something writhing to be free. "Alma could be back any minute."

Sarah froze, and the vibration in her skin subsided.

"Better listen to your girlfriend. Don't want to end up shipped off to another outpost, do you? I've heard long-distance relationships are tough." The girls behind her started laughing.

Leah let go of Sarah's arm, feeling her own anger build up in her chest.

Isaac jumped in front of Paige and raised his hands. "Guys, stop, we're all in this together, remember? Alma wants us to—"

"Shut up, hobbit." Paige straightened her back and slipped her hands behind her. Before anyone could react, she kicked, throwing a wave of energy forward, slamming into Isaac and flinging him backward, past Sarah and Leah.

Anger uncoiled in Leah's chest and filled her entire body, the pressure building beneath the surface of her skin. She straightened her back and placed her hands behind her, mimicking Paige.

The girls laughed, while Harry and Buck glanced back at the cabin before joining in on the trouble.

"Aww, Look Sarah, your girlfriend wants to fight. Too bad she doesn't know how."

The pressure inside Leah kept building, and she did

nothing to stop it. She needed more pressure, wanted more pressure. She took in a sharp breath.

An icy wind streamed in around her, and the pressure nearly doubled, pressing hard against her flesh. Anger seeped into every fiber of her being, and with it, Leah heard whispers carried on the wind, egging her on.

Kill. Let it go. Blow her away. Destroy.

She spoke through gritted teeth, the power strong enough to make her teeth chatter. "Apologize."

Paige smiled, holding her straight-backed stance. "Make me."

The energy inside Leah tore out of her like an uncontrolled tempest. The brunt of the force slammed into Paige. She took in another breath, and the cold wind flooded around her, forcing Paige to stumble backward. Pushing again, Leah felt a weak barrier. A force opposing hers. But she pushed harder.

The force vanished, and with it, Paige and her friends behind her flew backward into the practice dummies.

The power ebbed and flowed off Leah in waves, and others around her stumbled back and forth before they were flung away, tossed like rag dolls away from her. Only Gabe resisted, pulling Sarah back and pushing against the tempest that emanated from Leah.

Voices screamed, *Murder! Kill! Die, die, die!* in Leah's head. The power surged on, tearing deep gouges into the ground.

A voice shouted from behind her. "Leah! Leah, stop!"

She turned and saw Gabe maintaining a straight-backed position as blood dripped from his nose. "Stop! Please!"

The sound of his voice, the fear in his voice, pulled Leah back. Anger fell away in an instant, and the power emanating from her faded. The voices fell to a whisper. "*Kill, murder, die,*" still carried on the air.

Gabe looked around, and Leah's eyes followed. The dummies lay scattered across the yard, thrown yards away.

"What . . . What did you do?" Gabe asked.

Leah looked at Paige, who bled from her nose while she looked down at a broken arm. "I . . . I don't know," Leah whispered. "I didn't mean to."

CHAPTER 17

CONSEQUENCES

Alma slammed her hand on her office table. "Do you know what you've done?"

"Black Bishop Sachs, please. I didn't mean to. I . . ." Leah's voice trailed off.

She knew she deserved every punishment Alma had waiting for her, having injured nearly every other student. The energy in her was too strong to control. Something inside of her told her it could've been worse.

"You've put my other students at risk. I clearly instructed no use of *Malchut*, yet you managed not only to do that but also use *Nehemoth*. You hurt others, Square Ackerman. You broke Paige's arm! I'm not even sure I should be calling you a Square anymore."

The door swung open, and Sarah rushed in, standing next to Leah. "Please Black Bishop Sachs, she didn't mean it. It was Paige; she egged her on."

Isaac peeked in from outside the door. "Paige used *Malchut* first, on me."

Alma pursed her lips and stared at Sarah and Isaac. "Squares. What gives you the right to come running into my office?" She folded her hands and waited before staring at Sarah. "Well?"

The two bowed their heads, and Sarah said, "We're sorry. We just wanted you to know the entire story."

"If Paige's misgivings come to light, then that will be a separate matter. It does not excuse Square Ackerman, especially when I have Square Jones lying downstairs on the sofa after I healed her broken arm and cracked nose. Not to mention the handful of scrapes and cuts I've had to treat on the others. Had I known Square Ackerman was so willing to delve into the Tree of Death, I would have been certain to not leave her unsupervised."

Tree of Death. Leah hadn't heard that before. Had that been the opposing force Alma mentioned?

"But Paige attacked Isaac first," Sarah said.

"Enough!" Alma shouted, her voice booming over Sarah's pleas. "You two, out. And for your insolence, you'll be doing laps until I come and get you. Now!"

"But . . ." Sarah started, then froze, Alma's eyes locked on her, daring her to open her mouth again.

"One more word, and I'll see that neither of you gets bonds within the Infinity Board. You'll be scrubbing pots or cleaning toilets for the rest of your lives unless you get out of my sight now."

Isaac entered the room and wrapped his arm around Sarah, pulling her out of the room and closing the door behind them.

Leah looked down at her hands. "I didn't do it on purpose. I was just so angry. It happened so fast, like it sort of exploded out of me."

Alma sighed and leaned back in her chair. "Square Ackerman, the Tree of Death is not something to trifle with. You've become a danger to my other student." She cleared her throat and looked at Leah in the eyes. "I have no choice but to discontinue your training here at the outpost."

A brick settled deep in Leah's gut. *She's expelling me?* She shook her head. "But it was a mistake. I didn't mean to. I won't—"

Alma raised her hand, cutting Leah off. "You won't what? You won't do it again? You can't guarantee that, and I cannot, and will not, risk the lives of my other students. The Tree of Death is addictive. It yearns for you to use its power, and you've already dived in headfirst. Touching it so early in the process, even if you do not quite know what it means, makes you a threat."

Leah dropped her head, tears dropping from her face. Just when she thought she was safe, when she thought she could find normalcy, she was being cast out.

Alma stood up and crossed the room. "I've called for your uncle to return and pick you up. You are not welcome back at my outpost until you can get a better handle on your energy. Sit in this room and wait for your uncle. Understood?"

Leah kept her eyes on the floor. "Yes, Black Bishop Sacks." Alma left the room while tears flowed from Leah's eyes, dripping down onto her hands as she sat in silence. The tears slid down her knuckles, dampening her gray sweatpants.

She blinked, and a line of fresh blood slid down the top of her hand and her fingers, trailing a stream on her hand. Another drop of blood fell, and then another.

Leah sniffled and wiped at her face, but no streaks of red showed on her palms. She leaned back and furrowed her brow, then felt the warm breath rolling down from above.

Leah turned her head upward and met the smiling face

of her father. His lips stretched uncannily across his face, and blood dripped from his mouth. He spoke, his voice both a whisper and a deep guttural growl.

"I found you."

She leaped out of her chair, and Alma's office melted away, shifting and changing into a living room. The chair she had been sitting in was now a squashy leather sofa, Alma's desk now an entertainment center sitting next to a burning fireplace flickering light into an otherwise darkened room.

She locked eyes with her father while he crawled over the couch and stood in front of her, smiling. "You've been hiding, girl. Where are you?" He cocked his head and sniffed deeply. "Mmm, pine. Woods. A cabin . . . mmm."

Leah's chest tightened as she backed up against the wall. "What do you want?" she asked, staring into his blue eyes.

All she could see was her father's face, all the happy memories now splattered and torn. Her chest tightened more, this unfamiliar face of her father's burning its way into her memories.

She turned her head to see a woman lying dead in a pool of blood on the floor.

"I killed her too," the thing that was her father said. "More dead Knights to add to my collection. Revenge can be so sweet." He stepped closer to her, his hot breath rolling across her face.

Leah squeezed her eyes shut as an icy finger traced her cheek. "I hope I can add you to my collection."

Leah screamed as hands wrapped around her shoulders. "Leah!" a voice shouted. "Leah, wake up!"

Her eyes snapped open, meeting Eric's face as she stood pressed against Alma's desk.

Leah whipped her head around the room, expecting her father to lunge out any second, waiting for the right time to pounce. No one else was there. Only the two of them and Alma, standing in the doorway, staring at Leah.

Eric led her to the chair, sitting her down as he scanned her face. "Everything alright?"

She saw the worried look on his face. The same look her mother gave her when she'd scraped a knee. She felt the constriction on her chest unwind and nodded. "Yeah, I'm fine. Just a bad dream."

"A bad dream that makes you scream like that?"

Leah averted her gaze. "Can we not talk about this? It's nothing. I have nightmares like this from time to time."

Eric shook his head. "Fine." He turned his attention to Alma. "Black Bishop Sachs, do you want to tell me what this is all about?"

"Miss Ackerman has injured several students in a grand display lacking any self-control."

Leah wiped a tear that had streamed down her face. "I didn't mean for it to happen. Please, I can't be expelled. What if you train me, Uncle Eric? We can go somewhere else. Somewhere safe. Please?"

"I gave explicit instruction not to use *Malchut*," Alma said. "Not without supervision, and you let the Tree of Death lure you in. Atop that, this was only your first day and you used it on other students."

"Paige started it. Why aren't you expelling her?"

"Square Jones will be punished. Do not worry about her. However, your lack of control threatens the lives of my students, and I will not have it. I've agreed that your case is special, that because of the experience you've had, we should be more lenient."

Eric looked at Alma. "I could take her out into the field with me. I've got a lead on our case out in Starkweather. It could take a few days, and it might get us some of the answers we are looking for. Might be good for her to see."

Alma walked around the two of them to her desk. "Are you saying you're finally prepared for that responsibility again, Eric?"

Eric ran a hand through his hair. "I'm not saying that. But she's family. My family. If you're wanting to expel her, then at least give me a chance with her. She'll be safe, I promise."

Alma set her fingertips on her desk and thought. "She doesn't leave the car when you are in Starkweather. Understand?"

"Yes, Black Bishop."

"And you are prepared for the consequences? You know as much as I do that others who have delved so deep into the Tree of Death this early on are not always so lucky."

Eric nodded. "I'm prepared. It's time. I'm ready."

"What is that supposed to mean? Not as lucky?" Leah turned her head to look at Alma.

Eric rested a hand on Leah's shoulder. "Never mind that. You've got a second chance, okay? That's a good thing. You come with me for a few days, we practice a little, and if everything goes well, you come back."

Alma leaned back in her chair. "Black Knight Mizrahi, I won't guarantee that I'll accept Square Ackerman back. But I trust your judgement." She looked over at Leah and added, "Come back when you can show me some restraint. Otherwise, we might need to rethink your position here." Alma stood. "Now, if you'll excuse me, I have to tend to the injured students." She left her office, her footsteps trailing down the hall and creaking down the stairs.

Eric stood and held out a hand. "Grab some clothes and a toothbrush. We'll talk in the car." He helped her up and headed out the door, leaving Leah to collect her things.

As she walked down the stairs, she glimpsed Paige lying on the couch, smirking at Leah. Leah shifted her gaze to Sarah and Isaac, who sat in the living room.

Sarah mouthed the words, "I'm sorry," as Leah left the outpost.

CHAPTER 18
NEHEMOTH

They drove away in silence, Leah staring out at the darkening forest, choking back tears.

She tried convincing herself she didn't care about the outpost. Yet her mind fell back on Isaac and Sarah, the two students who actually cared and were nice to her. Did Alma really plan on taking her back in a few days, or was this the last time she'd ever see them?

"I get it," Eric said after he rounded another corner on the gravel road. "Wanting to show off, prove to the others that you're their equal."

Leah scoffed. "No, you don't get it." She breathed on her window, tracing her finger into a star in the fog.

Eric paused and chewed his lip. "Either way, you've been through more than any of them. All that energy inside you, the fear and rage . . . This power has a lot of risk, and it can hurt people, including those who wield it."

Leah shifted in her seat, wondering if he was talking about her or himself.

"Part of me feels guilty," Eric continued. "I should've known when you almost destroyed my car, but I ignored it. I figured Alma would know what to do."

The gravel road finally turned into pavement, and Eric pressed down on the accelerator. They picked up speed, racing down the road now.

"Ignored what? It isn't like you knew that was going to happen. Did you?"

"No, not exactly. But Knights are the Infinity Board's first line of defense. We scout potential Squares and determine if they belong with the Board. I couldn't do that for you. I knew you'd toppled a house and almost threw us off the road. But you were under duress in both instances."

"But what could you have done? Just left me at a gas station if I was too much for you?"

Eric cleared his throat. "From the moment I took you in, the Infinity Board has been testing you, seeking to find your limits and what level of connection you have with the Tree. If you could access the Tree of Death on your first day at the outpost, then I did a poor job determining the connection within you. If I had done my job properly, then I would have been able to get an exemption to work with you, alone. Instead, I rushed us to an outpost and dropped you off."

"You and Alma keep mentioning the Tree of Death. Is that like the opposing force, the temptation Alma mentioned? Can you tell me, or are you still sworn to secrecy?"

"Since you are a Square now, I have some leeway." He flipped open the middle console and pulled out a beef jerky stick, ripping open the wrapper with his teeth. "Want one? Help yourself."

She eyed the center console, looking at the clock and realizing how late into the evening it was. Her stomach growled as she riffled through a pile of prepackaged foods and what looked like a half bottle of whiskey. She picked out some jerky and peeled back the wrapper.

"This club is all a constant game," Eric said, ripping off a piece of jerky. "Remember that. Every test, every moment forward is all part of some bigger scheme."

She tore off a piece of meat, the hickory flavor sharp and sweet. "Well, that makes me feel a lot better, knowing I'm just some pawn in someone else's game."

Eric raised his index finger. "Technically, you're not a Pawn. Not yet. But yeah, in the colloquial sense."

"I just want to know what happened. I started hearing these voices. It happened before too. They say things, weird things, and then it just comes off in waves. You never answered me about the Tree of Death. Does that have anything to do with all these voices I've been hearing?"

He nodded and ran a hand through his hair. "What you heard was the Tree of Death, yes. *Nehemoth*, to be exact."

Leah bit her lip. "But I did the stance. It felt the same as *Malchut*."

"The Tree of Life is like one side of a coin, the side we Mystics connect to. Pure energy, refined and ready for us to use. The other side, the Tree of Death, is raw energy, unwieldy and corrupt. Most students only scratch the surface, and their instructor pulls them back. But you flipped that coin right away, to protect yourself. Whenever you pull on *Malchut,* your energy runs low, and you risk pulling the energy in around you using *Nehemoth*. These two energies are so closely related that the urge to use *Nehemoth* is the strongest of all energies in the Tree of Death."

"So, what, I'm like a full on evil space emperor with a breathing problem?"

Eric let out a laugh and nearly swerved off the road. "Your mom hated those movies."

Leah shrugged. "Dad and I would sneak off to the

theaters whenever they played it. She wouldn't let him buy any of them, so it was our secret."

Eric smirked and shook his head. "Well, no, young student, you are not turning to the dark side on me. Not just yet. The Trees are two sides of the same coin. No life without death, nor the other way around. The Tree of Death isn't evil, but we are living beings, so the more we use it, the more that death creeps into us."

"But it called to me. It wanted me to use it."

Eric nodded. "For us, the Tree of Death is temptation, and we must walk the fine line right beside it. That is the control you must have, and it's the control you must show Alma."

Badlands overtook the forest, and soon enough, the sun settled down behind them. Eric pulled into a small motel, its red vacancy sign and one streetlight the only source of light for miles.

"We'll get some shuteye here, then get up early and head into town," Eric said.

"Where are we going?"

Eric rubbed his eyes. "I've been trying to find out more about what happened to you. Alma helped me track down a demon case close by, and I could use some help."

"Really?" Leah's eyes opened wide.

"Just a minor demon. Nothing too bad for your first field trip. Hopefully, we can get some answers about what happened to your parents."

Leah nodded, then furrowed her eyebrows. "Minor demon? You mean there's more out there?"

Eric popped his door open and stepped out of the car. "Yep. There's quite a bit you still need to learn. You're only scratching the surface." He turned and headed into the motel's office.

CHAPTER 19

DEMON

A couple of days passed as Eric came and went from the motel, leaving Leah to fend for herself while surfing through the eight channels that worked in the motel room. He'd been scouting without her, leaving her alone in the motel while he came back every night smelling like whiskey. Now that he found their target, they drove down the road, headlights shining onto an old wooden sign with chipped orange paint peeling away at the illustration stating: "Welcome to Starkweather."

Leah drank the cold, and questionable, sludge of motel coffee and wondered who would name a town Starkweather. The town was settled in the middle of nowhere. Leah had thought she knew what nowhere was before, but after an hour of seeing no house lights or headlights, she had to reevaluate what it really meant.

She followed their headlights down Main Street, which seemed to all but end before she realized it. Leah had been to small towns before, but never anywhere like this. She counted two buildings that she'd call storefronts scattered among a fire department, post office, and a club building of sorts.

Leah broke the awkward silence. "So, what kind of demon shacks up in a place like this?"

"There's still a lot we don't know about demons," Eric said. "We know most of the stories we have on them aren't entirely true. Mainly we know they want the Trees."

Leah raised an eyebrow. "Both?"

Eric nodded. "They can't touch them since they aren't part of this plane. They have to possess someone who can connect to the Tree of Life and use them like a puppet. Mystics have the strongest connection, so the smart demons like to pick us. Even then, they are just a puppet master, unable to truly wield it."

"Why, though?"

Eric shrugged. "We don't know, exactly. It seems like they absorb most of the energy of their host, including the energy that keeps them alive. They don't last long, the host decaying quickly, except for the ones we think are more skilled and able to control the energy they absorb."

"How are they able to possess us?"

"They linger in the Astral Plane. We don't know where they really come from, but they are not from our plane of existence. They showed up long ago in ancient texts, which described them more like parasites than anything else. Out here, in the real world, you only need to know to be careful. Demons want what you have, and they will trick and worm their way in if you let them. It might even be one simple intrusive thought. So, it's best to stay vigilant and don't let them in."

After driving several blocks, they reached the edge of town. Eric pulled into the driveway of a small two-story home and parked next to two trucks.

"We're here." He unbuckled his seatbelt.

Leah observed the house, the sky a light purple, the morning sun still well below the horizon. It looked like homes she had seen outside of Lincolnwood, simple square houses with light blue siding. The grass was clean cut but with no frills. No designs in the grass, and no landscaping surrounding the concrete slab leading into the house. She nodded.

"I need to talk to the family," Eric said. "Stay in the car and keep an eye out for anything suspicious, okay?"

"Sure."

Eric stepped out of the car and back to the trunk. Leah popped open the passenger door and hopped out.

"I said stay in the car," Eric hissed.

Leah stretched her legs and walked around to the back of the car. "I will. I just want to see what you're doing."

"You're just like her," Eric said as he unzipped a duffel bag and pulled out a large Mason jar filled with dark red liquid. He opened it, and the scent of iron filled the air.

Leah gagged. "Ugh, what is that? Blood?"

"Sheep's blood to be exact," he said, pulling up his sleeves before dipping his fingers into the jar and drawing markings and Hebrew letters onto his arms. "Here's another lesson for you. Rituals, for us Mystics, can amplify our energy and help direct it in ways that some-times take decades to master. This here changes *Malchut* into something less physical and instead pushes away memories." He looked out toward the house. "This is the best way to get someone out of the house and keep them safe."

He hummed and muttered under his breath. The mark-ings glowed and sunk into his skin, leaving no trace of the blood. "With the right words, ingredients, and symbols, anyone can use rituals to get a taste of the Tree. Most Knights seek them out, determining if they are not a threat or if they are witches or something else, seeking to channel energy off the trees to do their bidding."

He grabbed the duffel bag and shut the trunk. "Stay in the car and honk the horn if you see anything."

Leah couldn't just sit there, not when she could be of use. "But I could help. I can come in there with you and—"

"No. It's too dangerous. Stay here." He turned and headed up the path before she could say anything.

She did as she was told, plopping into the passenger seat and crossing her arms while she kept her eyes on Eric. He reached the porch and rang the doorbell.

Leah spotted movement on the top floor, a curtain pulled back and one eye peering out. Goosebumps flushed her skin, as if the eye had pierced right through her.

The door swung open, and a plump woman stood in the doorway. She had curlers in her red hair and a thick robe a similar color as her curled ginger locks. She smiled as Eric spoke, the words too far off for Leah to hear. Then he placed a hand on the side of her head, and the air around Leah sparked to life.

The woman completely relaxed, her shoulders slumping and her gaze set far off in the distance.

What the hell was that?

The woman shivered and then smiled at Eric. She leaned backward and called into the house, "Riley!"

Moments later, a little girl in her pajamas came running. Eric kneeled down and Leah felt the spark again as the little girl relaxed for a split second.

The pair walked past Eric, onto the path and into the truck parked outside, unaware or uncaring about how they were dressed. The woman cranked the truck, its engine roaring to life in the quiet night, and backed out of the driveway.

Leah shifted her gaze back to her uncle. Well, where he should have been. Instead, there was only an open door and no one standing on the porch.

Leah shifted her eyes between the open door and the second-floor window, the face now gone from the curtains. *Stay in the car.* Leah replayed the memory of what Eric said, leaning against the door.

So she waited.

Silence prickled at her ears, an uneasy quiet that felt unnatural. She looked around—up at the trees, down at the bushes—and frowned. There were no early morning bird calls, no squirrels chittering away. It was silent.

The air outside grew stagnant and sickly, a faint humid pressure building up around her. She heard a creak from inside the house, then a whisper that skirted the edges of her hearing.

You won't survive.

The lights inside the house flickered, and a loud thud sounded from within. The thought of her mother's last few moments crossed her mind, and it sunk deep into her stomach. Her uncle was in danger, alone, while she waited out here.

She raced into the house, hearing Alma's warning to Eric playing through her head.

She doesn't leave the car.

The carpeted floor beneath her shoes muffled her steps as she creeped through the front door. Immediately, a smell of stagnant air hit her, like the smell of an old dusty attic.

She peered into the living room, noting the piles of takeout stacked on top of the coffee table and reclining chairs.

A crash sounded above her, and she froze. *Eric.*

Leah raced to the stairs, carefully testing each step, trying to prevent them from creaking. Her heart pounded in her ears, waiting for the moment something came descending on her, a crazed smile stretched across its face.

Photos lined the stairwell. They portrayed a happy

family, including the red-haired woman and a little girl accompanied by a tall man who Leah could only presume was the girl's father. The photographs showed the family joyful on a beach, at a waterfall, and inside a cabin. They seemed a lot like Leah's family, and something had invaded their home as well.

She reached the top of the stairs, her hands balled into fists when she could finally make out the murmurs coming from one room. The voice bore into Leah's head as it spoke, an ache in her jaw like a dentist's drill. "You Mystics think that you have everything figured out," it said, laughing and coughing. "You really have no idea."

Eric sounded different, more authoritative. "Deceivers, all of you! Tell me what I asked, or I promise this will hurt."

Leah sneaked across the hallway and peered through the small opening of the cracked door.

Eric's back faced her, and the man from the photos sat tied to a chair in front of him. The man, or demon, was in pain. Eric had hurt it, not the other way around.

Eric continued, his voice distant. "What happened to her? What happened to Elizabeth Mizrahi?"

The demon groaned again. "You already know. Not like she could hide from Asmodeus, even if she tried. Those little spells can't hold us away forever."

Eric stood up straight and formed a triangle behind his back with his fingers. The air grew dense, and in one swift move, he pulled out a hand and cut the air in front of him. The demon slid back in his chair, a red gash appearing across its face. "They used concealment spells; you can't just break those down. How?"

The demon groaned and coughed. "Carriers. We just need to hitch a ride to get in." It coughed and spat a wad of congealed blood on the ground. "Stupid Mystic, you're killing him. Killing him like that girl, Jade, was it?"

"Shut up!" Eric yelled, stomping his foot on the floor. Energy sparked in the air, and Leah saw the man fly backwards, out of view, but then heard a loud slam.

Fingers snapped on the other side of the door, and light flickered in front of Eric's silhouette. She pushed the door open a little more and peered through as Eric stepped closer to where the man lay. Fire formed in Eric's hand and dripped down like burning liquid, singing small marks into the carpet before fizzling out. The man, who was the father in the pictures, lay on his side, still tied to the chair, a dent in the wall above him.

The flames in Eric's hand sputtered, and the demon laughed. "Don't have enough in the tank, Black Knight? Kill this body or die. I have nothing else to tell you." The smile on the man's face grew wide, stretching across his face unnaturally, splitting his lips.

The man's eyes fell on Leah, and whispers buzzed in her ears.

We see you. We found you. He is looking for you. He will find you.

Eric wrapped his burning hand around the man's neck and pulled him up. The demon let out a howl that shook the house. Leah stumbled into the room and fell behind Eric. Pictures fell from the walls, and the man locked eyes on Leah.

Leah imagined the man's body on the floor, dead. She felt the grief that his wife and daughter would feel when they found him. She could feel the pain of another broken family, just like hers. Nausea rolled over her, a putrid feeling scooping the inside of her stomach and a taste in her mouth like vomit. She tried to look away, but the smile kept her, held her gaze.

"Speak!" Eric yelled.

Leah couldn't hold the nausea anymore. It pressed into

every corner of her body as the whispers grew louder and louder. She screamed, and with it, a force of energy burst out from her. It made a crack in the floor and up the wall, picking up Eric like a rag doll and flinging him headfirst into the wall.

CHAPTER 20
FLASK

Eric crumpled to the ground, and the demon looked over at Leah, smiling widely.

"Ah, I see he brought along the little Mystic Asmodeus has been fawning over." He pulled at his bindings and looked over his bloodied arms. "Hopefully this old, retired Knight has some energy still."

The demon cocked his head unnaturally. A force rammed into Leah, picking her up and throwing her into the wall behind her. She slammed her elbow, a sharp pain blinding her before she fell to her knees, gasping for air.

"This is the best the child of Elizabeth Mizrahi has to offer?" A croaking, almost animal sound came from the demon's throat. "Her talents clearly don't run in the family."

The fear festered inside her, followed again by voices whispering in her ear. She couldn't hurt Eric, not again. Her gaze shifted to the man in front of her, imagining the energy inside her condensing down into the smallest of points. She threw her hand forward, letting out the force built up inside her. The energy came out in three short bursts, flinging through the air and cutting the demon on the cheek, arm, and slicing into the wall behind him.

The demon stuck out a long tongue that stretched up to his cheek like some horrific tentacle, lapping up the blood on his fresh cut. "Ah, much better than the drunk who brought you. Where have you been hiding?"

Leah stood up on shaky legs and held her elbow, the pain already subsiding. "Fuck off."

"Oh, don't be like that," the demon sniffed the air around him. "Ah, the scent of pine. It's close to here. Asmodeus is quite angry he couldn't finish the job." He looked over at the crumpled Eric and scoffed. "But now that you're part of their little club, that makes you even more delectable." He licked his lips. "Just like your mother!"

More anger grew inside Leah.

"You know," the demon said. "I heard she screamed when he cut her."

"Shut up!" Leah shouted.

In an instant, the demon leaped across the room, grabbing her by the throat and propping her up against the wall. She kicked him and clawed at his arm, but he stared into her eyes, baring his teeth. He brought his face closer, sniffing her hair. "Such energy. I wonder what fun we could have together."

Leah felt something pressing against the inside of her head, a pressure that was oozing into her skull, forcing its way into her mind. The pain seared through her body, and the room faded. She was going to die here, and there was nothing she could do to stop it.

The demon smiled, his eyes the last thing she may ever see as his grip tightened around her neck.

The push against her mind suddenly stopped, and she no longer felt the squeezing grip on her throat. Color came back to her as the demon freed her, clutching at his own throat, his eyes popping out of his head.

Leah slumped to the floor, out of reach of the man's flailing arms. She coughed and saw Eric standing behind the demon, his hands pressed together.

The demon couldn't move, except for his arms. The rest of him stood like a statue. His lips turned blue as he tried to claw at nonexistent hands at his throat.

Eric's hands shook, but his eyes stayed locked on the demon.

"Eric, I—"

"Get my bag!" He slowly stepped forward, rounding to the side of the demon, keeping his energy focused on it.

Leah clamored to the other side of the room and grabbed the duffel bag, unzipping it to see an assortment of glass flasks and other odd metallic instruments. "What do you need?"

"A flask! Small blue one!"

She turned back to the bag and riffled through it, spotting the blue flask. Leah came to his side and handed it to him.

Eric's arms shook, and the demon heaved a labored breath before whispering in a low melodic tone, "You don't know what's coming. You'll be dead before you even—"

Moving quickly, Eric dropped the demon, grabbing the flask from Leah and extending it forward. The temperature of the room dropped several degrees, and whispers buzzed around Leah's ear.

He found you. Sweet, sweet Leah. He comes. He comes for you.

Leah shivered, letting out a cloud of air as ice formed on the windows. Pressure built in the room, pushing against her senses, screaming in her ears.

Let me in! This Mystic won't help you find your father. None of them will help you. I can help you. I can bring you to him. You'd like that, wouldn't you? He'd like that. He wants to see you. Let me in!

Leah fought against it, slipping to her knees and covering her ears.

"You're mine!" Eric yelled as the lights in the room exploded. The pressure vanished in an instant, taking with it the whispers. He closed the cap of the flask, and heat flowed back into the room.

CHAPTER 21

A MATTER OF TRUST

Leah sat down on the porch and watched the sun come up over the horizon. She tried extending her elbow and winced from the pain. At least it wasn't dislocated. She probably only needed to press an icepack against it for a while.

Eric arrived beside her. "I notified the Board. They'll come clean this up. The father should wake up any minute, no memory, and he'll meet up with his wife and kid. Maybe they'll go on vacation or something."

Leah looked down at her hands. "The demon said he was a Knight. That he retired. Why would he need to forget?"

Eric sat down next to her and sighed. "He served decades. Up until his body couldn't take it anymore. Someone that lasts that long. They remember things they've done in service to the Board."

"What kind of things?"

"The sorts of things they'd rather forget." Eric stared ahead. "He did his time, so the Board respected his wish to forget. They'll wipe his memory for this too. His family will wake up tomorrow, no one remembering a thing."

She nodded and swallowed. "I'm sorry. For coming inside. I shouldn't have—"

He patted her on the knee and cleared his throat. "I should be upset, but you held your own in there. After you knocked me around, that is."

"I used it again . . . the Tree of Death." Leah said.

Eric nodded. "You did, and we'll work on that."

Leah looked up, unable to contain herself. "But you also used it, didn't you? When you trapped the demon in that flask?"

Eric hesitated. "There are two options when facing a demon. When we can, trained Knights and Bishops use *Nehemoth*, the opposite of *Malchut*. We pull energy, hence the cold. It pulled the demon out. Then we use *Malchut* to push the demon into the flask, trapping it."

Eric paused and held up the flask to the rising sun. "If we're outnumbered, and we have no other choice, then we kill the host before it takes any more lives."

"Kill them? Does that kill the demon? Wouldn't they just possess again?"

"It depends. We believe the weaker ones either die or go somewhere else, deep in the Astral Plane. Stronger demons seem to linger close, but it at least gives time for the Knights and Bishops to prepare to exorcise them or get out."

Leah paused, wondering if she wanted to know if her uncle or mother had ever been in that position. After a few seconds, she looked back at the front door. "Will the man be okay?"

Eric put the flask inside his leather jacket and said, "Should be. He was a lot like your mother. Great fighter. He'll think he wrecked his truck on the way to seeing his wife, but really, he'll drive it off the road, get a few bumps and bruises, and be none the wiser."

"But if he was such a strong Mystic, how'd he become possessed?"

Eric cleared his throat. "There isn't any surefire way to protect yourself. Stronger Mystics can detect them easier and use rituals or spells to ward them off. This Knight had those. Probably set them up before they wiped his memory. But they failed. Seems like someone sent this demon after him and it waited for the right moment to get in."

Leah looked back up at the road where the truck had driven off as the early morning sunlight washed over them. "So, you can choose to forget it all?"

"Some do, yes. If they earn it. It doesn't happen often, but sometimes it is for the better for everyone."

"And it involved him. Whatever my mother was involved with?"

"Yes, they used to go on missions together. My guess is whatever they got themselves into was worse than I could imagine. The Infinity Board placed concealment spells around here, the same thing they did with your family, but one still wormed its way in."

Leah's chest tightened, and a lump formed in her throat. "At least we got to him, you know, in time." Leah bit her lip to stop it from trembling, but she couldn't stop the tears from falling.

Eric wrapped his arm around her shoulder and pulled her in. "I know. You did good today. You protected them. They're safe, for now."

They sat for a while, feeling the morning sun on their faces before Eric stood and stepped off the porch. He turned around and held out his hand. "We'll head back to the motel and get a few more hours of sleep. Then we've got work to do."

Leah took his hand and nodded, turning back to the

house. Looming above her, still standing, as if nothing had happened inside.

Leah drifted off the moment she lay down on the motel bed. In seconds, she found herself beyond the walls of the room and far off, standing knee deep in cold water, darkness surrounding her.

A light beamed across her face, blinding her for a moment before passing by. Her vision focused, and she saw a lighthouse on the horizon.

Wary of the unseen depths below, she carefully waded forward, feeling the same smooth platform she stood on. Her eyes followed the beam as it passed over her again, tracing a light in the darkness before it stopped on two figures off in the distance.

Something inside her knew it was her parents, her mother resting her head on her father's shoulder, staring back at Leah.

She took another step toward them. "Mom? Dad? Wait for me!"

No matter how many steps she took, their distances stayed the same. She raced ahead, feeling the water push her back, pulling her farther away from her parents. They were right there, in front of her, less than a football field away, and she couldn't get to them. All she wanted was to feel their arms wrap around her, their warmth.

Pressure built in her chest as she sobbed, her tears even cold in this strange dark land. Something warm wrapped around her neck and squeezed. A hand, made entirely out of shadow, materialized, pulling her back from her parents.

A familiar voice whispered in her ear, "Not yet. Not until I get my turn." Something wet slid across her cheek.

Leah stepped out of the motel bathroom, squeezing her hair in a towel. She'd pulled on her clothes from the day before, but at least she felt somewhat clean.

Eric sat at the small table next to the window and stared at his half-eaten twinkie. "We need to get going. I've got to drop this demon off before heading to my next call, so we need to hit the road."

"Another call?"

He pulled out a map from his back pocket and unfolded it across the table. "Yep, some knights need help with a witch cult on the rise screwing up the sacred lands near Devil's Tower."

Leah raised an eyebrow. "Whoa, hold on. Witch cults?"

Eric nodded. "It's a weird world out there. There are shifters too. And Druids. And—"

"Okay, I get it." She peeked over Eric's shoulder at the map, noting the collection of red X's he'd marked. He'd taped the map together at some of the folds, and it had yellowed from age. Notes and marks had been scribbled all over it, alongside smudges from what looked like dried blood.

She imagined what it must be like to live on the road, taking cases from someone on the other end of a phone while pulling out a map and marking the next adventure. She wondered if he ever felt lonely. If he waited to be called to support other Knights like him.

Leah looked down at her hands, and her voice cracked

when she spoke. "This was her life. Wasn't it? Before me. Before . . . my dad."

Eric turned, meeting her eyes. His face hardened, and he nodded. "She was a fighter, and a good one too. She even had her own elite squad. Lizzy was far better than I could ever be."

Leah imagined her fending off demons and saving others from death. Leah could be just like that. She could be the fighter that her mother gave up being.

"What about you? Do you have a squad?"

Eric avoided her gaze. "Not anymore. I prefer to work alone. Scout and provide support to other squads."

She took a step back and cleared her throat. "Well, now I'm with you. We can work together. I'm ready to fight—"

"No."

The dream in Leah's head shattered, and she tilted her head. "Why not?"

Eric folded up the map and shook his head. "You need to get back to the outpost. It's too dangerous out here."

Leah bit her lip, the idea of following in her mother's footsteps becoming a distant glimmer of hope. She eyed the folded-up map on the table. "Is this how it's going to be? After the outpost. Living out of motels? Shut off from the rest of the world?"

Eric nodded. "For me, yes. You might end up doing something else. Lizzy didn't always do this if that is what you're asking. But there is always something, somewhere, trying to shift the balance."

Leah looked at her uncle's face. At the bags under his eyes. He'd sacrificed everything for this. Sacrificed knowing her and watching her grow up because of this cause. A cause she was starting to understand. She nodded, her face hardening. "And we're here to protect it."

The sun passed beyond the peak in the sky as they pulled into a rest stop overlooking Badlands National Park.

A few kids played at one of the picnic tables in front of them, their parents watching from the side of their RV. Leah checked her arm, tracing up and down the large purple and yellow bruise that had blossomed from her elbow.

Eric parked the car and sighed.

"Well, what now?" Leah asked.

"The map suggests it overlooks the Badlands just as good as any of the parks." He pointed toward the building. "There's some food in the vending machine if you want anything more than what I've got. Otherwise, you might be able to catch dinner at the outpost if things go well." He fished out a couple of quarters and handed it to her.

"And miss out on a honeybun? No way." Leah opened the door, noticing the flecks of blood staining her gray shirt.

She left him in the car, finding the vending machine and grabbing herself a honeybun. When she headed back to the car, she spotted Eric waving to her, leading her down a secluded path. Leah followed, picking away at the pastry, the icing sticking to her fingers. As she walked, Leah looked out toward the Badlands, peaks of rock streaked with reds, browns, and purples.

"So, what now?" Leah asked., while trying to catch up.

"We focus on you."

Leah paused, thinking of the others she'd flung around in the outpost backyard. "So I stop being a danger to everyone else?"

"So you stop being a danger to yourself. Take all this sleeping, for instance. I doubt you normally sleep this much."

Leah looked up, realization hitting her. She had been sleeping a lot more lately.

"You've used the Trees, both of them, a lot in the past few days," Eric said. "That sort of energy takes a toll. Luckily, for *Malchut,* that toll is only exhaustion. The other wells are not as kind. I think that it's time for a lesson."

Eric peered out to the open land. "Without months of training, most Mystics can barely push down a dummy, let alone an entire house. Do you know yet why you can do what they couldn't?"

She paced in the grass, finishing the pastry and licking her fingers. "Not really, no."

Eric steepled his fingers. "Out of all the times you've used it—the house, the practice yard, on the demon—what did you want? What did you *feel*?"

"Scared." The memory writhed, the feeling inside her again, a feeling she was growing accustomed to. "Well, scared at the house, and here with the demon. The time at the outpost, I was angry."

"What made them different? The time at the house and here. Did you think of me, or the demon? I was right behind it when you slashed it. The second time you tried using *Malchut.* How come you didn't hit me with it?"

She walked toward the edge of the overlook, peering down at the rocks below. "Because I wanted to protect you, but I also wanted to stop the demon before it got out."

Eric clapped his hands. "Exactly, and that's probably the same motive you had back at the house. Only you were protecting yourself in that case. *Malchut* easily changes to *Nehemoth* when all you want to do is to be stronger than the other person. When your intentions are to protect, *Malchut* will prevail. But the moment you fill that void with anger, *Nehemoth* entices you to absorb energy, pulling on more than you should before exploding it out with *Malchut.*

Where *Malchut* depends on what energy you have, *Nehemoth* adds to it, making it stronger and more chaotic."

Leah walked back to the picnic table, sitting down across from Eric. "Like what happened at the outpost?"

Eric stood. "You were angry at that girl, Paige. Your motive wasn't focused on protection. You wanted power so you could dominate the situation."

Leah thought back to the feeling, the voices, and the energy that came with it. "It was hard to tell the difference at first."

"Yes, but that difference matters. Your motive always has to be protection, and you need to hold that in your mind, never allowing it to waver. Otherwise, *Nehemoth* can sneak in and make your *Malchut* unstable and dangerous."

Leah remembered the feeling, the wave pushing against an invisible force in front of Paige before it shattered. "What if your opponent uses *Nehemoth*? How can you protect yourself from that if it is more powerful?"

Eric paced again. "Other wells. You could make yourself invulnerable and stop the opponent, like I stopped our car on the highway, or burn them to a crisp." He looked over at Leah, her eyes wide and eager to learn. He smiled and shook his head. "All in due time. You shouldn't have to worry when facing demons. Most don't have the energy to protect against *Malchut* unless their host is a Mystic. Once you get back to the outpost, and eventually get a *Yesod* bond, you'll have the upper hand."

Leah hopped up from the bench. "What if I don't want to go back?"

Eric rubbed the back of his neck. "Well, you can't stay with me. So, if you don't go back, then the Board will put you somewhere you don't want to go. Somewhere that will not help you get the answers and fight that you want."

She sighed. Did she really have a choice? Other than

running away, but Leah guessed the Board would find her one way or another if she did. "Fine. What do I need to do?"

"Show me you can control your intent. You already did it once, with the demon. Now again, without the threat. You ready to do that?"

Leah opened and closed her fists. She could do it. She *had* to. Her back straightened, and she faced Eric. "Ready, Black Knight Mizrahi."

He stepped back, closer to the overlook, and said, "Then strike me with *Malchut*."

She looked out past him, his feet mere inches from the edge. "What? Here? You said without a threat."

"There isn't a threat. Strike me and prove you have control."

"But you're so close to the edge. What if you fall?"

Eric fished around in his pocket and tossed the keys at Leah's feet. "Then drive off into the sunset. I've got a few hundred dollars in the glove compartment that could get you to the coast. I hear the Board might struggle to find someone like you in Vancouver." He shrugged. "But that won't happen. I know it. Just slide me back a few inches, nothing more." He placed his hands behind his back and stood still, staring at her.

Leah could feel her heartbeat loudly in her ears. She stared at the keys on the ground in front of her and back up at her uncle.

There was no going back now. She thought of Sarah and Isaac, two people who at least knew more than any of her friends back home. Two people she felt like she could trust.

She shook out her arms, relieving the tension before placing them behind her back, thumbs and index fingers touching. She breathed, imagining the pressure building in her chest.

"That's it," Eric said. "Just a little."

The energy uncoiled within her, a soft pressure slithering inside her skin, pressing against her, ready to be released.

She thought of Eric in front of her, the drop-off behind him. She didn't want him to fall, she couldn't let him.

Her eyes opened, and she kicked her foot forward, feeling the wave of energy expanding out like a breeze emanating off her body.

The gravel under Eric's feet crumbled and moved as his feet slid closer to the edge, slipping up onto the stone held in place on the edge of the cliff.

Leah let go of the energy, and the serpent inside her receded back, the pressure subsiding.

Eric smiled and stepped away from the edge. "Well done."

Leah gasped and clapped her hands over her mouth. "I did it!"

She ran up and hugged Eric. He stood frozen for a moment before hugging her back.

For now, she was safe. Leah had her uncle, her protector, holding her. Everything felt right with the world. "Thank you," she whispered into his coat.

Eric patted her on the back and broke away. "Okay, that's enough love for today." He stepped past her and scooped up the keys, heading back up the trail toward the car. "Record time, if you ask me. Time to head back to the outpost and show that Black Bishop what you can do. I'm sure Alma would sleep sounder knowing you're coming back."

Leah raised an eyebrow, but before she could ask about his next mission, he had already left her alone in the small inlet. She chased him up the path back to the car, ready to see her friends again.

CHAPTER 22
NEW BEGINNINGS

The sun dipped below the trees, the sky turning from blue to a golden hue as they drove down the graveled roads. Leah felt her stomach curl into knots, thinking about facing Black Bishop Sachs so soon, knowing how she had disappointed her before.

Eric eyed the small wooden signs as they passed. "Almost there. You ready?"

Leah let out a long sigh and rubbed her thumb in her palms. "I think so. I'm ready to get this over and face Alma, that's for sure."

"Black Bishop Sachs," Eric said, correcting her. "She'll be fair. And she'll take you back if I say you're ready. Don't assume you won't have a punishment, but it won't be anything you can't handle."

Leah rested her head against the window, feeling the warmth of the glass. "That's what I'm worried about. Do you think she has some dungeon in the basement where she flogs the terrible students?"

Eric laughed. "Well, no one in my class ever saw it if she had one. Be sure to tell me all about it."

Leah rolled her eyes. "Ha. Ha."

They turned a corner, passing the dilapidated cabin Leah had run past with the other Squares. Ahead, the light post illuminated the cabin.

Eric stopped the car and got out. Once Leah willed herself out of the car, they walked to the front door and Eric knocked. The same knock he'd done before: once, wait, then two more.

The crickets chirped loudly here, something Leah was happy about, knowing what a home with a demon had sounded like. She wondered if that was common, animals silent around homes where something evil lurked. A familiar voice cut through her train of thought as it spoke from the other side.

"Who's there?"

"B8 bringing back a lost Square."

"And who am I to care?"

"C8, responsible for shaping Squares into Sevens."

After a brief pause, Alma cracked the door open. "Why are you back so soon?"

"I contained the demon with Leah's help. She's proven herself capable of containing herself and using her abilities with intent. She's ready, Black Bishop Sachs."

Alma opened the door all the way and looked between the two of them. "It has barely been four days. I find it very hard to believe that she learned anything in that amount of time."

Eric smiled at Leah. "She's got the fight in her." He cleared his throat. "She, uh, joined me inside on that demon case."

Alma's eyes widened, and her face grew pale, all restraint lost. "You took an untrained Square to face off with a third level demon?"

Eric took a step back and lowered his head. "Well, no, she was supposed to stay in the car, but—"

Alma's eyes glared daggers into Eric. She then scanned Leah up and down. Leah stood, sweat forming on her forehead, worried about what Alma might do if the demon had injured her. But other than the bruised elbow, which Alma seemed to notice right away and huffed, Leah was untouched.

Eric stepped in front of Leah. "Regardless, she joined me and fought well. I'm pretty sure she managed some blades out of *Malchut*. After that, she passed my test. She can control it. With a little effort on her end, she'll be ready."

Leah felt certain Alma was thinking of all the ways she could kill Eric and hide the body, but the Black Bishop cleared her expression and stood straight-backed once again. "Fine. I'm willing to trust your judgement, Eric. But this is her last chance. I will not have her endangering my students. There will be no third chance if she harms any of my other students, understand?"

Eric stood straight up. "Understood."

Alma cleared her throat and stared at Leah. "You are welcome back to the outpost as soon as you apologize to the Squares you've injured. Once they accept, then you will resume classes and abide by my rules. And I mean it. Any foot out of line, and you will be out for good. Do you understand?"

Leah nodded and straightened her stance. "Yes, Black Bishop Sachs."

A slight smile peeked out behind Alma's stern look. "Good." She looked back at Eric. "Were you able to get any information from the demon?"

Eric shook his head. "No, but hopefully they'll get something when they process it for questioning."

"I see. Well, I have some documents regarding your next case you should review before you leave. That witch cult could have some information of interest. Both of you, come inside. Leah, wait in the living room while I collect the others."

Leah sat on the couch, her eyes on the floorboards as Alma led Eric upstairs and called for the others to join her.

They piled into the living room, including Paige, who glared at Leah the moment she saw her. They paused and looked up at Alma. "Square Ackerman has something to say."

Leah stood and walked over to Alma, spotting a glare from Paige and her friends before her eyes fell on Sarah and Isaac, who both shot a quick smile. "I'm sorry for what I did. I lacked control and discipline." She looked at Paige and her friends. "It was irresponsible and dangerous of me to lash out like that. I apologize for hurting you. I'll do better from here on out." Leah stepped back, staring down at the ground, feeling the eyes on her.

Alma rested a hand on her shoulder. "Squares. Do you accept this apology?"

Sarah and Isaac shouted a yes almost before Alma even finished, followed by Gabe, Buck, and Harry.

There was a long silence, and Leah looked up to see Paige and her two friends whispering to each other. Alma cleared her throat and looked at them. "Girls, do you accept Leah's apology?"

Paige looked at Leah, her blue eyes piercing into her.

Alma raised an eyebrow. "Remember, we rise together. The students of the Black Hills Outpost are a unit, and therefore, you must all work together."

Paige rolled her eyes, and she led her friends in saying, "Fine. Yes, we accept."

Alma tutted her tongue, likely holding back a comment on the eye roll, and nodded to Leah. "Then it is done. Welcome back, Square Ackerman. Check with Square Tate on dinner and please pitch in on night duties." She panned around the room. "Black Knight Mizrahi and I will take our dinner in my office. We have some business to tend to. I expect everyone up early for Saturday drills."

Everyone stood and clicked their heels together as Alma and Eric turned toward the stairs. "Yes, Black Bishop Sachs!"

Gabe walked over to Leah and smiled. "Glad you're back. You can join Isaac and Sarah on cleanup. Everything else is taken care of. Hope you're hungry for my Friday night special: spaghetti."

Leah's chest tightened. "It's Friday?"

He tilted his head and raised an eyebrow. "Yes?"

"Oh. I, uh. Never mind."

"What?" Gabe asked.

"My mom used to make this dish on Fridays. Moroccan Fish. It was sort of a Jewish tradition. It was usually my dad who cooked, but my mom made this one. I don't know if it was because she was in the kitchen, or the spices she used, but it was special." Her lips trembled at the memory.

Gabe nodded. "Oh, I see. Well, I'm pretty sure we're out of fish. I'm sorry. The spaghetti is fantastic, though. I promise."

"It's fine. Don't worry about it. Spaghetti sounds good. It's just another thing I'll have to get used to, I guess."

Gabe said to the rest of the Squares, "Dinner will be ready in twenty."

He turned and headed to the kitchen, Buck and Harry following behind him.

Leah found Sarah and Isaac sitting on the couch behind her. Sarah hopped out of her seat and pulled Leah over to the couch. "How are you back so soon? Everyone thought you were—" She slid her finger across her throat.

Leah shrugged and sat down next to Isaac. "Guess you can't get rid of me that easily."

Isaac pulled a deck of cards from the side table and began shuffling them. "Everyone has been talking nonstop about what you did on the practice field. Alma keeps trying to silence us, but we can't stop."

Leah bit her lip, eyeing some bandages on Isaac's arm. "Yeah, things got a bit out of control. I'm sorry I hurt you guys."

Isaac dropped the cards and laughed. "Out of control? That was the coolest thing anyone has seen! No one could do an ounce of what you did."

"Yeah," Sarah leaned forward and whispered. "Paige keeps trying to come up with excuses, like you made a pact with a demon or something. Clearly, she can't handle when the competition blows her away. Literally."

The three of them chuckled and played three-way War as the aroma of basil and garlic filled the air.

While Isaac dealt cards, he said, "You guys know that was the Tree of Death, right? The thing you did, Leah? That energy wasn't something good. It was wrong."

Sarah waved her hand before flipping over her top card. "Yeah, yeah, but no one here has even got close to using the Tree of Death. So, be happy. You're now at the top of the food chain."

Isaac flipped his card, and Leah followed, winning against the three. "Great, just what I wanted, another target on my back," she said.

Leah looked over at Paige, sitting across the room, still whispering to her friends. Then Leah flipped over another card, winning against the three again.

"Dinner!" Gabe shouted from the kitchen.

They got up off the couch and sat around the table. In the center sat a massive bowl of noodles, a bowl of marinara, and a pile of garlic bread. Paige and Serena passed around plates, but before they handed a plate to Leah, Gabe cut in.

"So. I didn't think we had any fish, but I found some fish sticks in the freezer. They're still good, I promise. I also might have seasoned them a bit to just bring out the flavor. Anyway. If you don't like it, then there's still the spaghetti."

He handed over a plate of perfectly rectangular fish sticks and a dollop of tartar sauce. Leah stared at the plate, tears welling up in her eyes as images of her parents praying, laughing, and talking about school over their Shabbat dinners played in her mind. She muttered, "Thank you," before grabbing one and biting it.

It wasn't the same, by a long shot, but the gesture alone was enough. She smiled and ate her food as everyone else dug in.

After dinner, as they cleaned the dishes, Isaac elbowed Leah. "So, Sarah and I were wondering, where did you go? Alma said Squares never leave, at least not normally."

Leah looked over her shoulder, seeing that no one else was around them. She told them everything about both the demon and the rest stop.

When she was done, a pressure finally lifted off her chest, and she stared at her friends. She let out a snort, laughing at their dumbstruck expressions, glad she felt safe once again.

Sarah nudged Leah's shoulder and smiled.

"Hey, guess what?" Sarah whispered.

"Yeah?"

"I'm glad you're back."

"Yeah," Leah said, smiling. "Me too."

CHAPTER 23
A MYSTIC HISTORY

Pavement cooled her translucent, bare feet, and Leah's vision focused on the road underneath them. Another one, this time in the middle of nowhere. Darkness stretched for miles in all directions, the Badlands only illuminated by the stars above.

Lights flashed behind her, and she turned. The blinkers of a semi pulled over at the side of the road flashed into her eyes. She walked forward, noting that they had left the driver's door open.

"Hello?" Leah hugged her arms, the cool dry air sending a chill down her spine.

Her eyes focused on a hand hanging out the driver's side window, blood dripping off the fingertips into a pool on the pavement. She froze, her throat closing.

A head peered out from the driver's door, still hidden from the shadows, but she could feel the eyes on her.

Staring at her.

Smiling.

The eyes turned into Alma's as Leah opened hers. The Black Bishop quietly hovered over her bed. Leah blinked several times, wiping her eyes, trying to erase the dream from her mind.

"Downstairs in ten." Alma turned and walked out of the room without another word.

Leah sat up and stretched. "Who just stands over someone's bed like that?"

A soft giggle sounded next to her from Sarah's bed. "Better than dumping cold water on you," Sarah whispered.

Leah shrugged and headed to the bathroom before descending the stairs, dressed and ready for her lessons with Alma.

Sitting at her desk, Alma buried her nose deep in a thick book as she flipped through the pages. Leah cleared her throat in the doorway, and Alma sat upright. "Good morning, Square Ackerman."

"Morning, Black Bishop Sachs," Leah said, standing straight-backed and doing her best to stifle a yawn.

Alma gestured to the desks. "You know the drill. Front row."

Leah blinked a few times and walked over, claiming the front middle desk. "When do we get to the practice field? I'm ready to have a go at those dummies."

Alma stood up from her desk. "Not yet. It is my duty today to ensure that you have the knowledge and understanding of where the Infinity Board came from and how it works. I will have to condense weeks of history lessons in what little time we have together."

Leah leaned back in her chair, doing her best not to cross her arms and sigh. She looked to the door, wishing she could show Alma what she'd learned.

The Black Bishop paced the front of the room. "Mystics have shown up in history as witches, warlocks, or even prophets. For a long time, we were all separate, a few covens here and there. But it wasn't until we came together and formed a society that we began feeling safe from the inquisitions and witch hunts that nearly led to our extinction."

Alma continued, but Leah's mind drifted elsewhere, imagining facing off against the dummies that slowly turned into Asmodeus. She clenched her hands into fists, feeling her nails digging into her palms.

The thud of a book dropping onto her desk pulled Leah from her imagination, looking down at a portrait of a man. Alma stepped back and cleared her throat. "Maimonides, born 1135 AD in the Almoravid Empire. We call him The Great Eagle, who formed the society of Mystics. He was a man of many titles, including astronomer, philosopher, chess player, and a Jewish scholar who shared what he learned, so no one had to learn on their own."

Leah leaned forward, instinctively reaching for her necklace. She paused, remembering that she had taken off the Star of David ages ago, ever since . . .

"So, the Infinity Board is a Jewish Society?" she asked.

Alma stopped pacing and shook her head. "No, the society has no religion. It pulled tenants from the Kabbalah, but the Tree of Life shows up throughout history, not tied to any one religion."

Leah dropped her hand and rested it on the other. She looked at the portrait, tracing over his arched eyebrows with her eyes. She took in a breath and asked. "Are there religious people in the Infinity Board?"

"Yes. There is no rule against it, and for those seeking higher knowledge, a breadth of religious understanding that spans over multiple religions is encouraged. I suppose while on that journey, some may settle into one that calls to them."

Leah couldn't help herself. The question bubbled to the surface before she could stop it. "What about you? What do you believe?"

Alma paused, glancing out the window and smiling. "If you had to give it a label, you might call me agnostic. I believe all religions lead back to the Tree, so I look there for knowledge and truth."

She turned and pulled down the same diagram Leah had seen in her first lesson, the image of the tree with ten circles joined by intersecting lines. Alma pointed to the top well, with Hebrew lettering within the circle that spelled:

כֶּתֶר

"The highest well, *Keter*, comes from the Hebrew word 'crown.' I suppose if I have anything to believe in, it comes from there. The essence of the divine. No one from the Infinity Board has accessed it since the founding."

Leah eyed the top circle. "No one? Then how do you know what it is?"

"Centuries of study. Religions were mapped and old texts scoured over until 1837, when a war broke out in the society." The Black Bishop grabbed her mug and took a sip, wrapping her hands around it while she paced the front of the room. "A group of power-hungry Mystics rose against the Scholars and Protectors. Their desire to rule beyond the bounds of the society led to the downfall of the Society of Mystics. Based on the records, it was the bloodiest event Mystics have faced in history."

Leah envisioned how a battle between Mystics might look, with invisible forces flinging everyone left and right and balls of fire streaming through the air.

Alma continued, "Mystics are the living embodiment of self-sacrifice. We might have to sacrifice our lives, or even worse, the lives of our comrades, for the greater good. For the safety of humankind. Never forget that."

Leah nodded.

Alma carried on. "After the war, Branch organizations, like the Infinity Board, grew in place of the Society of Mystics, maintaining a balance in their designated locations and awaiting the member who can access *Keter*."

Leah tilted her head. "So, the Infinity Board isn't the only one?"

Alma nodded. "But only the Queens know the other societies by name and location."

Leah glanced out the window, seeing the morning sun light up the tops of trees.

Alma pulled up the chart and looked at Leah. "One last bit for today, then we'll break for breakfast. You are a Square on the Board. Simply a potential place for a piece to sit. Pieces scale up in ranking as Pawn, Knight, Bishop, Rook, and Queen. Rankings also alternate from Black to White. Meaning that your first promotion will be as a Black Pawn. Through trials, you can earn a promotion to White Pawn, while bonding you to a Knight or a Bishop. Further promotions are based on skills and mastery of the wells from the Tree."

Leah nodded. "That makes my uncle a Black Knight. That's a lower rank than you, right?"

Alma tilted her head and nodded. "Technically, yes, but the Knight and Bishop rankings are staggered. A White Knight outranks me."

Alma waited a moment before continuing. "Where Knights and Bishops are ordered on missions and teach the Pawns. Rooks maintain order in the outer council, which organizes the overall direction for the Board, among other important duties, on and off the field. Then, the Queens make any final or crucial decisions. Both Queens and Rooks survey the Infinity Board for corruption and possession and snuff out any internal threats."

Leah raised an eyebrow. "You missed the Black King and White King."

Alma smiled. "The King, which has no color, is an empty position, open to anyone who successfully masters *Keter*. The King will lead the Infinity Board, and all the other societies, out of secrecy to bring balance to the Earth. Though no one has come even close, not even the Great Eagle."

"And what happens when you have a King. What will he do?"

Alma smiled. "Or she. The roles of the Infinity Board are based on skill. If a woman were to access *Keter*, then she would become King."

Leah ran her fingers through her hair, processing everything Alma explained. "I don't know if I'm going to remember it all."

"You will, in time. We'll go over it again."

Noises sounded from above, and Alma looked at the clock.

"Time to join the others for breakfast. Perhaps you'll remember some of this when I quiz you this evening."

CHAPTER 24
TEST

During Leah's private lessons over the next week, Alma drilled the history of the Board over and over in Leah's mind. She repeated the structure of the society, adding in more bits and pieces of history that stuck in her memory.

In the mornings, they ran, raced through obstacle courses, and practiced maintaining control while pushing and sliding the practice dummies away with *Malchut*. In the afternoons, she sat in the classroom with the others, going over history and practical uses of *Malchut*.

Eventually, Paige's mutterings and side comments became part of the background. Leah had become one of them. They were a functioning unit, led by Alma.

After another week of lessons during every waking moment, from history to basic rituals, Leah's evening lessons changed. She then became more like a personal assistant to Alma.

She filed away missions and took notes while Black Knights, none of whom were her uncle, came to the outpost to report back to Alma on their cases.

One rainy morning, Sarah and Isaac quizzed Leah in the kitchen.

Isaac leaned in and rubbed his hands. "Okay, *Hod*?"

Leah looked up at the ceiling. "Uh, it stops movement, but can cause insomnia and jitters."

Isaac nodded. "And *Netzach*?"

Leah bit her lip and Sarah jumped in. "Invulnerability at the cost of thinking you can take on anything, even after it burns out."

Steps sounded behind them as Alma descended the stairs carrying a bag, Gabe following right behind her.

The three of them stood and in unison with the other Squares said, "Good morning, Black Bishop Sachs."

Alma glanced outside at the rain. "Good morning, Squares. Join me in the classroom. Lessons will be inside today."

Alma took ten candles from her bag and placed them on her desk while the Squares took their seats. She pulled a lighter from her drawer and stood at the front of the class.

"Square Ackerman, join me up here."

Leah's face flushed, and she stood, slowly heading to the front, next to Alma.

"Square Ackerman has proved her restraint on the practice field this week, so I feel it is time to take our practice up to the next level." She held up the candle and lit it, the flame shining a faint light on her face. "While she was away, Square Ackerman refined *Malchut* into what we call blades. Today I want you all to blow out these candles, doing just that."

A small murmur broke out, but Alma's hand quickly silenced it. She placed the candle at the front of her desk and signaled Leah to the other side of the room.

"When you are ready, I want you to let out the tiniest gust of *Malchut*, directed at the wick."

Leah nodded and stared at the candle. She replayed the memory of the demon, the thought of her uncle getting hurt, and her need to protect him. This was no different. Alma stood next to the candle, and Leah could strike her if she wasn't careful.

She drew in a long breath and put her hands behind her back. She faced the candle, her eyes locked onto the wick below the flame. Leah could feel the other Squares staring, waiting for her to do something.

Paige scoffed, breaking Leah's concentration. She glanced over, spotting Paige leaning over and whispering into Serena's ear.

Alma cleared her throat, and Leah snapped her head back to the candle, her mind drawing attention to the wick.

Eric's voice played in her head. *Keep calm and focus.*

She shifted into the stance, and the energy inside her uncoiled and pressed against her skin. With Alma in her peripheral, Leah focused on keeping her safe from the pressure within her. She only needed a sliver of energy, thin as a blade and as wide as the candle. The pressure sunk into her fingertips, and she shifted her leg forward, pulling her hand out from behind her back and slicing through the air, pointing at the wick.

The flame on the candle snuffed out, and Leah stood frozen, her finger pointing at it.

Sarah and Isaac clapped, forcing the others into a round of applause. Leah looked around with a slight smirk until she found Gabe's eyes locked on hers, as if studying her. Leah quickly looked down, feeling her cheeks getting hot.

Alma stepped out from behind her desk and over to Leah. "All right, class, settle down." She gave a quick approving nod to Leah before turning to the class. "Thank you, Square Ackerman. I hope the rest of you noted her stance. Line the desks up along the wall and stand with your backs to the windows. I don't want any of you blowing out one of them. I'm looking at you, Square Baccus." Alma glared at Buck.

The others stood, moving their desks and creating a line of candles on one side of the room while they lined up on the other.

"Why did you pick me to do that first?" Leah asked Alma. "Gabe, or even Paige, could have done it."

Alma shifted her gaze to the other students, noting Buck had already splattered hot wax all over the wall. She rolled her eyes. "I picked you because you're quite the natural. From what your uncle told me, you formed the blades instinctively. I was curious if you'd be able to do it again. Besides, had I picked someone like Square Baccus or Square Douglas, I'd be scraping wax out of my clothes for weeks."

Leah laughed and looked over at Buck and Harry, who'd already splattered hot wax on each other.

Leah turned, readying herself to join Sarah and Isaac, when Alma rested a hand on her shoulder.

"Perhaps I see myself in you, Square Ackerman. You've been pushed to your limits a few times now, yet you keep persevering. You've got something to prove, and that will take you far." Alma dropped her hand and marched toward Square Baccus. "No, your form is all off. Let me show you again."

Leah lay in bed, woken by the faintest whisper of, "Leah," which trailed on the whistling sounds from the wind outside. "Leah."

She sat up in bed, looking around the dark room. A

silhouette stood in the door frame, a shadow she couldn't make out from the starry light coming in from the window.

"We have little time. Follow me." The voice rang a familiar tone, a woman's voice.

She squinted at the silhouette before clearing out the lump in her throat. "Mom? Is that you?"

The silhouette glowed, and the features of her mother showed in the dark. "Yes, my love. Hurry and follow me. We have little time."

"But . . . you're . . ."

"Dead. Yes. Come, I need to show you something." The silhouette turned, gliding out of the room and through the door.

Leah furrowed her brows and got out of bed, slipping out the door on her tiptoes. Her mother's silhouette floated down the hallway, glowing dimly in the pitch black. Leah followed, butterflies fluttering in her stomach. Her mother was here, somehow, and all she wanted to do was hug her once more.

The ghostly figure floated through Alma's office, casting Leah into the dark. Leah raced up to the door and tested it, unlocked, and turned the handle, slipping into the room and closing the door behind her. Her mother's spirit hovered in front of the wall of books, her hand tracing the bindings.

"Mom? What is it?"

Her mom faced her and smiled, gliding toward her and brushing Leah's face with warm fingertips.

"You've grown so much already." She paused and looked away. "I'm sorry things went the way they did."

Leah reached out and grabbed her mother's hand. "Mom . . . I—"

Her mother cut her off. "We don't have the time."

"What is it? What do you have to tell me?"

"This connection is weak. Come. Over here." She led Leah to the wall of books.

Her hand passed through a few books Leah had seen a bunch of times already when she would pull them for Alma. *Early Renaissance Architecture* and *Gardening Homesteads,* books that Leah would never look twice at unless she was looking for good sleeping material.

"Behind those, pull them out."

Leah slid the books out of the shelves, revealing a small compartment in the wall. "What is it?"

"She keeps her most prized books in there. Ones she doesn't want others to see. Open it, see for yourself."

Inside sat a small black leather-bound book. There were no insignias on the outside, and the pages looked hand bound.

"A black tome, full of rituals. There's one in particular you could use to see me." The glow on her mother dimmed, and she looked at her hand. She sighed heavily and looked at Leah. "There is a page on Astral Projection. Learn it so we can meet again and with more time." She paused and looked around the room, landing her gaze on Alma's desk. "You can't trust her, or any of them. Why do you think I left? I had to keep you safe. Learn the ritual. Use it and see me on the other side."

"Why can't you just tell me now? Why show me this?"

"They listen. And I can't stay here long enough this time to show you, but time on the other side is longer. You'll see." She tapped the book. "When you wake, take this book. Keep it hidden and use it the moment you learn." She winced and flickered as if for a moment she wasn't even there. "I can't stay. Please, do what I ask." She stared into Leah's eyes, her honey-colored eyes reddened with tears.

Leah nodded, tears slipping down her face. "Okay, Mom. I will."

"That's my girl." She smiled and leaned in, kissing Leah on the forehead before fading away.

Leah jolted upright in bed, cold sweat seeping out of every pore. She touched her forehead and still felt the warmth from her mother's kiss.

She lay back down, staring up at the ceiling, feeling the warm breeze coming in from the open window. If it hadn't been a dream, then there was a book in Alma's office that would prove it. A book her mother wanted her to have.

CHAPTER 25

DREAM SECRETS

Leah slipped out of bed long before Alma came to wake her. She prepared herself for the day and sitting through the private lesson, wondering what her mother had to tell her.

The day blurred together. History lessons and training passed Leah without a single thought. All Leah could think about was the dream and her mother. The dream had rattled something inside her, and the sooner she could get up to Alma's office, the better.

On the porch, after dinner, she sat away from the others until Sarah and Isaac squeezed in next to her. Sarah nudged Leah, snapping her out of her daze. "What's with you today?"

Leah blinked a few times and looked over at Sarah. "What are you talking about?"

"You've been acting all . . ." Sarah mimicked a zombie, with her arms outstretched and face slack. "The entire day. What is it?"

Leah bit her lip. She'd considered telling them about what had happened to her, but what they might say worried her. It'd be easier, though, with a lookout or two.

She ducked her head lower as her friends leaned in. "Fine, but what I'm about to tell you stays between us. Got it?"

Sarah leaned back and slapped her knee. "Aw man, I planned to spill the beans to my bestie Paige."

Isaac rolled his eyes and laughed. "The day that happens, I'm pretty sure hell will freeze over."

"I'm serious, guys," Leah said. "This isn't the time to joke around."

"I'm sorry," Sarah said.

"Yeah," Isaac added. "You know we've got your back and your secret is safe with us."

Leah took in a deep breath and nodded. She told them about her dream, about her mother, and the book. When she finished, she looked at the two of them. "I just want to know if it was real, you know?"

"What was in the book?" Isaac asked.

Leah tried remembering the contents of the book. "It was something that would let me see her again. Face to face. Some kind of ritual."

Isaac looked out toward the practice field, scratching his head. "I dunno, Leah. I don't like this. Rituals like that can't be good. And breaking into Alma's office, over a dream? She'd have our heads."

Sarah smiled and rubbed her hands together. "But if we don't, we'll never know. It has to be a message from the other side. We've heard of stranger things. What's saying this can't happen?"

Leah stepped off the porch and paced in the grass. "I know it's a risk. I was worried about telling both of you because I know what it could mean if we get caught. Sure, it could've only been a dream, but I'm not willing to believe that. Not yet."

Sarah hopped up and shrugged. "There's only one way

to find out." She couldn't hold back a grin, and Leah was certain Sarah was just looking for a chance to do something dangerous.

Leah looked up at the second-floor window above them, chewing on her bottom lip. "My private lessons at night are usually in her office. Maybe I can rig the door and sneak in after."

Isaac shook his head. "It's pretty quiet at night. One creaky floorboard and she could know someone was moving around. And then trying to rig a door. When would you have time?"

Leah paused and crossed her arms. He was right. Her plan likely wouldn't work. "I don't know when else we could do it. I just need that book."

Isaac shook his head. "I don't like it. It's too risky."

"Oh come on," Sarah said, "We can pull it off."

Leah met Isaac's eyes. "Please? For me?"

He let out a long sigh and shook his head. "We'd have to do it during lessons when she's distracted by the rest of us. I could ask her a ton of questions, more than the usual to keep her busy. That would buy you two time to get in and get out. Only problem is the door. I don't know if she keeps it locked or not."

Sarah put her hands on her hips and shook her head. "Isaac! I didn't know you had it in you."

Isaac smirked and looked up at the second floor. "There is more to me than I let on." He looked at Leah. "And you don't want to just tell Alma about your dream?"

Leah shook her head. "I want to be certain. In the dream, Mom said not to trust her. There has to be a reason."

Sarah stepped in between Leah and Isaac and wrapped her arms around their shoulders. "Okay, I'm all in. Isaac will be the brains, and I'll be your guard. Yeah?"

Isaac paused, then shrugged. "Well, we've got to know the truth, right?"

The plan took three days to devise. Isaac insisted the girls let him map out all the variables any moment they had free time. "To ensure everything goes according to plan," he kept saying.

By the third evening, Leah and Sarah had had enough of it. That day had been composed of a grueling practice, using all they learned with *Malchut* to roll a single marble into a contraption that would launch a disc they had to shatter. Buck had broken the contraption entirely on his second attempt, while Gabe had been the only one who'd gotten it right the first time he'd tried. Shifting between *Malchut* forms had proved exhausting, and now Leah and Sarah laid on the floor of the living room as Isaac opened a small diary he hid from Alma.

"Let's run over it one more time," Isaac said.

Sarah rolled over onto her stomach and groaned. "Leah will ask to go to the bathroom ten minutes before class lets out. I ask five minutes before class ends and stand guard at the top of the stairs. You pester Alma, and *voilà*." Sarah rolled her eyes. "Not that hard."

Isaac shut his diary and glared. "You skipped a few things. And if we don't follow every detail, then everything falls apart."

Leah smiled at Isaac. "We've got this. Promise. You made a solid plan."

Isaac watched Alma ascend the stairs. "I hope so."

Leah reached the top of the stairs, slipping off her shoes and tiptoeing down to Alma's office. She tested the knob and wasn't shocked to find it locked.

Shit.

She didn't have time for this. At least Isaac had a back-up plan.

Leah knelt and checked the lock, a simple pushpin lock. She pulled the bobby pin from her hair and bent it, fishing around the lock until she heard the pop of the lock coming free.

She slipped in, shutting the door gently behind her. Tiptoeing along the edges of the room to avoid any creaks on the floor, she made it to the end of the bookshelf.

Leah scraped at her memory, trying to remember the names of the books her mother had pulled out, but none seemed to resemble those from the dream. Instead, she removed the books from the shelf, one by one, looking behind them until she spotted the small door.

Her heart pounded in her chest. Emotion welled up inside her, loss, fear, and excitement all bundled into one. She raised a shaky hand, testing the small door, but it wouldn't budge.

Creaks from the stairs echoed down the hallway.

Fuck.

She raced to get her fingernails into the little door as the steps creaked closer.

Please don't be Alma. Please don't be Alma.

The next creak in the hallway came, and she yanked on the door, popping it free. She listened, waiting to hear more footsteps headed up the stairs, but nothing came.

Inside, the black book rested on top of a set of other

books, each with worn names, or no names at all. She wrapped her fingers around it, and a feeling washed over, pulling her stomach into knots.

The dream was real.

Her instinct was to throw the book back in the compartment and slam it shut, the feeling inside her that strong. Yet, she held onto it, knowing something inside would take her to her mother.

Leah opened it to the first page where a brownish ink spelled out the words *Grimorium Aeternum*. She flipped through the other pages, seeing sketched rituals and notes. The rituals inside contained rites to bind a foe, to peer into the future, and to enhance power. Someone had gone through it and crossed out the text, scrawling notes in the margins on how to do it better.

She finally came to the page she'd been searching for: *Chapter Twenty: Astral Projection Rites and Rituals.* Through the notes and text, she determined that the ritual required herbs, a ton of salt, and bones. A symbol filled the next page, and from the notes, she'd have to draw it on the floor. The markings were all foreign to her, but she traced them over and over in her head, committing them to memory.

Sarah sounded out from the other side of the door. "Uh, Paige, what are you doing up here?"

Paige huffed. "Could you move? Alma asked to check on Leah. She wanted her for something. Leah, you in there?" She shouted toward the bathroom at the end of the hall.

Leah felt the blood drain from her face.

Why did Alma send Paige of all people?

The book was too bulky to sneak out, but she wasn't ready to go yet. The ritual was too complex. She tore the pages out, slowly, to not make any noise, and slid the book back into the compartment, restocking the shelf.

"I said I'd get her for you," Sarah said. "She isn't feeling well. Those pizza rolls last night didn't sit right."

"Why are you acting weird? You two sneaking off to make out or something?" Paige laughed at her own joke, and Leah clenched her jaw.

Don't do anything stupid, Sarah.

Shuffling sounded outside the door, and Sarah said, "Yep, obviously. Fine, go to the bathroom and see for yourself since you don't believe me. Just don't tell me I didn't warn you."

"Gross," Paige said. Footsteps sounded closer as they walked down the hallway to the bathroom, nestled between Alma's office and the girls' room.

Leah tiptoed around the office and to the exit, listening as the door to the bathroom swung open.

Sarah pulled open the door to the office, her face pale, and waved Leah out of the room.

Leah turned to head down the stairs, but Sarah grabbed her arm and pointed to the dorms. Leah followed her friend's instruction and raced down the hall.

Sarah stood in front of the bathroom doors as they opened, coming face to face with Paige.

"She's not in there," Paige said.

"Oh, strange. Maybe she went and laid down?"

Paige glanced over at the girls' room and spotted Leah with her hand on the door handle, her shoes in her hands. Paige looked at the two of them, then her eyes widened. "I was right! You two *were* making out!" She grinned.

"I don't know what you're talking about," Sarah said, trying to stifle gasping for air from racing down the hall.

Paige raised her hands and smiled. "I was only joking before. But I'm cool with it, just so you know." She focused on Leah. "Alma's looking for you. Maybe you should, uh, freshen up a bit? I'll just let you two be, then."

Paige stepped out of the bathroom and headed down the hall, passing by Leah without a word.

When they heard her reach the bottom of the stairs, Sarah asked, "Was it there?"

Leah pulled the folded-up pages partway out of her pocket. "Yeah, I got it."

"Holy shit. Wait, the dream was real?"

Smiling, Leah nodded.

"I can't. Holy shit. Leah. Your mom . . ."

"I know," Leah said, smiling.

"And you ripped the pages out of the book?"

Leah shrugged. "I was in a hurry. The book was thick and already in terrible shape, so unless she needs this specific page, she won't notice."

Sarah looked back down the hall to Alma's office. "Well, good. I don't know if I'm ready to break in again anytime soon."

Leah smiled and slipped on her shoes. "We should do the ritual tonight, before she notices someone found the book."

Sarah grinned, a mischievous light flickering in her eyes. "Hell yeah we should."

CHAPTER 26
ASTRAL REALM

Leah and Sarah found Isaac standing in front of Alma's desk, still bombarding her with questions after the lecture. "But why doesn't everyone use *Yesod* to bond to the Tree? Wouldn't it be easier?"

"We bond with each other as part of our tradition. Not only is it easier, but it helps maintain the structure that we have established within the Board."

"But . . ." Isaac started, but Alma raised her hand and stood up from her desk.

"I think that is enough for now, Square O'Conner. I appreciate your curiosity, but we will continue our lessons on *Yesod* tomorrow. Please, do you mind clearing the board before dinner?" She grabbed her things to leave, spotting Leah and Sarah on the way out.

"Square Ackerman, I forgot to mention that I don't need your assistance this evening. I need to make a run for supplies."

"Do you need me to go with you?" Leah asked instinctively.

Stupid, why would you ask that?

Alma shook her head. "No, I'll be going alone. I expect

you Squares to be civil while I am away. You'll take charge of nightly duties and getting everyone to bed on time, understand?"

Leah sighed and stood at attention. "Yes, Black Bishop Sachs."

Alma nodded and exited the room, leaving Sarah and Leah alone with Isaac.

Sarah slapped Isaac on the back. "Good job, Isaac! I'm gonna make a rule breaker out of you yet!"

Isaac smiled. "Was it there?"

She patted her pocket. "Yep. Had to tear out a few pages, but it looks like we can get most of what we need from the kitchen."

He looked up to the ceiling, hearing Alma's footsteps as she entered her office. "So, it's true then? The dream?"

Leah nodded.

Sarah rubbed her hands together and looked at Isaac. "We're doing the ritual tonight while the Black Bishop is gone."

Isaac dropped his gaze from the ceiling and stared at her, his face paling. "Tonight? We should study it so we don't mess up. Why rush it now?"

Leah pulled the pages from her pocket and held them up to Isaac. "My mother wanted me to do this as soon as I got it. She doesn't trust Alma, and I need to know why. Tonight is our best shot."

Isaac paced the room, rubbing his finger over his lips.

Sarah sat on top of a desk. "We'll both look after her, alright? She'll be fine."

Isaac leaned against the wall and let out a deep breath. "How do you know? You don't. I don't think this is right."

Sarah groaned and pulled at her curls. "You're right, I don't know. But I think we can both agree that she is going to do it with or without us. So, the least we can do is to be her lookout."

Isaac looked at Leah and then down at the ground. "Fine. I don't like it, but what do we need?"

Leah unfolded the pages on Alma's desk while the other two huddled around her. "We need salt, sage, rosemary, thyme, matches, and a bowl. Isaac, do you think you can pinch the herbs and a bowl from the cupboards? Salt, we need about a pound. I think we can use the pickling salt. Yeah?"

Isaac eyed the pages and nodded.

Leah continued. "Next, animal bones. It isn't specific, but the freezer in the cellar has to have something in it, right?"

Sarah nodded. "Alma gets meat from a butcher every few months and stores it in there."

"Good." Leah paused and found the last thing on her list. "Last thing I need is a knife. I'll take one from the kitchen when we clean up. I'm sure Serena and Paige will switch dish duty with wiping down the tables. We'll have to wait until everyone is asleep, then sneak back down here. The nearest town I saw was nearly three hours away, so Alma won't be back until late. We need somewhere we can do this ritual away from everyone."

Sarah looked around the classroom. "If we sneak back in here, no one will bother us."

"What about the mess it'll make?" Isaac asked.

Leah paused, thinking. "I'll grab a bucket and some cleaning supplies from the kitchen, too. We'll clean up once we've finished."

Isaac nodded. "That should work, as long as we don't destroy the place."

"Alright," Leah said. "We'll get the supplies and sneak

them in here when we can. We'll meet back around midnight."

They joined the others in the kitchen, Leah siding up next to Gabe. "Can I help you with dinner?"

Gabe looked up from the cutting board, cubing raw chicken. "Actually yeah. That'd be great. Harry and Serena are on dinner duty, but they're useless."

Leah looked over, spotting Harry leaning up against the counter, eyeing Emma before he shot a glare at Gabe. "Hey, who're you calling useless?"

Gabe set down the knife and turned to Harry. "Do you know how to make a roux?"

"Well . . . uh, no. But I can make a mean ramen."

Gabe shook his head. "Can you and Serena just set the plates or something?"

He turned to Leah. "How about you?"

Leah racked her brain, remembering the nights she'd spent cooking with her dad. She half-smiled and said, "Flour and butter, low heat until it browns?"

Gabe smiled. "Wow. I might have a new sous-chef here!"

Leah got to work, easily pocketing the herbs she needed for later while working on the stovetop. When the coast was clear, she opened the door to the cellar so Sarah could slip in with no one noticing.

Gabe turned her roux into an Alfredo, and shortly after, their chicken Alfredo served a table full of hungry Squares.

Leah sat up and looked out the window, confirming that Alma hadn't returned before she slipped out of bed. She lightly shook Sarah's foot, checking to see if she was awake as the other girls breathed heavily, deep in slumber.

She slipped her hand into her pocket, confirming the paper was still there before creeping across the room. She tensed, her hands shaking. Tonight, she'd see her mother again, get to hug her again and tell her how much she loved her. Leah would finally admit the accident had been her fault. That she'd brought Asmodeus to them with the Ouija board and that she should have listened to her mother and stayed home.

She tiptoed out of the room, waiting for Sarah to emerge before they closed the door behind them.

Leah whispered to Sarah, "Okay, now we wait for Isaac."

Moments later, a silhouette rounded the corner at the end of the hall, and Isaac joined them, yawning and rubbing at his eyes.

They crept down the stairs one by one, keeping to the edges of the steps and pausing at any hint of a creak.

The door to the classroom slid open, and a waft of raw meat blew over them. Leah turned to the others, stifling a gag.

Sarah brushed past the two of them and ran to the windows. "Ugh, help me open these. I didn't think the bones would reek this bad."

With fresh air to clear their senses, Leah grabbed the supplies from the corner and carried them into the center of the floor. She pulled one of the practice candles from Alma's desk and lit it, using the candlelight to peer over the torn pages. She stuck her arm out to the chalkboard and whispered, "Hand me the chalk," and she reviewed the notes again.

Isaac dropped the chalk in her hand and hovered over her shoulder. "We have to make sure we clean up after. If she sees chalk on the floor, she'll have our heads."

Leah nodded and began drawing two concentric circles around where she sat. In the spaces to her left and right, she drew symbols unfamiliar to her. Then, in front of her, she drew a word in Hebrew. It wasn't familiar, and the word felt strange on her tongue. "*Th . . . Thagirion?* I wonder what that's supposed to mean."

Sarah shrugged. "Maybe a well she hasn't taught us?"

Isaac kneeled and looked at the symbol. "What if it's one from the Tree of Death?"

Leah turned around and inscribed a different Hebrew word opposite of *Thagirion.* "*Malchut.*" She looked up at Isaac. "See? Whatever *Thagirion* is, it probably just enhances *Malchut,* just like what my uncle inscribed on his arms to push away memories."

Sarah pulled Isaac back up to his feet and brushed her hands. "*Voilà!* Mystery solved."

Leah grabbed a handful of salt and poured one thin continuous circle around her, following the chalk line. She placed a small pile of bones on either side of her, and then sprinkled crushed thyme, rosemary, and sage into the bowl and lit a match, igniting the herbs. The scent of burning spices permeated the air, and a buzz filled Leah's ears.

Leah repositioned herself in the circle and flattened out the paper in front of her before looking up at the others. "Okay, it says here to never break the circle. I should be able to hear you on the other side if you need me to come back."

Sarah nodded and checked the doorway. "Okay, we'll keep an eye out. If Alma comes back, we'll let you know."

Leah let out a long breath. "Here we go." She cleared her throat and squinted at the inscription. "*Taob,* I call on you to transport me to the astral realm. Take me to the far reaches, to the place between wake and dream. *Taob*, heed my call.”

A breeze flickered the candle, and Leah looked up at Sarah and Isaac. A few moments passed, and she was about to say she didn't think it worked when a pressure exploded out of her chest. It was like a serpent inside her, striking without notice, and she felt her mind expand with it, beyond her body.

Everything churned and changed in an instant. One moment she was sitting inside a dark classroom with Isaac and Sarah, the next she was standing in the same classroom but with a dull orange glow filling the room, and no Sarah or Isaac in sight.

Everything was different and stale. She turned around, noting a dark orb floating in midair. The portal, she recalled from the pages, would take her back to her body.

Her eyes adjusted to the sickening light, and she spotted the hole immediately. Half the wall of the classroom was completely torn off, and tufts of yellowed grass and moss flowed into the classroom like some slow overtaking from the forest outside. Even though the hole in the wall must have been missing for ages, the wood hadn't rotted, left preserved from the dry stale air that Leah breathed in.

“Okay,” Leah whispered, feeling eyes on her from all directions. “I'm here, Mom. Where are you?”

She heard movement above her, where Alma's office was, and she jumped. “Mom?” Her voice echoed in the space.

Silence was the only response.

She walked over to the classroom door and reached for the handle. She paused, noticing something strange on her left arm: a jet-black handprint, like a bruise wrapped around her forearm. Flashbacks of Asmodeus grabbing her in her dream, the searing pain pulling her out of sleep. He must have done something to her, bruised her spirit.

A child's giggle broke her train of thought, sounding from the other side of the door, followed by the padding of feet. A shadow ran past the door, and Leah jumped back, her hand recoiling from the door handle.

"Leah," a voice whispered. A woman's voice. Her mom's voice. "Come upstairs."

She braced herself and opened the door, prepared to throw her fist into anything that might pop out, followed by a swift thrust of *Malchut* to send them flying.

But nothing was there.

She stepped out into the hallway and glanced in both directions. The place was a mirror image of the outpost, aside from the lack of furniture.

Chirping sounded from outside the front door, a melodic tone followed by another. It lulled her closer, turning her on her heels, away from the stairs and to the front door. She leaned against it, her ear pressed to hear better.

The two sources chittered back and forth as if they were talking to each other. The sound changed and morphed from the tones of a cricket to the low rumbling of a bullfrog.

She'd heard nothing like it before, and it drew her in. She wrapped her hand around the knob, ready to open the door and see what was on the other side.

An odor filled the air, metallic like iron, and the memory of her home flashed in her mind. She backed away, dread filling her veins.

Whatever was behind the door was luring her.

She stepped back farther, and the low tones stopped. A bang thudded against the door.

Leah turned and ran, not waiting for the thing to come crashing in.

She raced to the top of the stairs, layers of dust on them blowing up in the air. Her feet padded against the wooden floor, as if nothing had set foot on them in decades.

The hallway was even worse, warm stale air making her gag. Her footsteps kicked up dust, and a cloud formed around her, obscuring the path down the hallway.

She could make out a faint silhouette in the dull orange glow standing at the end of the hallway. It had the same glow as her dream, the same shape as her mother.

"Mom!" she yelled and ran down the hall, escaping her dust cloud and seeing her mother standing there, wearing the same dress she had been wearing to the wedding. Leah's heart raced as she wrapped her arms around her, her mother returning the same gentle squeeze.

"Mom, I'm so sorry. I didn't mean to." A lump formed in Leah's throat, and tears fell from her eyes.

Her mother lifted Leah's chin and smiled at her, her face as radiant as ever. "What are you talking about, love?"

"You and Dad. You're both gone." Leah sniffled, trying to catch her breath. "And it's my fault . . . I led him to us . . . Ashley's party . . . I used . . . a Ouija Board."

Tears fell from her mother's face as her expression changed, a look of pain spreading across her face. She wiped away Leah's tears, pressing hard on her face. "You're right," she said, her voice lowering. "It is your fault I'm dead."

CHAPTER 27
TRICKS & LIES

The words cut deep, and a chill tore through her. Leah pulled back, trying to wrench free from her mother's grip, but her mother only squeezed tighter.

Leah clenched her jaw and frowned, her mother's arms seeming to stretch and grow longer as her face contorted deeper and deeper into rage.

She strained to breathe. "Mom? What are you doing?"

A slight cut formed on her mother's forehead, and blood trickled down her face, dripping onto Leah.

Leah tried pushing away again, wriggling her arms between her and her mother. She could feel her mother's body shaking and see her eyes bulging out of her head. A laugh sputtered out of her mother—or whatever this thing was that wore her face—more cuts and fissures forming in her face as she threw her head back and cackled.

It leaned in close to Leah's face, the scent of blood strong in Leah's nose. "Why don't you come here and give your mommy a kiss?"

A piece of skin dangling on its face peeled and landed with a plop on Leah's cheek.

Leah screamed and pushed with all her might, *Malchut* releasing from her. The force let out a beam of light that pulsed from Leah, thrusting the creature impersonating her mother down the hallway. It crashed through the door at the end of the hall, and Leah stumbled back, exhaustion pouring over her. She looked at her hands, her vision passing through her now translucent skin. Whatever she'd done with *Malchut* must have done something to her, too.

The creature jerked. It rose, stretching its limbs until its head brushed the ceiling and twitched to one side. A smile stretched wide across its face, teeth falling out and razor-sharp spikes taking their place.

"What . . . What are you?" Leah asked, her voice trembling.

"He comes for you, Leah. Our fallen Kyjak will finish what he started. How pleased he'll be to see you here, caught in my web." Its voice hummed and spoke in a melodic tone, the same one she'd heard outside the door before.

Leah stood and backed away, glancing behind her to locate the stairs.

The creature stepped forward. "There is no escape. Not here." It steepled its long fingers and let out a high-pitched giggle. "Don't you want to see your father again? The flesh our Kyjak still wears, you know. Oh, Asmodeus will be most pleased with me." It giggled again.

Pressure grew in Leah's chest, and with it whispers sounded in her ears. She thought for a moment to calm down, to find the calm within her, but the whispers egged her on, and she listened. If Asmodeus was on the way, then she needed to use every ounce of energy she could to protect herself, even if it meant the Tree of Death.

A voice cut through the whispers, Sarah talking in her ear as if she was standing right next to her. "Leah, get back here now. Hurry! Alma's here, and we can't save you if you're unconscious."

She looked at the creature, the anger inside her clawing to get out. Knowing that Asmodeus was still inside her father, still using him like a puppet, enraged her. Sarah's voice reminded her of something her uncle had said. She realized she had to protect her father, save whatever was left of him from Asmodeus.

That thought deafened the whispers. The idea of protecting her father cleansed the energy building up inside of her in an instant, and with it, she threw her hand forward, thrusting out a fine slice of air that flew across the hall and cut through the creature's left arm.

The monster howled as its arm fell to the ground, flailing on its own accord.

Leah's hands were almost completely clear now, save for a faint outline. Whatever was happening to her, she was fading away, and she didn't think she could use another one of those attacks.

She turned and ran the rest of the way down the hall-way, making it to the stairs. She glanced over her shoulder to see the creature stepping forward, gaining speed down the hallway.

"Ah, little Leah wants to play,

"But will she make it through the gray?

"Or be trapped and have to pay?"

Another set of arms and legs exploded out the back of the creature, and its abdomen expanded like a grotesque spider, clinging onto the floor and walls, dragging its body after Leah. Its elongated face still had a faint resemblance to Leah's mother, calling out as it moved across the floor.

Leah's eyes stung from the tears streaming down her face as she tore her gaze from the thing that pretended to be her mother. Her heart pounded heavy in her chest as she raced down the stairs, hearing the creature closing in on her. It skittered on the ceiling above her and landed right in front of her, blocking her path to the classroom. A disgusting fleshy spider partially morphed from her mother.

"Little Leah's just not fast,

"Guess tonight she will not last."

It closed in, its jaws opening wide, drool oozing out of its mouth. Leah backed away, her back pressing against the railing leading upstairs. She took a slow breath, her knees buckling, sure that this was going to be her end.

Light shone from behind the door to the classroom before it burst open, and in an instant, all four legs of the spider creature were sliced clean off by a blade of light. It howled in pain, and Leah saw Alma standing behind it. The Black Bishop thrust her hand upward, blinding light shining from her palms. The ceiling above the creature cracked and came falling down on it. The creature struggled under the weight, and Alma pursed her lips. "Why won't you things just die?"

She snapped her fingers, and blue fire burst to life in her hand. It moved like a snake, twisting and writhing in her hand. She aimed her palm at the creature in one fluid motion, ejecting a ray of fire that engulfed it.

It gave way to the debris above it and collapsed to the ground, spraying out blood and viscera.

Alma wiped away a hair that had fallen out of place and looked to Leah. "Get over here, now. They reform fast."

Leah already noticed the chunks of flesh rolling back to the debris. She pushed off from the stairway and raced around the heap of flesh, meeting Alma in front of the class-room. "How did you—"

"Shut up and get back to your body!" She reached for

Leah's shoulder, but her hand slipped through the girl. Alma shook her head and pointed to the black orb. "Now."

Leah rushed inside, then froze. Cracking wood sounded in front of her as another creature wriggled its way in through the hole in the wall, a massive eye locked on Leah. She stepped back slowly, her back pressing against the wall.

Blue fire erupted around it and Alma, now partly translucent, stepped in front of Leah. Leah leaped forward and touched the black orb. Darkness surrounded her, and her mind slipped into unconsciousness.

CHAPTER 28
DEMON MARK

The world churned once again, and she felt her mind slip back into her body. Aches and pains surfaced as her senses condensed and settled, her numbed legs and arms firing off pins and needles.

Leah lurched up, gasping for breath. Bright incandescent light shone down on her and she squinted, her eyes adjusting as she felt around an unfamiliar bed. A warm hand rested on her shoulder, gently pushing her back down.

"Take it slow," Alma said, standing next to her. "Gather your bearings first." Alma helped prop Leah up on the bed.

Leah looked around the infirmary at the other two empty beds and noticed it was just her and Alma in the room. "How long was I . . .?"

Alma walked to the closet, returning with a damp cloth that she placed atop Leah's head. "A day. Your spirit was nearly gone. It takes time, coming back from that. Had you used any more energy, you may not have woken at all."

Leah studied her hands, solid now instead of thin translucent outlines. Had she really been that close to dying? "I'm sorry, Black Bishop Sachs, I—"

Alma patted Leah's hand, a mix of both affection and concern that Leah didn't expect coming from her. "Square Turner and Square O'Connor told me everything."

Leah's eyes widened. If they told her everything, then were they kicked out? Did she miss her chance to say good-bye? And herself, did that mean she'd be out too?

Alma looked up at the door. "I see the concern on your face, but your friends are fine. They're in their rooms with the others."

Leah averted Alma's gaze, tears welling in her eyes. "It was my idea. Sarah and Isaac were just there to help pull me out. I didn't give them a choice. Please, if there is anyone you should punish, it should be me."

Alma leaned back in her chair and intertwined her fingers. "I'm not throwing you, or anyone, out into the woods, if that is your concern. You'll have extra duties, no doubt about that, but if Square Turner and O'Conner were correct, one of those . . . things . . . coerced you."

Leah swallowed. "What do you mean? I was stupid. I took pages out of your book."

Alma tapped Leah's left arm. "I spotted a mark on you in the Astral Realm. Did you notice it too?"

Leah looked down at her left arm. The black mark was missing now, but she wouldn't forget soon. "There was a mark, like a handprint or a claw print."

Alma stood and clasped her hands behind her back. "I suspect the night he attacked you, the demon in question, Asmodeus got a hold of you and marked you. Demon marks are all different, but I am certain of what I saw. It makes sense that this one would stay hidden, Asmodeus being one of the strongest demons out there.

"Great, so how do we kill him?"

Alma shook her head. "It would be best if he were captured again. Killing demons only sends them back from where they came from. I'd hoped the last time we dealt with him, he would have stayed banished."

Leah tilted her head. "Last time?"

Alma exhaled. "Twenty-five years ago, there was a war between the Infinity Board and demons. They'd always been a nuisance, but Asmodeus led an assault like the Board had never seen before. An attempt to take over this world. It lasted nearly a decade, and it was relentless. We lost many good Mystics from it. But your mother was a part of the team that eventually took him out."

A wave of grief overcame Leah. "That's why he wanted my mom. And why he wants me, right?"

Alma nodded. "She was the most skilled White Knight I'd ever seen. So much potential . . . same as you."

"But how did he get back? You said the Infinity Board banished him."

Alma shrugged. "Banished demons can take generations to return, if they ever do. At least, that's what our records show. But it would seem Asmodeus has circumnavigated that."

Leah looked down at her arm, rubbing at her skin, hoping that would somehow get rid of the mark her family's killer left behind. "So, about the dream I had. That wasn't my mother?"

Alma shook her head. "I'm afraid not. It is likely that Asmodeus commanded these lesser demons to find you using that mark. This outpost has strong concealment spells, but after this infestation, I don't know how much they can hold." She tilted her head. "These dreams. When did they start?"

Leah felt a pit in her stomach grow. She had been used, tricked into thinking that it was her mother who'd wanted her to take the book and meet her on the other side. "He hasn't stopped, not since . . . not since . . ." Tears formed in her eyes. "Why did he have to do that? Why did it look like her?"

Alma grabbed Leah's hand. "We'll sort this out. You must be strong because I fear the worst is not over. I need you to tell me everything that happened. Can you do that for me?"

Leah nodded and took a deep breath, starting all the way back to the first dream she had in the room with the silhouetted figure sitting in front of the fire and the gravelly voice that clung to the walls.

Alma listened in silence, letting Leah speak without interruption. Once done, Alma leaned forward and placed Leah's chin in her hand. "Thank you. I will need to make some preparations." She stood and smoothed her clothes. "Until then, this information must be kept between you, me, Square Turner, and Square O'Conner. We are dealing with a very strong demon that is fixated on you, so anyone else who knows could become another pawn in his little game to get to you."

Leah wiped away tears and nodded.

Alma drew in a deep breath. "Good. I will make you some chamomile tea." She turned and paused, looking out the window. "I'll need to call in some Knights to keep nearby while we figure this out, just in case. As for us, we'll go on a field trip in the morning."

"Where are we going?"

Alma made her way to the door. She glanced back at Leah, her eyes dropping to her arm. "We're going to put that mark to good use and track down Asmodeus."

CHAPTER 29

FAMILY PAST

Isaac knocked quietly in the doorway to the infirmary and whispered, "Hey, Alma's been adamant that we leave you alone, but we can't. We're worried. How are you?"

Leah stretched, feeling the aches and pains from the night before, and waved them in. "I'm . . . okay, I think."

Sarah moved past Isaac to stand at the foot of Leah's bed. "What happened? Alma sent us to our rooms right when you two came back from the Astral plane."

Isaac stepped through the door and closed it, elbowing Sarah as he stood next to her. "We're just supposed to check in on her, not come in. Alma said she needs her rest."

Leah sat up. "It's fine. I'm just a little sore." Her eyes welled up before she could stop herself, and her voice wavered. "It wasn't her. It was just another demon trying to use me."

Sarah sat on the edge of Leah's bed and grabbed her arm. "I'm sorry," she said. Then, after a moment, added, "It was still worth a shot."

"And you made it back in one piece. That's what

matters," Isaac said. "We were worried. The moment you went over, you got all rigid and your lips turned blue."

"Then you let out a weird, creepy scream," Sarah added. "Lucky Alma showed up when she did."

Leah looked down at her hands. "I just wished it was her, you know? So I could see her one last time."

"I get it," Sarah said. "If I knew my parents better, I probably would have done the same."

Leah's face flushed. She realized then that she didn't know anything about her friend's past. "I'm sorry. I've been so caught up in my own problems, I never asked either of you—"

"You've been through a lot," Isaac said. "I don't think either of us blames you."

Leah looked at Sarah. "Well, mind helping take my mind off all this? What happened to get you here?"

Sarah stood up off the side of Leah's bed. "Well, not much there. They died when I was young."

"Oh. I'm sorry."

"It's fine. I don't even remember them."

"Well, then what? How did you end up here?" Leah asked.

"My aunt and uncle raised me. Sent me to a private school, which they thought would be better for me, but didn't realize me being the only Black girl there was going to cause problems."

Leah let out a laugh. "Yeah, I get that."

Sarah raised her eyebrow.

"Well," Leah said, "I mean, it isn't the same, but I was the only Jewish girl at my school. Luckily, I could just hide my Star of David necklace, but when people found out, I was always the butt of jokes."

"Well then, it's official. We're the band of outcasts here

at the outpost. But I guess it's that or be friends with Paige," Isaac said.

"And no one wants that," Sarah said with a laugh.

"So, what then?" Leah asked.

Sarah rubbed her hands together. "Well, I was in my room, replaying something someone said to me. I don't even remember what it was, but I remember that my aunt kept trying to tell me it wasn't a big deal. It was. I couldn't get it out of my head. Then, *Malchut* happened. My closet door got the brunt of it, and that was the last straw. My aunt and uncle grounded me 'forever' and started looking at military school. Two days later, a Knight showed up and offered to take me to some boarding school on a scholarship. They took the offer, and here I am."

"They just shipped you off? Just like that?" Leah asked.

Sarah shrugged. "I left out all the fights, both at home and school. I didn't fit in."

"And they believe you're at a boarding school? It's the middle of summer."

"Yeah. I mean, I think the Knight that picked me up might have done something to their memories, but Alma had me call them a week ago. As long as my grades are up and I sound happy, they don't care."

"And are you?" Leah asked.

"What?"

"Happy?"

Sarah smiled, "Well, I met two dorks that actually see me, so yeah. I guess I am."

They laughed, and a warmth filled Leah. She was happy too, even among the chaos that had destroyed everything she knew in an instant. At least she'd found friends that pulled her out of the darkness.

Leah swung her foot out of the bed and nudged Isaac. "And what about you?"

Isaac looked down. "It's not all that exciting."

"Oh, come on," Sarah rolled her eyes. "You can't keep secrets forever."

Isaac smirked. "Fine. My parents are still alive. I think."

"You think?" Leah asked.

"Well, I don't come from the best of families. Both my parents were in and out of prison growing up. I sometimes think they were more interested in using us kids to help them steal than actually care for us."

"Hold on a minute," Sarah said. "You have brothers and sisters? You didn't tell me that."

"I didn't tell you much of anything. Two sisters and two brothers, all older, and none of them were nice. I found a chance to run when the police raided the house. I got out, and a Bishop found me and brought me here."

Leah frowned. "Wait, but *Malchut*. How did that wake in you?"

Isaac looked down at the ground. "Ah, well, I went into the basement one night. My parents forbade us from going down there, but they were gone and the smell was so bad. It was some type of makeshift lab. Then they came home, and I had nowhere to hide, so it happened. Everyone figured it was just whatever they were cooking in the basement, but I was the reason the cops came."

"Oh, I'm sorry." Sarah said.

The three sat in silence once again until Leah leaned back in her bed and said, "Well now we have each other."

The door creaked open, and they all nearly jumped out of their skin. Alma stepped into the room, her lips pursed as she looked at Isaac and Sarah. The two shot up out of bed and stood at attention.

She nodded at their form. "What are you two doing here?"

Isaac stammered over his words. "I . . . We wanted to check on Leah."

Alma stepped past them to Leah's bed. "At ease," she said to Sarah and Isaac, then she checked Leah's forehead with the back of her hand. "Good thing you're awake. Feeling any better?"

Leah nodded. "Yes, much better."

"Good. We're leaving in an hour. I've brought in your uncle and some other Knights to watch over the house while we're gone. Get ready and meet me in the living room." She turned and grabbed onto the door handle.

"Wait, my uncle's here?"

"Yes, you can talk to him when we get back."

"Where are we going?" Leah asked, looking at Sarah and Isaac.

Alma glanced over her shoulder. "Just you and I, Square. Hurry, please. I'd like to make it there before sundown."

CHAPTER 30

LE SYNDICAT

Leah sat inside the old sedan, shifting in the lumpy seat to find a comfortable position. Rain had come in as they drove away from the outpost, and she watched it fade away in the passenger mirror.

She looked over at Alma and noticed dark bags under her eyes, her hair now messy and tangled. The Black Bishop had left the radio off, leaving Leah to her thoughts and the sound of rain on the windshield.

After an hour, Leah finally asked, "So, where are we going?"

Alma kept her eyes on the road, turning off the gravel and onto the highway. "A place we call a gray zone, or no-man's-land."

"What's a gray zone?" Leah turned and looked at Alma.

"It's where others who are not on the Infinity Board can talk to us freely, without fear of retribution."

"Retribution, why would we—"

"You've heard of Voodoo, yes?"

"You mean like voodoo dolls and zombies? Stuff they do in New Orleans?"

"Close, yes. But Voodoo is a religion, a way to respect

ancestors and gods. And a way that uses the energy of the Trees differently from us."

Leah raised her eyebrows. "So, Voodoo is real?"

Alma nodded. "Many things in this world are real. The Infinity Board keeps everything in check."

"But how does it work? How can they use the Tree differently?"

"The energy of the tree passes down through their ancestors. They use rituals similar to the one you stole from my book, that call on their ancestors for power. That power is the energy of the trees, but different from what we can do with the wells."

"Are you saying we're going to a place full of voodoo witches?" Leah asked.

"Priests, priestesses, and practitioners. Best not to use the word witch. Some of them may take offense. Witches are *very* different."

"Everything I've ever heard about voodoo is bad. Sacrificing goats, chickens, and even people. Why would the Infinity Board let that exist?"

"Their ways are not ours, and what you see on TV or hear from those that don't practice it is full of fear and falsehood. They practice a balance, much like the Board. However, they take from and respect the energy in the Tree of Death as much as the Tree of Life, something we cannot do without corruption." Alma paused, exiting off the highway before continuing. "We've fought with them in the past and suffered many losses, but now we keep our distance and let them handle their own unless they ask for our help. Or, in our case, when we ask for theirs."

From what Alma and Eric had told her, Leah knew there were others who could use the energies of the Trees. Yet, it never crossed her mind that there would be entire underground societies scattered around. This strange world grew even larger.

She stretched and rubbed her palms against her eyes. "So, who is right then? If we call ourselves the guardians of the Tree, but they access it, then are they wrong in how they do it?"

Alma hesitated, choosing her words carefully. "We have a direct connection to the wells, something most others don't have. We not only protect the Trees but our world's balance as well. They practice through rituals passed down through generations, using the energies of both Trees to perform their rites and magic. They do not harm the Trees, so we do not need to protect the Trees from them. If they ever cross that line or put the balance of energies of our world at risk, then they break our treaty."

"What treaty?" Leah asked.

"The Treaty of Lyon, 1892. Both parties agreed they would govern over their own, and every few years, a representative of both parties would meet. That way, we keep each other in check. Other than that, there is to be no formal communication or surveillance."

"Why are we going to them, then?"

Alma pointed to Leah's arm. "Their magic works well with the Astral plane, so I hope we can use that to our advantage."

Leah kept the rest of her questions to herself for the rest of the ride, imagining up ideas of what this bar would look like in person. Skeletons, stacks of dolls, and chicken feet were at the top of her list.

The sun rose high into the sky as they passed a mile marker outlined in purple instead of the usual green. Alma turned down a bumpy road and onto a dirt path surrounded by forest. Branches hung over the road, scraping the top of the car as they drove deeper into the woods.

A wave of nausea hit Leah, and the dry air turned hot and humid in an instant. The trees seemed to lean in closer, scraping against the windshield. And then the car broke free, and they faced a sign.

"Sekrè Fami," Leah read off the flaking, brightly colored painted welcome sign. "Where are we?"

"We've made it to our destination," Alma said.

Leah rolled down the window, and hot air rolled in, caking onto her. "How is it so hot here?"

"Because we're not really in South Dakota anymore," Alma said.

"What? What does that mean?" Leah asked.

"We're in a space that many roads lead to if you know where to look. A place that was once a part of New Orleans but has since changed."

The forest melted away into homes that grew closer and closer together. They were like what she'd seen in a travel show about New Orleans, some with large columns and massive windows, others with porches and balconies supported by posts. She'd expect these homes much farther south than they drove. Each home was painted just as bright as the welcome sign, and nearly everyone had neon lights in the windows stating "Readings" or "Love Spells" intermixed with markets, restaurants, and pharmacies.

Leah couldn't believe this place. She shook her head and muttered, "But how?"

"Old magic," Alma said. "When these people sought freedom, they found it here."

They stopped as a procession passed by them, people dressed in strange clothes. Some wore massive papier mâché heads, dancing while marching behind a group of trombone players blasting an upbeat jazz Leah had never heard before.

"This place is amazing. Why haven't I ever heard of it?" Leah asked.

"Well, for one, you'd never find it on any map," Alma said, eyeing the people as they passed by.

She drove farther through the town, passing more marches and people crowded on the sidewalks. Leah noticed that some of them sat or stood inside chalk markings on the ground, surrounded by bottles and candles, and she suspected they were openly performing rituals, as if they didn't have a care in the world who saw.

They stopped in front of a building painted a bold red, a color that made it stand out differently from the other places surrounding it. A small yellow sign glowed above the door.

"*Le Syndicat.*"

They got out of the car and walked to the front door. A large dark-skinned bouncer sporting a shaved head, tattoos, and a look that made Leah want to lunge back to the car opened the door for Alma, nodding at her to enter.

Alma patted the man's chest and said, "Thanks, Ralph," before walking in.

The man eyed Leah for a moment but didn't stop her as she followed Alma into the bar. She thought she'd need to show him an ID at the least, but no, Alma had been the ultimate fake ID.

Scents of cinnamon and rum filled the air, and Leah felt a strange buzz in her head as she entered. Her nerves untangled, and a slight smile grew on her face the farther in she followed Alma.

Music caught her ear, and she looked over to see a live jazz quartet playing in the corner, the sound gently flowing into the rest of the bar. Red booths and tables filled the bar, and she immediately noticed that everyone there was dressed up. She also realized just how underdressed she and Alma were, on top of the fact that they were the only white people there.

Alma walked through the bar as if she'd been there a thousand times, ignoring the stares from patrons. Her eyes locked on the bartender in front of them. Leah struggled to follow, trying not to get distracted by every little thing. There were no skeletons or voodoo dolls. Instead, there were portraits of people. A Black man playing a trombone, a woman holding a microphone, and another woman wearing an intricate headdress, her painted eyes locked on Leah's.

Leah bumped into Alma. She then rested her hands on the bar as a tall bartender with a firm jawline approached. "*Bienvenue*, mademoiselle Alma. Would you be wanting the usual?" He towered over the both of them, his white shirt and black vest tight against his muscles.

"Not tonight, Jack. I was thinking something sweet, with a hint of cinnamon."

He paused, staring at Alma with a look as if he were about to throw her out before his face changed to a broad smile. "Ah, yes, of course." He turned and walked to the back of the bar and down a flight of stairs.

"Usual? I thought you said the Board is supposed to leave them alone?"

Alma placed her back against the bar and looked out at the band. "They do. I, on the other hand, come here often. Keep your friends close and all."

"Is cinnamon like the secret code, then?"

Alma nodded. "Did you notice the scent in the air when you came in?"

Leah nodded.

"It changes from time to time. Sometimes rum, other

times pineapple, but that's the trick. If you ever come to one of these for business, that is."

A man's voice sounded behind them. "Follow me." Leah jumped, and they turned to see Ralph, the bouncer, eyeing them from behind the bar.

They walked to the back, down the stairs and through a hall. The scent of cinnamon grew stronger, and Leah had to take in shorter breaths to stop herself from coughing. They stepped into a darkened room, and before they could turn around, Ralph shut the door, muting the sounds behind them and leaving them alone in the dark.

Leah tested the doorknob. When it wouldn't budge, she pounded her fist on it.

Alma grabbed her shoulder and turned her around to face the darkened space. A dark figure moved forward, and candles bloomed to life around the room, small flickers of light illuminating a woman dressed in white.

"What are you doing back in my bar so soon, Alma?" the woman asked.

"Nice to see you too, Madeline." Alma stepped forward, crossing into the circle of candles.

"I didn't expect you for another month or two. Perhaps you have news of my granddaughter?" She walked over to a small circular table in the corner of the room and pointed to the chairs. "Have a seat."

Alma sat. "No, nothing new. She is still rising the ranks, as expected since she was best in her class. I come here today because these are odd times."

Leah met Madeline's eyes, brown and tinged with yellow. She smiled, and Leah saw three gold teeth flickering among her smile. "Odd times indeed. And my gift? Was it where I told you?"

Alma nodded. "It was. And it has answered many questions, and spawned even more. That's not why I'm here, though."

"Yes." She rubbed her hands together and turned to Leah, pointing a crooked finger at her arm. "Mizrahi's daughter. Quite the potential, this one. And that mark of yours seems especially interesting."

"I'm sorry, how do you know about . . ." Leah trailed off, gazing at the woman.

The woman shrugged. "What sort of Voodoo Queen would I be if I didn't know everyone who comes to my land?"

"The mark," Alma said. "Can we use it to track him down?"

Madeline's eyes pierced through Leah. "This demon . . . they call him Kyjak, yes?"

The name rang a bell in Leah's head, and she nodded.

Madeline raised an eyebrow, then turned to Alma. "Bringing attention to something like that is going to cost you."

Alma nodded. "I know. Whatever it takes."

Madeline stood and brushed her hands together. "Dark magic begets dark magic. Fetch me a chicken. Ralph will take you."

Alma stood and left the room without a word.

Madeline pulled some jars off the shelves and handed one to Leah, full of some type of red sand. "Line the doors with this. Start over there, then finish with that door when Alma gets back. Do not to leave any gaps."

Leah took the jar and got to work.

Alma stepped into the room moments later, a small red chicken resting in her arms.

Madeline filled a bowl with water, adding in powders and spices she pulled from the shelves. The odor in the room magnified, the sweet scents of herbs mixing with something foul, making Leah nauseous.

Leah set the half-empty jar on the table and looked at Madeline.

"Strip to your undergarments," Madeline said.

Leah narrowed her eyes. "Excuse me?"

Madeline nodded at the bowl. "I need you covered in that. You should be stark naked, but you all like your modesty. Hurry, the oils start really stinking the longer they sit out."

Leah turned to Alma, who nodded. She looked back at the door, confirming it was closed before stripping down.

Madeline guided her to the middle of the room and gestured her to sit, putting down yellow, orange, and white candles in a large circle around them. She rubbed her hands together, letting out a low guttural sound as the candle flames shot high into the air. Then she went to work, pouring the oily mixture over Leah, rubbing it in her hair and under her arms. It was foul, a scent that made her gag a few times before she focused on something else.

Madeline pointed to the chicken in Alma's arms. "Hand it over."

The bird clucked and crowed as Madeline took it from Alma. Leah looked at it in horror as Madeline held it up by the legs.

"What are you going to do with that?"

"You've got a stench on you, child," she said, staring into the chicken's eyes while cooing softly. "Not the one I put on you, but a stench only demons carry." She held the chicken up to Leah. The protests from the chicken stopped altogether. It hung slack in Madeline's hands, completely entranced. She brushed its body against Leah's from head to toe. "This chicken will pick it up, then we use it to find your demon. Better it than you."

The Voodoo Queen stopped, looking over the chicken and nodding. She drew a knife and cut off its head in one swift motion as Leah did everything she could not to scream. Blood poured out at Leah's feet, and Madeline crouched down, staring at it as it pooled.

Leah gazed at Alma for direction, her eyes wide, but the Black Bishop stood still, as if all of this was normal.

Madeline sighed and shook her head. She tossed the chicken corpse onto the table and brushed her hands. "You're too late."

"What's that supposed to mean?" Leah asked.

"He's well on your *odè*—your scent—and he's already made his first move." She looked to Alma. "He has already dealt his first blow."

"What does that—" Leah started, but Alma threw a towel at her and scooped up her clothes.

"Wipe that off. We have to go, now!" Alma said. "*Merci* Madeline, I will send you payment upon my return."

"*Pa gen pwòblèm et bon chans,* Alma. May you find what you are looking for."

CHAPTER 31

OLD BONDS, NEW BONDS

Alma's knuckles were white on the wheel the entire way back. The sun skirted along the sky while Leah kept her thoughts to herself, focused instead on pulling the chunks of herbs out of her hair.

They pulled out of the city via a different route, after Madeline gave them directions, the thick humid air turning cold and dry through the trees. They reached the outpost faster than Leah thought was possible, and from the opposite direction, just as the sun rested at the tops of the trees.

The outpost looked normal, nothing out of place as they approached. Then they drove past the first dead body.

It was a Knight, torn apart, blood sprayed against the trees.

Alma put the car in park and unbuckled. "Stay by my side. Whatever happens."

They stepped out of the car, and Alma stepped in front of Leah, looking left and right into the woods as they approached the house.

As they got closer, Leah noticed something large propped up against the door of the outpost.

"There's something there," Leah said.

Alma nodded and approached, her hands balled into fists.

Once they had a better angle, Leah realized it was a body wrapped up in a shredded brown coat.

Oh no. No. It can't—

His face came into view. Eric slumped against the front door, surrounded by a pool of blood.

No. No. No, she repeated to herself over and over.

She took in sharp breaths, and the air grew cold and icy. Her body felt like it was vibrating, and blood pounded in her ears.

Then the voices started.

He's dead. You're dead. You did this. You killed him. Murderer. Killer. Orphan.

Alma kneeled down beside him, placing two fingers on his neck.

"Is he . . .?" Leah stuttered.

"He's alive. I've got a pulse. Help me take him inside. Quickly!"

Her breathing slowed, and a ray of hope silenced the voices. She moved at Alma's command, opening the door and helping lift him inside.

Blood drenched his shirt, covering Leah's arms.

"What about the others? Are they. . .?" Leah asked as she looked around the empty outpost.

Alma's eyes flared a bright yellow, and she looked down, her eyes locking on some unseen object. "They're fine," she said. "Now, get me a bowl of hot water, bandages, salve. Hurry!"

Leah ran off to grab the supplies while Alma dragged Eric past the classroom and into the infirmary. She heaved him onto the bed and grabbed a pair of scissors, cutting his shirt free. Several holes and gouges deep in his side oozed thick, congealed blood.

Alma ran her fingers along his side, finding the largest wound and resting her hand on top, pressing down. Blood seeped between her fingers. She shut her eyes tight and sweat formed on her brow as heat radiated around her. The air continued to grow hot and dense as Alma's face turned paler by the minute.

She pushed harder on Eric's wound, and the blood soon stopped. She lifted her hands, and Leah saw the wound stitching itself back together. Alma repeated the process on several other slashes on his chest, each one stitching as she moved on to the next.

By the fourth wound, Eric gasped, his eyes opening as he let out a scream. He clutched Alma's wrist. "It's here. It killed them. Leah! Protect Leah!"

Alma took his hand with her free one to comfort him. "Yes, we know. We're all inside the outpost. It's safe, for now. Lay still." Alma wrenched her wrist free from his grasp and held her hands above his wound again.

Eric's eyes rolled around in his head as his hand moved to his side, shaking. "Save your energy. It's too late. Protect them. Message . . . He left me a message. Leah can't leave the outpost. He wants her. He said he'd kill them all. Protect them."

He looked up at the ceiling, the color draining from his face. Blood flowed from his wounds again.

"No," Alma said, her voice breaking from her usual calm. "You have to fight it. Stay with us."

Eric's eyes fluttered and closed, his breathing labored. Alma rested her hands at his side, the dense, hot air subsiding while a tear slipped down her face.

Leah shook the bed. "What are you doing? Help him! He's still alive! Please, help him!"

Alma looked at Leah, her eyes distant. Leah felt the

tears flowing down her face, but she stood firm, searching Alma's face for any hint of hope.

Something sparked inside Alma as she looked between Leah and Eric. She checked his pulse and said, "There is something. The Board won't like it, but it just might save him, or kill you both."

Leah raised her eyebrow, eyeing his wound. "What is it? Please."

"He doesn't have a bond. If he did, he could heal faster. There is an old ritual. It's forbidden, and crude, but it will get the job done."

Leah looked at her uncle's pale face, his breathing slower by the second. "And if he dies with a bond?"

"It's an old ritual, missing the proper precautions we have in place today. So, you'd probably die too."

Leah stared at his bleeding wound. "I can't let him die. Do it."

Alma extended her palm. "Give me your hand."

Leah did as she was told, and Alma took her hand.

The Black Bishop then used the scissors and sliced Leah's palm in one swift motion. She then did the same to Eric, who didn't even wince.

Leah stared down at the jagged cut, blood dripping down onto the floor. Alma dipped her finger in Leah's blood, using it to draw יְסוֹד the Hebrew letters of *Yesod* onto Eric's chest. Then she did the same to Leah, drawing between Leah's clavicles.

She took both their cut hands and brought them together. Leah pulled, eyeing the blood on her hand and on her uncles, but Alma held it firm.

"The Board forbids blood rituals like this, but we have no time," Alma said. "His blood should be mostly clean after what I did."

Alma squeezed them together and began muttering

words in a foreign language, faster than Leah's ears could pick up.

Heat steamed from her palm, growing hotter and hotter until she wanted to pull away. Alma's grasp kept it in place. The pain shot up her arm in pulses, reaching farther and farther into her body, until it felt like molten lava coursing through her veins. The serpent inside her uncoiled, pressure building as it intertwined and curled around the searing heat. She squeezed her eyes shut to get away from the pain, but she couldn't hide from it.

Darkness bled in from the edges of her vision, and the pain became numb as she slipped into unconsciousness, a dull heartbeat pounding in her ears.

"Disgraceful. So humiliated," a voice growled in the dark.

Leah stood inside a house dimly lit by one flickering incandescent bulb hanging from the ceiling. She glanced over at the boards covering the windows, blocking any light that might come in from outside.

"I am a Kyjak! How dare he chain me to him? Damn you, Legion!" The roar echoed throughout the entire house, sending a chill to Leah's bones.

She spotted the black silhouette crouched down in the corner of the living room, hidden in the shadows.

"Little sheep, little sheep, where is my little sheep?" the voice mocked, every word exaggerated.

Leah recognized the melodic sounds, similar to the ones she had heard in the Astral Realm. She backed into the wall. "This can't be him," she muttered to herself. "This can't be—"

"I am Asmodeus. One of seven Kyjak. Not some low

valley dweller who obeys your every little wish." He clawed at the wall next to him, digging his fingers into the drywall, leaving behind large, bloody gouges. He rocked back and forth, his head on his knees. "Once she's dead, they'll see. They'll *all* see. Starting with you, Legion. As soon as she comes out of that outpost, out from those protections that little Bishop made, I'll have my chance."

Leah stepped backward, fear coiling tight in her chest. If Asmodeus could take down four Knights, what chance did she have against this thing?

Her hand brushed up against something and she turned, noting a broken chair leg resting against the wall. Reaching out, Leah saw her translucent hands and remembered the last time she'd faced a demon on the Astral Plane. She leaned back against the wall, feeling the wooden leg pass through her hand. It felt odd, cold even, before it twitched and fell to the ground.

"Who's there?" Asmodeus asked, a shadowed figure lurking deep in the room, pacing back and forth. Eyes glowing like a predatory animal in the night squinted and fell onto her. "Ah, my dear, sweet Leah. I was hoping you'd come in the flesh." Eyes glinted from the shadows, locked on her like a wolf. "I left you a little message. I hope you got it before he died."

"What do you want from me?" She stuttered, her voice echoing strangely off the walls.

Asmodeus laughed, his glowing eyes looking right at her arm. "What do I want? You. Dead. And if I don't get what I want, everyone in that outpost will die until I get to you."

Rage boiled up inside her, vibrating her bones. "I'm here now, aren't I? Let's finish this."

Asmodeus grinned and ducked back into the shadows.

"You aren't here. You are a wisp—a ghost. Come to me in the flesh, and we will settle things."

Leah looked down, seeing the black handprint wrapped around her left arm. She looked around the inside of a dilapidated house. "And where is *here*?"

The beast clicked his tongue. "That energy in you is wasted by your sheer stupidity. Simply follow the road to the bend. Come alone, or not at all. You have one hour."

"And you'll leave them be, all of them, in the outpost?"

"My bond is my word."

"Yet you're a demon. A liar. How can I trust what you tell me?"

The silhouette stood and approached the dim light. The remains of her father stepped out from the shadows, his rotted breath rolling over Leah. "I suppose you can't, but don't you want to see this face again? You could still save him, you know."

His face changed. The fissures in his face stitched together and the rotted flesh shifted to look more human. His expression shifted from something like a predator looking at his prey to confusion. He looked around and dropped his gaze on Leah. "Leah? Where . . . Where are we? Are you okay?"

He froze for a second, and then a snarl grew on his face. "One hour."

CHAPTER 32

INTO THE NIGHT

Leah sat up with a jolt, knocking over a tray of food as a rush of adrenaline flowed through her. Exhaustion melted off her, replaced by an energy like she had never felt before. She looked at her palm, noticing a thin pink line where Alma had cut her.

Alma appeared in the doorway, her face pale. "What is it? Are you okay?"

Leah looked at the clock and shook her head. "I. I had a dream. He's giving us an hour."

"An hour for what?"

"For me to turn myself in. Or else everyone dies," Leah said.

Alma straightened and entered the room, kneeling down and picking up the spilled food. "Absolutely not."

"But if I don't—"

"He killed three of my Knights and almost killed your uncle. I'm not allowing him to just take what he wants without consequences," Alma said.

"He'll kill everyone. I can't let that happen. Not again."

"The outpost has rituals in place to protect and hide us.

He is a demon; demons lie. What makes you think this isn't all just a trick to pull you away from the outpost?"

"My family's home was supposed to be hidden too, but he got through. I can take him. You said yourself that I was stronger with *Malchut* than others. I fended him off once before. If he's weak—"

"Enough!" Alma shouted. She stood and tossed the tray of food onto a small counter behind her. "I will not allow a child, with minimal training, to fight off a fourth level demon by herself. We do not negotiate with them, and we do not trust them."

Leah opened and closed her hands. "I feel it. The *Yesod* bond. I'm stronger. I could—"

"The *Yesod* bond has gone to your head, as expected. We stay inside the outpost and wait until morning. Do you understand?"

"But—"

"My word is final. You will go to the basement with the other Squares, where you will be safe." She pointed to the door and waited for Leah to move.

Leah huffed and clenched her jaw. She turned toward the infirmary when something from her dream tugged at her. "He mentioned a name. Legion. Does that mean anything to you?"

Alma froze mid-step. "What did he say?"

"He was mad at him, cursing him."

"Good," Alma said, her shoulders relaxing as she gestured Leah to the basement door. "Stay put here. You'll all be safe. I'll make sure of it."

Leah took a step down the stairs, but Alma's hand grabbed her shoulder. She turned and met her glare. "I'm warning you, *do not* leave the outpost."

Leah looked down at the ground and nodded. "Yes,

Black Bishop Sachs." She turned and walked down the wooden stairs.

She met the other Squares at the bottom of the basement steps, sitting on top of crates of canned goods, all looking out toward her. Sarah rushed up from the corner, her hair pulled back in a tight bun.

"Leah! You're ok!" She immediately backed up and gagged. "Ugh, you smell kinda funky."

"I got covered in some oil and chicken blood by a voodoo priestess." Leah shrugged, as if saying those words were normal now. In this environment, they strangely were. "I'm sorry I didn't think to bathe. We've been a little busy."

Sarah smirked, and Isaac ran up behind her. "They attacked us in the middle of the day. We were all inside studying when they came. The Knights ordered us to get in the basement. We heard the fighting, but then everything went quiet. The Knights. Your uncle. Are they . . .?"

"The Knights are dead except my uncle. He'll make it. We got to him in time."

Paige walked over and crossed her arms, Serena and Emma standing behind her. "So, what? Is Alma bringing in reinforcements, or are we just trapped down here until those demons find a way in?"

"Alma said they wouldn't be here until sunrise," Leah said. "We're just supposed to all wait in here until then."

Harry frowned at Leah. "And where were you two?"

"We went to a Voodoo town."

Paige tilted her head. "I'm sorry, what? Why?"

Leah looked at all their faces, pale and wide-eyed. "I haven't told all of you what happened to me. This demon attacked me. Attacked my family, possessed my dad, and killed my mom. He's been following me. Stalking me in my dreams. Alma thought we could track him down and get ahead of him."

Serena scoffed. "Why is a demon after you? What makes you special?"

Sarah stepped forward, shoving Serena back. "Hey, why don't you—"

Leah grabbed Sarah's shoulder. "Stop. It's ok." She took in a breath. "His name is Asmodeus. I think he's after me for something my mom did to him. He's not going to stop until I'm dead."

A moment of silence filled the space as the rest of the Squares gathered around. Isaac rested a hand on Leah's back.

Harry and Buck avoided Leah's gaze, while Gabe kept his eyes locked on her, an unspoken pain across his face.

Emma bit her lip. "Well, it wants you, right? What about the rest of us?"

Leah nodded. "You're right. It wants me. None of you should get hurt because of that. That's why I'm going."

"No. Leah, you can't," Sarah said.

Paige threw her hands up. "Why not? If that thing wants Leah, and it killed those Knights, then what do you think it'll do to us when it finds out she's back?" She glared at Leah. "We aren't safe with you here."

Sarah turned and slapped Paige across the face. "Shut up, Paige. What? You want to just throw her out to fend for herself? She's one of us."

Paige lurched forward and punched Sarah in the nose. Before she could get in another swing, Gabe slipped between them and grabbed her fist. "Guys. Stop. Fighting isn't going to—"

Sarah wiped the blood off her face and shoved Gabe aside, attempting another swing. One second her fist was closing in on Paige's face, the next Sarah was shoved backward, into a shelf, by an invisible force.

Paige glowered at Sarah. "Why can't you just let her go?

What is so special about her? Just because she's your girl-friend, you think the rest of us should die?"

Buck and Harry pulled Paige back while Gabe wrapped his arms around Sarah. "We aren't going to solve anything if we just keep fighting," Gabe grunted.

Moments passed while Sarah and Paige glared at each other.

"I have to go," Leah said.

Sarah dropped her shoulders and shoved off Gabe. "No, Leah, please," she said.

Leah bit her lip. "Asmodeus gave me an hour. The Infinity Board won't be here in time. If I don't show up, everyone dies."

Emma peered from behind Paige, and after an awkward silence, said, "Well, what are you waiting for?"

Sarah took a step toward her, reeling up for another slap when Isaac grabbed her hand. "We need to figure this out. Ignore them."

"There is nothing to figure out. Emma's right," Leah said. "I have to go."

Sarah huffed and turned back to Leah. "Then I'm going with you. We can catch it off guard."

"Are you stupid?" Paige said. "It killed three Knights. What makes you think—"

Leah shook her head. "No. I have to do this alone. He said he'd know if I brought anyone with me. I can't let you all risk it."

Isaac started pacing. "You're safer here. We have protec-tions all around the outpost. If he was strong enough, he would have come in here already."

"But he's weak right now," Leah said. "That last attack took a lot out of him. If I wait, he'll get strong enough to break through."

"Well, I'm not helping you walk to your death," Isaac said.

Leah shook her head. "I think I have a chance."

"How?" Isaac asked. "You might be strong in *Malchut,* but he's killed full-fledged Mystics."

Leah looked down at the pink scar on her hand. "I'm bonded now. He wouldn't see that coming."

"Wait, you're bonded?" Isaac said.

Leah nodded. "Eric was going to die. Alma did it. And I feel . . . stronger. I could fight him."

Gabe stepped forward, his face emotionless. "Then Leah might be on to something." Everyone turned to look at him. "I know what it's like to be targeted by a demon. It gets into your mind, tricks you into doing their bidding, and torments you." He winced, looking past the others toward a distant memory. "But it never lets up, whispering in your ear until you give in, until it becomes a part of you. If Leah says it is weak, then she knows. And she could use that to win against it."

The room fell silent for a moment before Paige cut it. "It's what I'd do. If I was in her shoes."

Sarah groaned. "You're just saying that."

Paige shook her head. "I'm not. We are Mystics. Protectors. If Leah thinks that going at it alone is going to protect the rest of us, who would certainly die, then who are we to stop her?"

Everyone stared at Paige. Leah nodded, an unspoken understanding between the two girls.

"Then it's settled. Tell us how to help you." Gabe said.

"If I go out the basement door, Alma will know. So, help me get out of here, for starters."

Buck snapped his fingers. "Hey, Gabe, come here and help me."

He walked over to the shelf against the stone basement wall and pulled.

Gabe joined him, pulling the shelf from the wall as quietly as they could, revealing a small window near the ceiling. "Think we can boost her up?"

Buck nodded and looked at Leah. "Looks like we found your escape."

Leah turned to Isaac and Sarah. "Alma can't know I'm gone. Keep everyone talking. If she gets suspicious, then we're screwed."

"Leah," Isaac started, "I don't like this."

She looked at Isaac and gave a shrug. "I have to try. I can't let him keep hurting everyone I love."

"Just come back," Sarah said.

Leah looked at her friend and smiled. "I promise."

She turned and faced Buck and Gabe, who hoisted her up and out the window.

CHAPTER 33

MIDNIGHT STROLL

Leah headed straight into the woods, hiding in the shadows of the moonlight until she reached the road in front of the outpost.

A chill ran up her spine, and her thoughts trailed to the trees opposite the outpost where she'd buried the photo of her parents. *If I make it out of this, I'm coming back for you.*

A breeze blew past her and with it a trail of fog that seemed to seep out of the woods like thick white tendrils. The wind pushed up against her back, as if something were there with her, encouraging her to go on. "I wish that was you, Mom," Leah whispered.

The path down the road to the bend was quiet, with only the rustle of leaves in the woods around her and the crunch of gravel from her own feet. The fog rolled past her, slithering up the road and obscuring the path ahead of her. Once engulfed, she truly felt alone, as if nothing else existed in the woods. Nothing but the breeze, which was still there, like a gentle hand on her shoulder.

"I don't know if you can hear this wherever you are. But, Mom, I hope I make you proud. I'm . . . I'm sorry this happened. I wish I could just see you one more time."

Leah reached the bend in the road and broke free from the trail of fog for a moment. The familiar home, a dark log cabin covered in moss with sheets of plywood concealing the windows, stood in front of her. Half the roof had collapsed, and the other half seemed to be ready to fall any second.

She could feel him inside the building, like a pair of eyes were watching her from somewhere in the shadows.

Leah took in a breath, a buzz of energy flowing in her, pressing up against her skin, ready to be unleashed.

She stepped toward the house, feeling her chest tighten the closer she got. Her eyes warmed, and her vision seemed to brighten. The house appeared to sharpen in her view, and all the shadows appeared to emanate from the first floor. He was there, waiting.

The wood beneath her groaned as she stepped onto the rotted porch, the smell of moss and dried leaves filling her nose.

Murmurs sounded from inside. Quiet mutterings of a madman crouched against the wall, waiting for her.

The wood beneath her cracked loudly, and the muttering stopped, followed by a strange giggle.

Her heart thrummed in her chest, and her breathing all but stopped as she wrapped her hand around the door handle. She took one last look back toward the gravel road and opened the door.

CHAPTER 34
A FATHER'S WISH

Leah stepped inside, immediately spotting a broken wooden chair leg resting on the floor where it had fallen. The space looked exactly the same as in her vision. The dusty old entrance with a dim yellow glow from the light above her. It was musty, like the scent of moss intermixed with rotting wood.

Her senses felt sharp as she took a few more steps inside, peering into the darkness, expecting Asmodeus to leap out. She stepped forward, and the floor creaked beneath her.

"Leah? Is that you?" A voice echoed from the living room, a dark silhouette standing up. "You're really here?"

She froze, confused. "Dad?"

The shadow limped forward into the light. Her father stood before her, ghastly thin, with bruises around his neck like a choker, heavy bags under his eyes, and clothes in tatters. What remained of his clothes was crusted in either mud or blood, something Leah didn't really want to figure out.

Bloodshot eyes looked down at her, filling with tears. "My beautiful Leah, you're alive. It . . . it kept telling me you were dead. Just like . . . just like your mother." He fell to his knees and sobbed into his hands.

She realized then why he was doing this. Her mind screamed to run to him and console him, make him feel better. Yet another voice, the one that knew Asmodeus was still in there, still sitting inside her father, held her back.

She bit her lip, wincing from the pain. "Is that really you?"

He nodded. "It's still here, though . . . still inside me." His sobs grew louder. "He made me to do it. Forced me to watch. I didn't want to. I didn't mean to . . . I didn't mean to kill her. I didn't mean to kill her!" He screamed and started hitting himself in the head.

Leah grimaced, watching her father, now a broken thing, something less than human, crying in front of her. The voice inside her head told her to stay put, but a softer voice yearned to hug him, to tell him everything was going to be alright.

She couldn't bear it, not anymore.

She rushed to his side and wrapped her arms around him, putting herself in the way of his hands. "Stop, Dad, please. It wasn't you, okay? I know that. I just need to kill the demon. Then you'll be back to normal."

"You . . . can't. Kill me. Kill me now, while he's gone." His hand darted to her shirt, and he pulled her to meet his wild eyes. "Kill me now before it's too late! Before he kills you!"

He thrust her away, throwing her into the wall behind her and sending a shock of pain through her back. She fell to the ground and caught her breath, eyeing him from the floor.

He twitched and contorted in front of her. His eyes flit wildly, and he let out a guttural scream that roared through the house. His body was flung upwards, and he stood, his head rolling to face Leah with a wide, toothy smile. Blood trickled from his mouth. "Such a lovely brief reunion. Too bad we have to cut it short." Asmodeus picked at his fingernails, tearing off one that dangled from the skin. "No matter. You'll see each other again soon enough."

That this demon had trapped her father inside his own body, forced to endure whatever it put him through, enraged her. Pressure filled every inch of her body, a surge of energy that carried to her fingers. "You're going to pay for what you've done."

Asmodeus stuck up a bloodied finger and wagged it at her. "Ah, ah, ah. Do anything to this meat sack, and your father dies. Me, on the other hand . . ." He lowered his head, a line of drool pouring out of his mouth as he grinned at her. "You can't kill. I'll just keep coming back."

Leah stuck out her hand, ignoring the form and focusing on the flow of pressure. She imagined a trickle of energy, just enough to keep him back, yet the energy had a mind of its own, fueled by the bond she'd forged. It pulsed out of her like a tidal wave, crashing into Asmodeus and slamming him back into his corner in the shadows of the living room.

Roaring laughter came from the shadows as he stood, cracks and pops sounding from his limbs. "I see you're not in the mood for games. Let me cut you a deal then. I'll let your father go, even assuring he gets the care his body desperately needs in exchange for you."

Tears flowed uncontrollably from Leah's eyes. She'd seen just how broken her father had become. Would he even survive this if he made it out? "What about everyone at the outpost?"

"That deal remains. I won't touch them. They are to leave me alone, and I will go my own way. You let me kill you, and I will leave this meat sack that is your pathetic father." He stepped into the light, blood dripping from a slight cut on his forehead.

"Why do you want me so bad?"

"Let's just say is not really my choice. I have to obey a command, and once I'm through with it, I can attempt my escape."

"Escape? From whom?"

"Does it matter? Your friends, your father, they'd be alive." He leaned back and stared at her, his eyes unblinking.

She shook her head. "It matters! Is this just some sick revenge because of my mother?"

"Maybe. Maybe not. We are all just someone's dark pawn in a game we can't control, aren't we? You are special to me. And we now have a similar enemy, one I wish to eradicate. But for that to happen, the first step is for you to die." He paused and stared into her eyes. "Your life for the life of your father and your outpost friends. That sounds like a good deal to me."

Leah's heartbeat pounded in her chest as she stepped back, instinct telling her she should keep him talking. "You didn't answer me. Eradicate who?" A faint memory came to mind, one of a dark room, a roaring fireplace, and the scent of scotch in the air.

"I'm trapped. Marked, just like you," He nodded to the demon mark on her arm. "A different demon went well out of their way to force me into servitude. Me, of all the demons! A Kyjak, no less, treated like a pawn. No. Not anymore." He finished while rubbing his bruised neck.

Leah stared at her father's neck, noting a patterned set of marks. The outline looked more and more like the outline of a shackle around his neck. He could be telling the truth, but could she risk it? What if he was lying just to take her life before going for the others? Was it worth believing him? Her father's words resonated in her head.

Kill me now before it's too late! Before he kills you!

She shook her head and stepped forward, looking at the ground.

"You made an excellent choice," he said, resting a bony hand on her shoulder. "I'll make it quick. You can know that you saved your father."

She looked into her father's eyes, feeling the pressure of *Malchut* sink to her fingertips. "I'd never trust you."

She swung her hands to his neck, energy surging at her fingertips.

He moved faster, leaping backwards and attempting to miss the blow to his neck. Instead, her fingers met his chest, unleashing a force that crashed into him and flung him into the living room wall across from her.

The entire house shook, dust pouring out from above.

A shriek sounded out of her father, followed by loud, labored gasps. Leah readied herself for a second attack, energy forming in her hands as a dizziness settled in her mind.

"You bitch! I'm going to tear you to pieces when I'm done with you, just like I did to your mother." Asmodeus wrenched himself out of the hole in the wall, wiping away the blood sputtering out of his mouth. "You're willing to kill your own father?"

Leah shook her head. "My father's been dead since the moment you took him from me."

She stepped into the living room and kicked her foot forward, the floorboards rattling and cracking before the sofa launched into the air and slammed into Asmodeus. He threw it to the side and stared up at her, his eyes wild with rage.

"You think showing me my broken father would soften

me? He's already dead after what you made him go through. You wear his body like a puppet, and I'm going to make you pay!" Leah shouted, aiming her hand once more.

Energy burst out from her hands, not thin blades but bullets of *Malchut* shooting out directly at his neck.

Blood splattered the wall as Asmodeus took a bullet through his arm but contorted out of the way of the others, more animal than human. He climbed onto the wall, digging bony fingers and toes into the drywall as *Malchut* bullets followed him.

He skittered across the wall like a spider and onto the ceiling. She could feel the *Yesod* bond feeding her as the energy in her sputtered out. She was going to die, her energy spent. Fear flooded her body one instant, and the next it siphoned away, carried into the new bond she had.

She focused back on Asmodeus and fired off blows of *Malchut* at him left and right, but she was too slow for his speed.

Asmodeus screeched and leaped toward her, hands outstretched like claws, aiming for her neck.

CHAPTER 35

ASMODEUS, KYJAK OF THE VALLEY

eah dived out of the way at the last second, slamming her shoulder into the ground and rolling to the side. Asmodeus crawled on top of her, his arms and legs bending in impossible ways while drool poured out of his mouth. A clawed hand dangled above Leah, sharpened bones protruding out of her father's fingers, ready to strike.

She kicked him hard in the stomach, kicking again and again until his body rolled off her.

He sunk one of his clawed fingers into her shoulder, the pain searing through her like a hot poker.

Another wave of energy blew out of Leah on instinct, a blast that thrust him off her and smacked him into the ceiling. Asmodeus shifted in the air, landing on his feet, staring at her like a wolf staring down its next meal.

Leah backed away, holding her hand to her shoulder, feeling the blood slipping between her fingers. She called the energy, but the pressure in her was weak, unresponsive.

Energy sparked just out of her reach. She needed more. She needed to kill him. Leah took in a quick inhale, and the air around her cooled. Voices whispered at the edge of her mind. *Kill. Eat the Flesh.*

She pointed her finger at him, forcing out raw energy that cut through the air.

He dodged them easily and slipped into the shadows. "All you Mystics are the same. You think you are so powerful against us? Yet, you are still only bags of flesh that can be torn apart."

Her eyes couldn't find him in the shadows, and his voice bounced off every wall. She backed up into the light, readying herself for an attack.

Shadows came to life, creeping closer to her, engulfing everything the light touched. Fear crept over Leah, pulling out every dark thought she had. She'd failed her father, failed her friends, and she'd never live to avenge her mother.

"Why don't you just show yourself then, you coward!" she screamed.

The darkness spread up the walls, covering the boarded windows, until it slowly consumed the dim light above her.

"Why, when I'm having so much fun?" The voice echoed, sending an icy wave through Leah.

The whispers grew louder. She needed the energy, and the pressure inside her grew like a pit of writhing vipers. She could feel anxiety building within her. Fueled even more as the light above flickered out, casting her into darkness.

The shadowed energy lulled her, fueling her rage and hatred.

Kill. Tear. Consume.

At that moment, everything stopped. As the Tree of Death tried to trickle into Leah's mind, an image came to her: Eric, with both arms opened, inches from an overlook.

Strike me and prove you have control.

She shook her head and thought of Sarah and Isaac. They needed her protection. All her friends at the outpost did.

The image of her mother's hand, protruding from the rubble, surfaced in her mind. She'd never see her again. Never get to tell her she was sorry.

Leah shook her head again. She had to focus on her friends, on the fact that others depended on her, needed her to protect them from this demon. Anything that would calm the tempest inside her, urging her to draw deeper on the Tree of Death, urging her to kill Asmodeus and revel in this hatred.

Things inside her changed, the writhing pressure calming, but the energy remained. The voices lessened, the power inside her cleaned, purified by the Tree of Life.

It pulsed out of her with a massive force, throwing back the looming shadow and tearing apart the remains of the wall in front of her.

For a moment, she was safe, surrounded by warmth. But then the shadow flowed back and thrust her into darkness. The whispers surrounded her, clawing their way in and turning to shouts inside Leah's head.

A little girl's voice cried at her side, pulling on her shirt, asking for her parents. She looked, and nothing was there.

An old man shouted behind her, making her jump as he yelled about young people invading his home. The energy called to her, every voice beckoning to pull on the Tree of Death and feel the tempest surge within her.

A crash sounded in the distance, followed by a shriek that pierced through Leah's ears. She covered her ears, wishing for it all to stop, wishing for it to end.

Don't fight it. Give in. Use it. You can't win without it. He'll kill you, like he killed your mother.

"Get up, Square. Fight it and get up!" A new voice pulled her attention from the whispers.

She shook her head, focusing on the voice that cut through the others.

"Come on Leah. I need you," Alma shouted, and Leah looked up.

The Black Bishop stood in front of her, cast in moonlight from the massive hole in the wall. She wore a long black leather jacket down to her knees, the inside lined with long metal spikes, two of which she held in her hands. Black markings lined her hands, glowing a soft blue in the dark.

Leah stood up on shaky legs, cold sweat running down her forehead, ready to face Asmodeus with everything she had.

Asmodeus shrieked, pinned to the wall opposite Alma by one of the metal spikes. He convulsed and clawed at the spike, tendrils of smoke pouring out from the wound. "Stand behind me. I need to pin his other arm down." Alma said, taking a few steps forward. Bursts of energy flung out of her, ramming into the demon, slicing deep into his sides. She tossed a spike in the air and pulsed *Malchut* behind it, projecting it like a missile deep into Asmodeus's arm.

Asmodeus shrieked again, writhing in place, contorting and popping his bones in and out of place.

He slumped down, held up only by the two spikes anchored in the wall, and looked up at Leah, his face gaunt, a hopeless look on her father's face. "Leah ... please ..."

Leah took a step forward, standing next to Alma, a deep hole forming in her stomach. "Is there any way we can save him?" Her voice broke as she asked, tears flooding her eyes.

Alma closed her hand around Leah's shoulder and held her in place. "Asmodeus is still in there. He's only trying to lure you."

"No, please, Leah. It's me. Your dad!" He sobbed, tears mixing with blood as they streamed down his face. "Please, I can't hold him off for much longer. Help me."

Tears streamed down her cheeks as she looked up at Alma, "Please. There has to be something we can do. A flask! We could use a flask and—"

"He's too far gone, and Asmodeus is too powerful. This is the only way." Alma winced and looked at Leah's father. She paused for a second before pushing Leah back and lunging forward, driving the metal spike deep into Leah's father's chest.

"No!" Leah screamed, stumbling to her feet.

Blood sputtered out of her father's mouth as he looked to Leah. "It's okay," he said between labored breaths. "It's what I want." He coughed up more blood. "Elizabeth?" His gaze fell off Leah, and he smiled, his eyes brightening for one quick moment before going still, his last breath wheezing out of his mouth.

Leah ran forward and Alma turned, grabbing her arm before she could reach her father's body. "No, don't touch him. We aren't done here."

Leah stared at Alma's face and spotted a shadow flickering in her eyes. The room grew dark, the moonlight lost in the abyss.

"Black Bishop? Alma?" she asked, feeling the grasp on her arm grow cold and tight.

Alma let out a chuckle before she spoke in a low growl. "I'm going to have fun killing you."

CHAPTER 36
ALMA

Leah jumped back, inching toward the hole in the wall.

Alma grinned. A smile stretched across her face inhumanly as she walked toward Leah, pulling out the metal spikes that lined the inside of her coat, tendrils of smoke hissing off her hands.

"You really cause more trouble than you're worth, little girl." Alma looked at her arms and repositioned her body. "I didn't realize how corrupted this Bishop already was. She practically let me slip in like a glove." Alma clapped her hands together and stared at Leah, a predator waiting for her prey.

Leah tried to harness energy, to feel that serpent inside, but nothing came. The pressure sputtered and died out, well beyond spent.

Another power called to her at the edge of her senses, the Tree of Death within reach, but her stomach churned at the thought of using it again, like chugging spoiled milk. The Tree of Life within her was empty. She was empty, facing Asmodeus inside her mentor's body.

Leah couldn't move, held in place either by fear or by

the sheer amount of pressure coming off of Alma. The Black Bishop stepped up to her, brushing Leah's hair out of her face, and grinned the same grin her father had given her. "Didn't think I could control someone so high in the Board without ruffling a few feathers. This body will be useful."

Alma raised the spike, the point glinting off the moonlight at the edge of Leah's frozen vision. "So long, Leah Ackerman."

The hold on Leah vanished, and she threw her hand up. Her eyes shut tight, and she tried to stop the spike from jamming into her chest. A moment passed, and the piercing pain never came.

Leah opened her eyes and found Alma's face contorted in a grimace of pain as one hand squeezed tight around the other holding the spike. Alma screamed, jerking and twitching backward, dropping the spike to the floor.

"You leave my Square alone." Alma's body seemed to be controlled by invisible puppet strings.

The Black Bishop reached into her coat, pulling out another spike and aiming the end at her own chest. Her hands fought over the spike, pushing and pulling toward her heart.

A growl sounded deep from within Alma, a voice that wasn't hers.

"You bitch! I'm going to kill you!"

Alma's body smashed itself against one of the living room walls, throwing the spike away while she struck and clawed at her body. Blood poured out of cuts, and the strikes and blows lessened.

Alma reached for the spike, but her other hand found it first, jamming the spike into the back of her hand.

"No!" Alma screamed.

Leah stood dumbstruck at the sight. How could she

help, even if she tried? A glint of light caught her eye, and she spotted the first spike near her feet.

Alma's voice played in her head.

"Mystics are the living embodiment of self-sacrifice. We might have to sacrifice our lives, or even worse, the lives of our comrades, for the greater good. For the safety of humankind. Never forget that."

Leah rushed forward and grabbed the spike with a shaky hand. Then she closed the space between her and Alma. She knew what the Black Bishop wanted to do and knew she was the only one who could do it now.

The spike entered Alma's chest with ease, sliding between her ribs. Leah leaped off her, stepping back while Alma gasped for air.

Blood trickled out of her mentor's mouth, and she growled. "You . . . What have you done?"

The snarling face of Alma shifted and calmed. Alma's smile shone up at Leah. "She did what she needed to do. You're coming with me, Asmodeus."

Emotions Leah had locked away surfaced in her mind. Images of her dead mother, the corpse of her father off in the corner, the rage at the demon inside Alma now. Pain, grief, sadness, love, guilt, everything surfaced at once, and Leah fell to her knees screaming.

Alma breathed rapidly, howling and shrieking as pulses of energy came off her. She slumped down, leaving a trail of blood on the wall, and the shriek faded and was replaced with haggard breathing.

The emotions inside Leah faded, like distant memories she'd locked away for another day. Instead, a glimpse of warm hope appeared with the silence. She took a cautious step forward. "Alma?"

Alma took in a slow breath and nodded. Her voice was

barely a whisper between breaths. "He's inside me, trapped. I don't . . . I don't have much time."

Leah rushed to Alma's side, holding her up in her arms while Alma coughed up blood. "I'm so sorry, Black Bishop Sachs. We can get help. I didn't mean. I don't want . . ."

Alma looked up at her, attempting to mouth words but coughing up more blood.

Leah looked at the hole in the wall and shouted. "Help! Help! Someone!" She pushed her hands around the metal spike, applying pressure while the blood leaked through her fingers.

Alma looked into Leah's eyes and struggled to whisper. "I trained you . . . better than that. It won't . . . make a difference."

"I'm . . . I'm sorry. I thought I could do this. I thought I could win." Leah's eyes stung, but no tears came.

Alma shook her head. "Don't apologize. You protected the others. He would have taken more." She wheezed and coughed.

"But I didn't want this, I didn't want to kill you . . ." Her voice trailed off as she looked at her teacher, her vision slowly getting watery.

Alma lifted her hand, showing off familiar markings made in black ink. "I bound him to me, and I'll take him into death. I can't hold him back for much longer. You did well. I . . . I'm proud of you, Leah." Her gaze trailed behind Leah, Alma's focus off beyond what Leah could see. "You will be a great Mystic . . ."

Tears trailed down Leah's face. "I'm sorry I let you down."

Alma shook her head and pulled back a strand of hair from Leah's face. "You were brave. But remember that bravery comes at a price. Make sure . . . Make sure you're . . .

willing . . . to pay it . . ." Her eyes dulled, and a slight smile twitched on her face before going slack and lifeless.

CHAPTER 37

BLACK QUEEN

Sarah peered into the home through the hole in the wall, gasping for breath. Behind her, Isaac and Gabe stood, their faces white and fists clenched, ready for a fight.

Crouched over Alma's body, Leah looked up at them and frowned. "Why are all of you here?"

Sarah crawled through the hole and ran to Leah's side. "We came with Alma. She made us stay back. Is it . . . is it done, then?"

Leah nodded and bit her lip.

Silence fell as all the students from the outpost piled in, looking at the carnage before their eyes fell on Alma.

Paige didn't have any snarky comments. Instead, she raced with Gabe to Leah's side, holding her face and looking her over. "It's over, okay?"

Everyone else surrounded them, Harry and Isaac helping to cross Alma's arms, Buck and Emma straightening her clothes, and Serena brushing back her hair. Giving Alma back some semblance of order, the way she would have liked it.

Sarah helped Leah up. She walked over to her father's

corpse, a mere pile of broken bones and flesh, barely a reflection of how she remembered him.

Leah kneeled and closed his eyes, feeling his cold skin and knowing he was with her mother now, somewhere better than here. Somewhere where he wouldn't be tortured anymore, his undeserved guilt stripped clean.

"Baruch dayan ha'emet." She whispered, a single tear sliding down her face.

Paige and Gabe instructed the others to help with both bodies as Leah and Sarah stepped out of the house. Sarah wrapped her arm around Leah's shoulder, the warmth calling her back from the abyss her mind was falling into. Isaac came around to her other side, hesitant to come close until she brought out her arm and he came in for a side hug.

The three walked together, in front of the somber procession, up the gravel road and back to the outpost.

Isaac looked down at their steps and whispered, "I'm sorry."

Leah squeezed his shoulder, unsure if he was shaking or she was. "For what?"

"I told Alma everything. There was a scream upstairs. I think your uncle, then Alma, came running down looking for you. I told her. I. I caused—"

Leah gave him a hug and squeezed tight. "You saved me, okay? You saved me."

Isaac raised his head and gave her a small smile. Leah looked past him, out to the forest beyond.

"What is it?" Isaac asked.

"I'll be right back," she said.

Leah stepped into the woods, the light of the moon guiding her path back to the knotted tree. She kneeled and dug at the dirt, loosening it until she found the plastic Flyby Donuts bag. Pulling the photo out, she stared back at the image of her younger self, covered in spaghetti, her parents on either side, smiling, happy.

"I promise I'll keep fighting," she whispered, gently tracing the image of her mother and father. "For both of you."

She joined the others back on the gravel road and back into the outpost.

Buck, Paige, and Serena gently rested Alma on the couch, placing a blanket over her while Gabe, Harry, and Emma did the same for Leah's father.

They all silently gathered around the dining room table, everyone transfixed by their own thoughts as their teacher lay dead in the next room.

Gabe was the first to stand, going into the kitchen and boiling water. Moments later, he started passing around mugs of hot cocoa before sipping on his own.

Time moved in slow motion, and finally, after what felt like hours, Leah broke the silence and shared what happened. She told them everything about the battle and Alma coming to protect her from Asmodeus.

The others cried the tears that Leah couldn't shed, all her tears already spent.

Once she was done, Gabe looked at the other Squares.

"So, what do we do next?" he asked.

Paige gripped her elbows and looked toward the exit. "Someone will come. Someone has to come."

"You don't know that," Sarah said.

Leah stood from the table. "We'll wait till morning then. If no one comes, then we can decide." She left the table, entering the infirmary moments later and sitting by Eric's side, holding his hand while she drifted off to sleep.

Leah stood in a pool of water, an unending ocean lapping up against her ghostly legs. The water was warm this time, and light filled her eyes instead of the gloomy shadows.

Her arm still had the mark on it, a blackened handprint. When she focused on it, it writhed. She reached to touch it, her finger hovering over the marked flesh.

"Leah?" a man and woman's voice called out at the same time.

Her gaze lifted from the mark, and she turned around. "Mom? Dad?"

Her mother and father stood behind her, smiling, their faces clear as day as they rushed over to her side. She could smell the perfume on her mother's hair and the scent of pancakes on her father.

She squeezed her eyes tight as she wrapped her arms around them for a moment that felt like eternity, and she was entirely fine if this was the last moment she ever had.

"Leah?" Another voice sounded. A man's voice, echoing from far away.

She broke free from her parents and looked off into the distance. A man waded in the water, a man who looked a lot like her mother.

"You better go to him," her mother said. "He's lost his way and will need help back."

Leah peered out into the distance, seeing her uncle flailing about as if he couldn't see them.

"Am I . . . Am I dead?" she asked, looking at her father and mother.

Her father kneeled next to her and shook his head, smiling. "Not even close." He nodded to Leah's uncle. "He can't stay here much longer."

She looked at the two of them, their smiles warm and kind. "I can't stay either, can I?"

They both shook their heads. Her father said, "It isn't your time. Not yet."

Her mother ran a hand through Leah's hair. "Many dark days are still to come, but keep your head up. I'm proud to have you as my daughter, love."

Tears flowed down her face, and she hugged them again. "I love you both so much."

They squeezed her tight and faded away, leaving her standing in the warm pool of water. She turned, seeing her uncle still pacing around, and approached. It was an odd feeling, as she came close to him and realized that for her this water was a shallow pond, but for her uncle, it was a deep black ocean.

"Leah? What are you doing here?"

"Time to go back." She held out her hand.

Golden light formed between them, emanating from each of their chests and forming a thin golden thread.

Eric stepped back. "No. I don't think I can do this again."

Leah felt at the string, feeling his fear flowing through it. "We'll figure it out. Together."

He looked at the thread, confused, but Leah kept her hand held out, waiting. He nodded and wrapped his hand around hers, and the world blurred into a soft white light.

Leah rested her back against the wall to the infirmary, comfortably sitting on her bed as the light from the sky outside streamed in. She sipped on a cup of juice Gabe had brought her and looked at Eric, who was still fast asleep.

A tall woman in a black pantsuit opened the door of the

infirmary. Her short blond hair was nearly white, and her reddened lips were a stark contrast to her pale skin.

She was younger than Alma, but her look of authority somehow surpassed Alma's in every manner. She stepped in and closed the door behind her, turning her crystalline blue eyes on Leah.

"Good morning, you must be the famed Leah Ackerman all the Squares are talking about." Her voice was entrancing, warm, and welcoming.

"Yes, that's me." Leah said, wiping away the sleep from her eyes.

The woman stepped over to Eric's side and placed a hand on his shoulder. "Eric Mizrahi, you may not hear me, but you did well, protecting these children when you could. You'll make a fine White Knight someday." She took a seat and shifted her gaze back to Leah.

"I'm sorry, but who are you?" Leah asked.

The woman laughed and placed her hands in her lap. "I am Helen Nielsen, Black Queen of the Infinity Board. It's nice to meet you, Leah Ackerman."

Adrenaline kicked in, masking the exhaustion, and Leah launched to her feet, ignoring the aching pain from her shoulder, her back upright in the best posture she could finally make. "I'm sorry, Black Queen Helen, I didn't know."

She waved her hand. "I get that a lot. My guess is, you figured the Queens were much older, yes?"

Leah nodded.

A small smile appeared on her lips. "Wisdom and power come in many forms. You'll see, eventually." She gestured to a chair next to Eric's bed. "Sit, please. I should salute you. Taking on a demon all by yourself to protect the outpost."

"That was all Black Bishop Sachs, she—"

"Would have left the demon to come into the outpost on his own terms, had you not taken it into your hands.

What she did was commendable, yes, but you took the initiative, and for that, I applaud you. I apologize that our reinforcements couldn't come any sooner. Our outposts are never in the most convenient of places." She snapped her fingers and a tall pale man wearing a crisp black suit stepped into the room, holding a notepad. "This demon has been tracking you since you were at your home. I'll need a record of what happened. So, please, when you are ready."

The memory of it all was shrouded in a deep fog, as if the events had occurred years ago. The harder she tried to focus on the details, the more abstract they became.

Helen stood, pulling her chair around Eric's bed and to Leah's side. She sat and held Leah's hand, warmth emanating from her, and her blue eyes felt sincere, motherly, as Leah stared at them. "I know it's hard. Trauma builds barriers for us, but it will help us piece everything together and determine our next steps."

Leah looked down at her hands and started with the first thing she remembered. The moment the planchette moved on the Ouija board. The rest fell into place, and she told it to Helen completely. She didn't know how long they sat there while she unlocked every box tucked away in her mind. Helen held her hand the entire time, staring intently into Leah's eyes.

When Leah finished, Helen turned and nodded at the man in the suit. He folded the notepad and stepped out of the room. The Black Queen turned back and patted Leah's hand. "You did the right thing."

"But my father . . ." Leah felt the tears forming, and she paused, wishing she could hold back the tears.

"You protected the lives of many for the life of one. That is a hard choice, especially when that one person is the world to us. But it is a choice we Mystics must make to preserve the balance."

"But I disobeyed direct orders, and Alma . . ."

"Black Bishop Sachs was right too, at first. She focused on protecting the Squares while she looked into the name you mentioned to her. Legion, it was?" Leah nodded and Helen carried on. "Either way, in the end, she defended all her students by making herself a vessel for possession."

"A vessel? Like a flask to trap demons?" Leah asked.

Helen raised her eyebrows. "I see you've learned well. Yes, it is a ritual that lures a demon and traps it within. Seems that Alma altered the markings to make herself the vessel. Then, Asmodeus was either going to die with her or be sent back to where he came from. I'm sure Alma was aware she might not be able to fight it, seeing as it took out four Knights, and failure wasn't an option. Not with the Squares she'd been trusted to protect. Bishops are always so cunning." Helen paused, thinking. "Did she tell you anything else?"

Leah shook her head. The weight of what Alma had really done, putting herself between Leah and Asmodeus, knowing she would not make it out alive, hit Leah then. She took in a sharp breath. "She sacrificed herself for us."

"Yes," Helen said, her eyes reddening. "Valiant, right to the very end. She trained many fine Squares. We will miss her dearly."

They sat in silence between Eric for some time until Helen took in a breath and said, "One more thing, regarding your father's remains. Back in your hometown, we have a plot for him, next to you and your mother. But would it be alright if we buried him here, alongside Alma and the Black Knights who didn't make it?"

This was the first time Leah had heard anything about her old life. They had made a plot for her next to her parents? Of course, they had to do something, but the thought had never crossed her mind.

She thought about what Helen had asked, then shook her head. "He belongs in a Jewish cemetery. He . . . He belongs next to my mom." Her old life was gone, something she could never go back to, but her father . . . He didn't deserve this.

Helen didn't skip a beat, instead crossing the room and kneeling next to Leah, resting a hand on her knee. "Then I will personally see that his body is laid to rest next to your mother."

Leah looked at Eric, lying in his bed, sleeping. "She would have liked that. They both would have."

Helen cleared her throat, stood, and backed up to the door. "I have some announcements I'd like to make to the others. Get yourself cleaned up and meet me downstairs. Take your time." She opened the door and turned. "The Infinity Board is proud to have you as a member. For all you've been through, we are happy you've stayed with us."

CHAPTER 38

THE LAST GOODBYE

"Leah!" Sarah rushed toward her the moment she stepped into the classroom, wrapping her arms around her friend and squeezing tight.

Isaac stood and crossed the room, standing behind Sarah, hesitant to join in. He waited until Sarah let go and Leah looked at him.

"You doing better?" he asked.

Lean nodded and reached out, pulling him into a tight hug.

She grabbed a desk, catching Gabe's gaze and giving him a nod before looking at the others. Aside from Paige, who kept her eyes trained outside.

Helen stepped into the classroom, flanked by two men, one the same tall pale man who had been in the infirmary, and the other muscular with dark skin and a gaze like a hungry lion ready to pounce.

The Black Queen stood at the front of the room, and everyone grew silent in an instant. "Today is a sad day for the Infinity Board. We will remember the Mystics who fell defending our most important asset, our future." She opened her arms, acknowledging the students in the room.

"You are our future. Our hope to perpetuate the society's goal to protect humankind and maintain the balance. Black Bishop Sachs knew this to the core. We protect what is most important to us, even if that means sacrifice." Helen's voice broke as she brushed away a tear on her cheek. "She was a formidable Bishop, and you should be proud to have been trained by her." The Black Queen crossed the room, running her fingers along Alma's desk.

"I believe the youth are the most important part of this society. I came as quickly as I could, ready to face this evil. Yet, it wasn't fast enough." She looked down and raised a hand to her chest. "For that, I am sorry."

Leah had the urge to run up and hug her, to tell her it was okay, but she sat in the discomfort as a leader of the Infinity Board shed more tears.

"It would be an insult not to honor her for everything she has done for the Infinity Board. So, I've motioned to rename this outpost after her, and to build a monument in her honor within the gardens of the headquarters." Her blue eyes rested on Leah for a moment. "We will lay her to rest here with the others we've lost. To always remember their bravery and sacrifice, and to send a message of strength to the future generations of Mystics." She paced the room, paused, and faced them. "I would like all of you to join me. Yet, I think there is something we must do before then." A half-smile appeared on her face. "You will no longer be Squares. By my decree, you are all promoted to Black Pawns. I understand it may be a bit early, but there is no sense in moving to another outpost. Besides, with a mentor like Black Bishop Sachs, I know you all have learned and seen enough to move on to one of our academies."

Everyone leaned and shifted in their seats, and Leah looked around to see the shock on all their faces.

Sarah nudged Leah and whispered. "I like this queen."

Leah nodded and looked back at Helen, not sure if being promoted should be something to celebrate or just another move made by an unseen hand. For all she knew, Asmodeus was right, and she was just a pawn in someone else's game.

Alma's voice echoed in her head. *There's always a price.*

The group stood in the woods beyond the outpost among four open graves, bodies wrapped in white cloth resting in them.

Leah stood by herself, a little further back, on the graveled road, next to the black truck that held the remains of her father.

"I'm sorry," she muttered. "I wish I'd told Mom sooner, about the dreams, the Ouija board, the whispers. Maybe this wouldn't have happened." She wiped away her tears and took in a deep breath. "I promise I'll do better."

Leah pulled the photo from her pocket, unfolding it once more to see the smiles on her parents' faces. She folded it back up and tucked it securely underneath her father's cloth. "I'll make you proud."

The sound of shovels cutting into dirt pulled her back to the graves, as the Squares started laying dirt atop the other bodies. Leah joined in, each performing a kind of one last form of respect to their mentor and the Knights who'd died protecting them. Once done, they gathered in line in front of the outpost. Queen Helen stood at the front and handed each of them black uniforms.

When it came to Leah, Helen handed her the pile of clothes with the symbol of a Pawn behind checkers, embroidered on the left chest. Black always suited her better, she thought to herself.

They dispersed, and she walked in line with Isaac and Sarah. "So, what now?" Leah asked.

Sarah ran in front of them and turned around, walking backwards like she did on their morning jogs. "We pack up and head out. The Queen wants us gone by tonight, on a bus to the academy."

Isaac scratched his head. "How do you know that? They didn't say any of that."

Sarah shrugged. "I eavesdropped on Queen Helen talking to Eric. Apparently, he's up and ready for duty. She's not too happy about the bond, so she says he needs to come with us."

Leah looked up at the outpost, thinking over the past few weeks she'd spent here. What was supposed to be her summer vacation was spent fending off demons. "Already on to somewhere new. I'm guessing nowhere will feel like home soon."

Isaac shrugged. "At least we've got each other, right?"

Sarah lunged forward and squeezed Isaac in a bear hug. "Aww, look who's being sappy."

"Hey, stop it!" Isaac squirmed, but a small smile broke from his annoyed face.

Leah let out a laugh and wrapped her arms around Isaac too, happy that whatever was going to come, she'd face it with her friends.

A Small Request From Us, The Authors

Thank you for reading the start of Leah's journey. We hope you've enjoyed it, so far.

As independent authors, reviews are so important to spread the word and reach new readers.

If you have a few seconds to spare, would you please consider leaving an honest review on the website you bought this book?

Your support helps so much in continuing Leah's story and the many others we plan to write in this world.

All the best,

A.B. Cohen & JP Rindfleisch IX

DEMON KNIGHT
LEAH ACKERMAN SERIES BOOK TWO

The story continues:

https://abcohenwrites.com/demon-knight

CURSED JADE
AN ERIC MIZRAHI NOVELETTE

Get it free using the link below:

https://abcohenwrites.com/cursed-jade

Acknowledgments

In January 2020 a group of authors journeyed on a train from Los Angeles to Oakland, California and stayed inside a haunted mansion. Two of those authors were us, A.B. Cohen and JP Rindfleisch. We were part of an author event called "Authors on a Train," which ended with a two-day workshop on co-writing and plotting a story led by the indie powerhouses J. Thorn and Zach Bohannon.

J and Zach have been instrumental in our collaboration, offering mentorship and guidance from the very first step. This book wouldn't exist without them, quite literally. J has been a wonderful developmental editor, aiding in strengthening our story and being the first pair of eyes to see our work. And Zach has been amazing as a copyeditor and launching coach to get this book off the ground. Both of you have been remarkable, and words could not convey our gratitude.

We also want to thank our Beta readers, who kept us on track and helped us make this story evolve into the tale it is today. Your input helped us tease out the confusing bits and add in a little more depth to our characters while keeping the story true to Leah's tale.

The last pair of eyes on our work was the amazing proofreader and fellow author, Lori Diederich. We were lucky to have met you in Salem, on another writing event full of witches, and can't thank you enough for the final polish you gave this story.

Another big thanks to our cover designers, at getcover

s.com. They understood the changes needed to make the striking cover you have in your hands today.

A.B. Cohen here; I would like to give special thanks to my parents for their continued support on this journey. My dad, Mimon, who did everything he could for me to immigrate to the United States. And my mom, Yojebed, my biggest fan, whose English is not perfect but that does not stop her from translating every paragraph on the kindle to read it in Spanish. My brother, Gabriel, for making me laugh every single time we are together, and for listening to my weird ideas at odd hours. A huge thank you to my wife, Raquel, for her unbreakable belief in me, even when I was feeling doubtful throughout this journey. Finally, to my best friend, Marcos Hirschfeld Z"L, who is no longer with us, but whom I carry in my heart and in every book I write, to always immortalize the wonderful, joyful soul he was. I love you all.

JP here, thank you to my partner, Josh, who has had to put up with this crazy dream of being a published author for more years than I want to admit. Your support and encouragement kept me pushing forward, even when things got tough. Thanks too, to my wonderful parents, John and Diane, who let me be the wild child I am. And to my friends and family, thank you for cheering me on through the years.

Last, but definitely not least is you, our dear wonderful reader. Thank you for giving Dark Pawn a chance and we hope you enjoyed it as much as we did writing it. We have more to tell with dear Leah, so get ready!

Thank you all.

A.B. Cohen & JP Rindfleisch IX

ABOUT THE AUTHORS

A.B. Cohen is an emerging author of freaky stories for weird people. He focus mainly on thrillers, horror and urban fantasy tales. Originally from Caracas, Venezuela, today he lives in San Francisco California. Along with his passion for writing, he also loves dancing, soccer, and traveling. You can find out more about A.B. Cohen's upcoming writing projects using the link below:

www.abcohenwrites.com

JP Rindfleisch IX is a horror, urban fantasy, and science fiction writer. They live in Rockford, Illinois, with their partner of eleven years, and a menagerie of animal children including a Siberian husky, miniature dachshund, African grey parrot, Quaker parrot, and a run of the mill cat. They love creating art, nerding out over science, video games, tabletop RPGs, and spending hours in the kitchen crafting delectable vegan grub. You can learn more about JP Rindfleisch IX by following the link below:

www.jprindfleischix.com